# Echo

## of the

# Moon

## The Will and the Wisp, Book 3

# James Armstrong

Echo of the Moon
The Will and the Wisp–Book 3
Copyright © 2023–James Armstrong
All rights reserved

~~~~

Cover Art–Hideaway–Copyright 2023 James Hussey
All rights reserved–www.jameshussey.com

~~~~

This is the third book of The Will and the Wisp series. This is a work of fiction based on the true story of the Armstrong family.

Sharon Kizziah-Holmes–Publishing Coordinator
Edited by: Sandy Armstrong

**Paperback-Press**
Springfield, Missouri
an imprint A & S Publishing, Paperback Press LLC

ISBN -13: 978-1-960499-48-6

# DEDICATION

To the Armstrong family.

# ACKNOWLEDGMENTS

Thank you to Mr. James Hussy for allowing me to use his beautiful artwork, HIDAWAY, for the cover of the original The Will and the Wisp and also for this second book in the series.

To Susan Armstrong, thank you for allowing me countless hours in front of me computer, writing, re-writing, editing and more. Without your support I may not have completed this project.

Sandy Armstrong, without you putting such great effort into the editing of this book, it may not have ever been finished. Thank you.

Sharon Kizziah-Holmes, thanks for helping me publish book 3. Without you, the original Will and the Wisp may never have come to fruition.

# PREFACE

Many years ago, in a musty storm cellar in southeast Missouri, light from an old kerosene lantern flickered off the faces of relatives and neighbors seeking shelter. The smell of kerosene permeated the air. Most storms that rumbled across the Missouri "boot heel" had the potential of harboring deadly tornados which lurked in pitch-black nights. The old dugout shelter was nothing more than a hole in the ground supported by wooden beams and covered by three to four feet of dirt, but since we had no modern warning system, we spent many hours huddled in that dark hole. And this is where I first heard the stories of a fortune in gold being found under a relative's ancient house in southern Mississippi. (My father knew the house well.) I was the youngest of eight children in our family, and we all looked forward to hearing those stories. These childhood memories inspired *The Will and the Wisp* and its sequels *A Voice in the Wind* and *Echo of the Moon*. Although the stories I eventually wrote down are mostly fiction, the story of the Wisp Gold is very true. It originates in an unforgiving swamp, then moves across the plains and leads to more dangers in a Wild West adventure.

Enjoy!
– James Armstrong

# CHAPTER 1

## The Triple A

The howling summer wind burned Nate's face as he pulled his bandana over his nose to block the dust. The day had been a long one and he could really feel the strain. Sliding from his horse to stretch his tired legs, he turned and suddenly became aware of smoke to the south. The grass was parched from the summer sun, and he realized that a prairie fire lurked in the distance. When he saw Pete racing toward him from the south, he knew they were in peril. Only about a mile from the ranch he could see tumbleweeds that looked ghostly in the distance as they skimmed across the prairie, totally engulfed in flames. The fireballs, big and small, were racing ahead of the prairie grass, something he had never in his life seen before.

Leaping back into the saddle, Nate urged his mount toward the ranch, with Pete not far behind. He passed the first several buildings and Levi's store, shouting as he rode.

Joe Armstrong's wife, Cindy, outside carrying a bucket of water from the water tower, heard the desperate warning. Turning toward the south, she stood unmoving, shocked at what she was seeing. The sun, sinking in the west, was reflected off a giant flume of smoke towering in the sky.

Most of the residents of the settlement had been indoors sheltering themselves from the howling winds and choking dust. Nate and Pete continued to shout their warning, banging on cabin doors as they raced from one to another. The fiery tumbleweeds had begun to hit the outskirts of the ranch buildings with blazing crashes of flames. By now the fireballs from hell were everywhere.

Frantic residents scrambled about, using shovels to throw dirt and forming a chain with water buckets, to save the buildings that were already on fire. Women rushed to gather the smaller children and herd them to the river. Thankfully, the panicked children instinctively headed toward the water on their own. Nate and Pete opened the corrals that held the milk cows and herd bulls, and the animals followed the children's lead and galloped toward the water.

Mingling with the wind and dust was the blistering heat of the inferno. As most of the buildings became engulfed, the heat became so great that the ranch hands finally had to give up their fight. At last, everyone was gathered at the river's edge, watching as their small village burned to the ground.

Joe, burned and black from smoke and ash dust, was one of the last to give up the fight. Finally, he became aware it was a hopeless quest. Most of the ranch was no more.

Cindy stood by the river with tears in her eyes and hands to her face as she watched her dream go up in flames. Slowly, Joe walked to her side.

## Two days later

The only buildings left standing at the Triple A Ranch headquarters were the school, Levi's Dry Goods store, and Charles Armstrong's small office. The south wind howled through the deserted street in the early morning sun.

Charles watched tumbleweeds dancing down the wind-blown street as he gazed through the dusty windows of his office. He looked at his pocket watch and lit his pipe, then sighed as he inhaled the sweet smoke. It had been a long road to success after the death of his father, and the prairie seemed almost empty without him. The last few years had been rough on the Triple A as the rainfall had slowly diminished, he mused. Then an onslaught of problems with rustlers, wagon trains, weather, and the management of a vast cattle empire, its employees and their families, had followed, one after another. Now the prairie fire had devastated the community. What could possibly happen next?

Movement in the dusty, still smoky, street caught his attention, and Charles recognized his brother Joe holding on to his hat as he leaned into the wind, making his way toward the building. He would be there soon.

As Charles reflected on the things the Triple A had endured through the years, and the toll it had taken on the ranch and the people there, he couldn't help but remember what Little Boy Horse and Johnny One Horn had told him about the curse of the gold they had found so long ago.

"Damn, that wind is howling. I could barely walk against it." Joe burst through the door, and it slammed shut behind him.

"Yeah, I watched you coming down the street, or what's left of it. We were lucky no one was killed." Charles paused. "Listen, I know it's probably not the time to bring this up, but you know we're out of grazing space, and I've been up most of the night trying to figure out some things. Have a seat."

Joe sat on the edge of the desk and looked at him curiously.

"About a month ago I found some land around Cheyenne Wells, and I've been thinking we should buy it. It has the Smoky River, some creeks, and better grass than we have here. There's about three thousand acres at a great price. It wouldn't be bad driving the herd there, according to Nate and Pete."

"Well, I don't know about that rattlesnake hole you'd have to go through. According to Pete, there's a snake behind every rock for about five miles through that one canyon." Joe took off his hat and ran his fingers through his tousled hair, shaking his head. "Let me ask you this, are we going to give up all the things we've built here and just go? This place was almost a town and we built it with our bare hands!"

Charles nodded. "Well, there's not much of it left now. We've got to get our people and children some shelter. I sent Nate and Shorty into Garden City to get tents and supplies. They should be back tomorrow. How many cattle and horses did we lose?"

"About fifty cattle and twenty good horses, but that's not bad, considering," sighed Joe. "That's good you're getting some tents. Everybody is all cramped up in the schoolhouse and Levi's store. If old Levi were still alive, he'd be tearing out his hair by now."

"Yeah, I sure miss that old goat. He was grouchy, but a heck of a man." Charles looked at his brother fondly. "You know, Joe, we can keep this place, and rebuild it, but this herd has got to be moved. With the drought, our cattle are starving. We need to move them now. Damn, man, we got to do what we got to do to survive!" He pursed his lips, considering. "Joe, I need you to organize the drive to Cheyenne Wells. We don't have much time."

"I'll do the best I can, Charles, but it's sure going to be hard with all this confusion going on."

Nate and Shorty returned the following day, and tents and medical supplies were distributed to the people who called the ranch their home. The wind had finally died down, and everyone rummaged through the debris to salvage what they could.

Charles planned to send half of the twenty-four ranch hands with the drive and keep the other half at the ranch to protect the women and children until they could rebuild sustainable living quarters. The men would have to volunteer, or a drawing would be held to determine who would stay and who would go. Men who had families would most likely elect to stay, while the others went to Cheyenne Wells. It seemed like a straightforward process, but bickering between some of the ranch hands made it difficult. Charles called them all together and informed them that they still worked for the Triple A, and if they were unhappy with the process, they were free to leave their jobs and go somewhere else.

After all the bickering was settled, four of the ranch hands decided they would resign. Privately, Charles thought they were lucky they still had twenty after all they'd been through. He thanked the four as they left, and they seemed satisfied, but he was sorry to see them go.

As he walked down the street of his once-thriving small community, Charles shook his head, tears streaming down his face. "My God, it's all gone," he thought. His favorite place had been the gazebo in the gathering park where everyone used to feast, play music and where Old Earl Stockman and Johnny One Horn used to tell them fascinating stories.

He headed down to the river cemetery, thinking about ways they might rebuild the little community. He opened the old wooden gate and walked among the tombstones, contemplating each one for minutes, though each held an eternity of memories. He stared at O.C.'s memorial and then glanced at the muddy river. Next was a memorial to his mother. O.C. had spent many weeks carving it from solid granite. Even though their bodies were not even there, he knew his parents were close in spirit. The tightness in his throat became unbearable. He swallowed. John Tunnie, Old Levi, the famous old mountain man Earl Stockman – visions of each returned with mind-soothing memories. Finally, he came to his little brother Carl's headstone. He thought about what Carl might have become and how witty he was. As Charles turned to leave, he noticed the marker for the woman who ran in circles. He said a silent prayer for all, glanced at Carl's marker one more time, and a gust of wind blew his hat across the cemetery and into the muddy river. Laughing out loud, he said, "Carl, you cut that out! That hat cost me two dollars!" Walking back toward the ranch, he glanced over his shoulder one more time to see his hat swirling around in the muddy current. A wry smile softened his face.

Joe had seen him in the distance and came down to meet him. "Hey, Charles, were you visiting the family, brother?"

"Yes, I was, and that little dickens Carl threw my hat into the river!"

Joe, bewildered, turned his head slowly and observed his brother, who was still smiling. Then he grinned. "Are you sure it was Carl? Maybe it was that lady that ran in circles or old mountain man Earl Stockman."

"No, I know exactly who it was and so do you," smiled Charles. He slapped his brother on the shoulder. "You know, Joe, I changed my mind. This time I think I should go with the herd out to Cheyenne Wells. How about you staying here and working on rebuilding the ranch? Cindy and the boys will need you here. Besides, I need to stop wearing this big city suit and get back to my roots. I'm asking you to run the operation for a while."

Joe nodded, musing. "Well, do we actually own the new property now?"

"Yep. When he was there, I had Pete wire the money from Garden City to the landowners in St. Louis! Those three thousand acres now belong to the Triple A."

"Well, I guess we don't really have a choice, do we now, Charles? Hell, brother, we've took chances before and it worked out, so moving on from this is the best thing we can do."

Charles tipped his hat back and stared across the plains

to the south. "Damn, you know, Joe, all this bad luck lately sure makes me think of the curse that Johnny One Horn and Little Boy Horse used to warn us about. There's a lot more to it than we know."

"Charles, you've always been the practical one," Joe shook his head. "But now you're starting to believe in hocus-pocus? Now that is funny, man."

"Well, makes you think, don't it, brother? You know we haven't touched that gold since we came here but one time. We did this all on our own and life has been a lot more rewarding that way, if you ask me."

"You're right about that for sure. It sure was a lesson though. You just keep on thinking, Charles. You're good at that," Joe laughed. "I'll make a trip down to Garden City and send word to Abilene that we're taking on hands. I'm going to need a lot of lumber shipped here, and the hands to build with. If I'm going to stay here and do this, I'm going to do it right."

"I know you will, brother, I know you will." Charles shook his head. "I've got to go over and pick me out a horse to ride on the drive I'm leading now. I hope I can pick a good one for my ass's sake – it's been a long time since I've ridden."

"Yeah," Joe laughed as he walked away. "Take care of that ass, Charles! It's the only one you got! Ask for my son Carl – he can hook you up with a ride. He knows all the horses on a first name basis.

### Two days later

Nate had ridden to the top of a hill and was watching the ranch hands finish cutting out the cattle for the drive. Most were experienced hands led by Jose Luna, Triple A's appointed drive foreman. Jose also served as an interpreter for Nate and Pete for workers that couldn't speak English or had selective understanding of it. Pete and Nate had become very close to Jose through the years and trusted him.

Surveying the sprawling herd, Nate felt very proud to be a part of such a great undertaking.

It wasn't long before Pete and Jose saw him on the hill and trotted up to meet him. "Hey, Nate, did you know that Charles is coming on this drive with us?" Pete asked breathlessly.

"Yeah, I just heard that," Nate drawled. "I never would have believed it, but I guess it's true. Wants to get back to the ol' wild west, does he? Well, Carl picked old Sachi to be his ride. I told him that it was a dirty trick, but he just laughed, and you know how he is."

"Oh, I do, and Charles will too before this drive is over," laughed Pete. Then he got serious. "I sent the Coyote Woman ahead to scout and told her to check back every three days. She took ol' Slick Harry with her. He follows her around like a lost puppy – she'll have her hands full for sure. I told her to check out that canyon of snakes to see if they're still there or was it just a fluke last time."

Pete paused before he spoke again. "Ol' Earl Stockman used to say that canyon isn't too far from a place that holds a fortune in gold. He called it a dark place and said if you ever took any gold from it, you would surely die. He said it was called the 'Echo of the Moon' and it was a forbidden place, even for the Natives. It's been said evil lives there in the form of wolves with glowing red eyes that can't be killed. As for me – I'll go around it if I can!"

Nate reflected. "Well, you know, Pete, ol' Earl used to tell stories all the time. Only thing is, you could never tell if they were true or if he was just trying to get attention."

"That place is real," Jose affirmed as he reined his horse closer. "I know people who have seen these wolves. We never want to go there, my friends."

Nate shifted in his saddle to look at Jose and saw that Jose had his hat over his heart. This surprised him. He turned and gazed northward for a few seconds, intrigued with what he had heard. Finally, he kicked his mount and headed down the hill. "Well, I've heard enough about all these boogers!" Now let's get these boys to work down there! We leave at first light."

# CHAPTER 2

### Scouting the Valley

Retha, the Coyote Woman, followed by Slick Harry, was about ten miles ahead of the herd and things were looking good for the drive. It seemed it would be easy going. But the morning winds had started to rise very quickly and blowing dust from the valley floor was making travel extremely difficult. She decided to travel north toward the hills and use them as a wind block. Just ahead of them next to the hills was a small line of trees that looked green and vibrant waving in the fierce winds.

When they reached the small offshoot of the hills, she saw that her intuition had been right. There was a small creek of clear water trickling down the gulch into several pools of nice blue water. "This place is damn pretty," she thought. "It's a great place to clean up, get some rest, and wait out the wretched dust storm." She called to her companion, "Slick Harry, let's make camp here on the sand – it's away from that damn wind and we can get some rest and get some of this dust out of our throats."

"Yes, Miss Retha." He obediently trotted up alongside her. "Can I lay down beside you?"

"Hell, no! And stop looking at me that way or I'll put one of these forty-four slugs right between your eyes. You know it's always no, so quit asking."

Slick Harry stomped away from his horse and kicked the

sand several times in a frustrated rage. After he calmed down, he began gathering wood for cooking, all the time mumbling in a low voice to keep Retha from hearing him.

Retha walked to the creek's bank and reached into the cool water to wet her face and hair. "Slick Harry, I'm going to ride around the creek line to see if I can get us a rabbit or two. You stay here and build us a fire."

As she mounted her horse, she could still hear Slick Harry mumbling. She covered her mouth to keep from laughing. In her heart, she really did know that ol' Harry loved her, but it was just a game for her. She had no memory of her past, and until she found it, she would never love another man.

As Slick Harry waited for Retha's return, he rambled around by the creek until he found a few skeletal remains and two saddlebags next to the body. He quickly opened the bags, and saw the contents seemed to be gold ore. Thrilled at the thought of being rich, his mind wandered to a grand life awaiting him. "Should I take the gold and leave while Miss Retha is gone?" he thought. He loaded the saddlebags onto his mount, but before he could climb into the saddle, Retha rode up behind him.

"Where are you going, you old fool?" she laughed. "And where did you get those saddlebags?"

"I wasn't going to leave you, Miss Retha, but I found a fortune in gold in these."

"Yeah? Well, let me see, Slick," she said, grabbing one of the bags from Harry's horse. She burst into laughter as she dumped the contents on the ground.

"What the hell are you doing, Miss Retha? It's gold!"

"It's fool's gold, you ol' goat. You know I am smarter than you, and I know the difference. Now skin these rabbits and I'll cook 'em."

"Yes, Miss Retha, but I wasn't going to leave you."

"You better hurry up! Those wolves from hell smell them raw rabbits, they'd make short work out of a fat boy like you!"

"What wolves from hell?" Harry stuttered.

"You know the ones that guard the 'Echo of the Moon?' You mean you never heard of that?" Retha retorted.

"Yeah. But I always thought it was just a story! You mean they're real?" Harry said, shaking. He remembered the skeleton he'd seen.

"Yeah," whispered Retha. "And they've got a lot of ol' boys like you."

It wasn't long after they had their rabbit supper that they started bedding down for the night. Pretending to be asleep, Retha was watching Harry all the while as he propped himself up against a small tree with his six-shooter ready for action. She laughed to herself and gazed up at the celestial light show in the sky. Suddenly, a strange feeling of *déjà vu* swept over her. As she looked at her surroundings it seemed like everything was somehow familiar. It was unsettling, and it took some time for her to fall asleep.

The following morning Retha was up at sunrise to see Harry still sitting, but sound asleep and snoring. His gun had slipped into the soft sand and lay halfway buried. She nudged him with her boot, and he came wobbling to his feet.

"Damn, woman, you scared the daylights out of me! It's a wonder you didn't get shot," he yelled.

"Shot?" Retha laughed, "Why, that old gun of yours is full of sand, and anyway you're not quick enough to shoot me." She turned on her heel and walked briskly away. "I want to get to the west hills of this valley by noon, so get your ass on your horse and let's go. I saw some tracks yesterday around the bend a few hundred yards from here. I need to check it out, but I also noticed some smoke by the hills to the west. I think we better look."

The two had ridden for a few hours northwest of the creek when Retha noticed the frame of what used to be a dwelling. The charred remains of a settler's cabin were outlined in the white sand. "This is not what caused the smoke I saw," she mused. "That was a little farther north of here."

"Look at all those arrows, Retha! Something bad has happened here, but I think it was probably a long time ago."

Retha dismounted and walked slowly to three stick crosses she noticed in the rubble. She felt sadness as she kneeled and shook her head slowly. "These arrows are Pawnee," she said as she stared with disbelief. "I didn't think they roamed this far northwest; their territory is farther east. I wonder who buried these poor folks? It was probably somebody just passing through, I guess."

She shook her head as if to clear it. "I'm getting this strange feeling I've been here before and said these exact words. Something just don't seem right about this whole thing."

She sighed. "Slick Harry, you better head back to the herd and tell Nate and Pete what we've found so far. It will be three days by the time you get back and I told Nate that we would report every three days. Ya hear me?"

"Well, you think I ought to just leave you here alone, Miss Retha? These parts are a might dangerous, if you ask me!"

"Harry, it's about twenty miles, I figure, back to the herd, so you better get started early as you can come morning. As for me being alone, hell, I was alone for a long time before you came along. It's hell when more than half of your life is missing, and you don't have a clue as to what or where it was. I'll be fine, Harry – you just do your job for Triple A."

Harry slumped in his saddle. He knew there was no winning this. Looking down and tipping his hat back in disappointment, he just answered, "Yes, ma'am."

## The following morning

The morning sun was just breaking the horizon over the hills when Slick Harry bid Retha farewell and started his journey back to the herd. Retha didn't say much as Harry left, but only tipped her hat. He repeated his goodbye several times trying to get a response, to no avail.

"I'll be riding north to the west side of the valley, Harry. That's where you'll find me when you come back."

As she turned from Harry, she spoke quietly to herself. "I never say goodbyes. It's just not what I do."

Harry watched for a few minutes as Retha's horse slowly ambled away from him. Then he turned his mount, shook his head, and headed south.

He had gone about two miles when he noticed smoke across the barren landscape, below one of the peaks. He thought he had better check it out before continuing. In a small wash several feet deep, he dismounted and led his horse down inside. The wash gradually ran up to a rocky peak in one of the highest hills. He spotted several rattlesnakes and proceeded very carefully. Then he stumbled upon a derelict makeshift campsite. As he surveyed the rubble and ragged old tarp-covered dwelling protruding from the wall of the wash, he heard something behind him and whirled around. The stock end of a buffalo rifle crashed into his face. With blood streaming from his face and mouth, Harry dropped to the ground. Another blow to the back of his head sent him face first into the sand.

Harry regained consciousness after a while to find himself tied to an old tree stump in a sitting position. An old man with ragged clothes and a scraggly white beard stood in front of him laughing. Harry was still regaining his senses when he realized most of his front teeth were gone. His head intensely pounding from the blow to the back of his head, he had a tough time speaking.

The old man was still laughing, though it sounded more like an evil, maniacal screech. "Why, it seems I caught myself a thief, don't it?" he shrilled. "So, you thought you'd steal my dead brother's goods, huh, mister? You know I just skinned a man a few days ago for doing this same damn thing."

"Mister, I'm not a thief," Harry pleaded. "I'm a scout for a cattle drive, and I wasn't meaning no harm, and I wasn't going to steal anything, mister. Just, please, let me go and I'll never come this way again, I promise."

Harry spent an hour or so trying to convince the old man to free him, to no avail. The old man just kept rummaging around his supposed brother's campsite, singing and mumbling things that Harry could not understand.

"Ahh, so you're a rich cattleman, huh? I hate cowboys, but I can use you to work for me, up there by the old Goat Head Rock. You see, the last four hands I had all acted like they were sorry, too, but now they're buried over yonder by the bluff. That is, if you ever had a mind to talk to 'em."

Harry was very aware by now that the old man was crazy, and if he didn't do everything he could to placate him, he would surely be killed. The old man had stacked what Retha called fool's gold at least eight feet high up the wash a short distance away. Harry could see another campsite up the wash by the glittering pile.

Slick Harry had been tied to the old stump all day in the hot sun without water or food, and now he was glad to see the sun sink in the western sky. He had asked the old man for water several times, but the old man would just laugh and tell him to shut his mouth. As the sun was setting, the old man waddled down the canyon to where Harry's horse was tied. Harry heard a loud shot from a buffalo gun and realized the old man had just killed his horse. It wasn't long before the old man came back with some bloody horse meat. Harry hung his head in sorrow. The horse he had ridden for many years, the horse that had often served as his best friend, was dead.

After the sun set, the snakes from the rocks started to emerge from their dens. Harry realized with horror that the snakes were everywhere. This must be the place that Nate and Pete had talked about. He used his feet to kick dust at the deadly slithering reptiles and stayed awake most of the night, dozing off just a few minutes at a time.

When sunrise arrived, he had just dozed off when the old man poured some water over his hair and bloodstained face.

"I'll give you some water every time you bring back a bag of gold ore from the Goat Head Rock," he chuckled. "You should have had supper with me last night, cattleman – I had some real good horse liver."

Harry couldn't hold his anger and cursed the old man. That didn't go over too well, and the old man grabbed his hair, cutting off a piece of his scalp. Harry screamed in pain as he begged for forgiveness.

The crazed old man seemed to feed off the pain he inflicted. He pitched Harry some sacks and ordered him to go to the top of the wash to the large rock and gather the gold he had mined. Harry dared not say it was fool's gold.

The old man cut the bindings on Harry's hands, but not before he hobbled his feet. "Now you remember, cattleman, I've got this here buffalo gun aimed right at your ugly face and if I see you shirking, I blow it off, you hear?"

With just a slight nod, Harry began to scale the rocks. Many trips were made up and down the steep hillside before the sun finally began setting. Harry's hands and knees were seeping blood, and his trousers were shredded from the jagged rocks. As soon as he finished the last trip down, the old man shoved the barrel of the Hawkins buffalo gun to Harry's head and tied him back to the stump.

His captor had an iron pot boiling over a fire. Harry noticed him putting a couple of dead rattlesnakes in it. But while the man was preoccupied, Harry began working the rawhide behind his back until he eventually got a little slack in it. He had found the source of the old man's water at the Goat Head Rock, and he'd gorged himself with the cool liquid. Now, as he rested, he slowly began to get his strength back. As his head cleared, he devised a plan to be free. Very slowly working his hand free, he sat patiently and watched as the crazed old prospector shuffled around the camp. The old man took a snake from the pot and cut a portion of it off with the skin still attached. Hobbling to the tree stump, he forced it into Harry's mouth. Harry, figuring this was his only chance, grabbed the old man by the legs and struck him in the head with a rock. It knocked the old man unconscious, and Harry quickly made his way to the buffalo gun. He picked up the gun, placed it to the old man's head, and pulled the trigger.

"Now, you old bastard, I don't have any teeth and you don't have any damn head!" he yelled. Suddenly Harry felt a stinging in his right leg. A large rattlesnake was hanging by its fangs just below his knee. He grabbed the viper and slung it into the brush. The snake had bitten him in the back of his leg in a place he couldn't reach. Desperately looking around, Harry spotted the old man's mule by the side of the hill and pulled himself to it. The mule was very gentle and allowed the exhausted scout to mount him. Harry thought his best chance of survival was to head back in the direction of where he'd left Retha, but his mind was beginning to fail him. He hung onto the mule as long as he could, but finally succumbed to the poison and fell into the hot sand. The mule slowly walked away into the moonless night.

# CHAPTER 3

**Three days later, back to the herd**

Charles, who was not used to riding, was taking a break in the cook's wagon, trying to heal his sore bottom, when Nate rode to the side of the prairie schooner.

"How's the raw ass doing, boss?" he smiled.

"Well, it's doing a little better day by day, I guess. I ought to fire you, Nate! If I didn't love you like a brother I would," he said, grinning ruefully. "Where is that Carl, anyway? He's the one picked out that horse, ol' Sachi – that's the meanest damn horse I ever seen. He starts stamping his feet and if you don't watch him close, why, he'll bite a plug out of you somewhere! I'm going to skin that boy when I see him, nephew or not."

"Well," Nate nodded his head southward, "you won't have to wait long, boss, 'cause there he comes."

Carl, Joe's oldest son, was quite a man now. Quicky picking up the cowboy skills, he had developed a way of carrying himself unlike the rest of the hands. He had seen a photo of Bill Hickock in a saloon in Abilene and he so much liked it he mimicked the style. His hair grew long, and he kept it in a ponytail. He clad himself in a cowhide jacket that resembled those he'd seen in the photos of the wild west show. He had become a very cunning individual, and funny, but when crossed he was quick to lose his temper. Some of the ranch hands gave him the nickname of Quick Fuse. He had a forty-four that had been left to him by O.C. Armstrong, his grandfather, and he was quickly getting exceptionally good with it. Every day he would ride away from the herd to practice – far enough not to spook them – and fire off a few rounds. At knife throwing there was no better, as he had been taught at an incredibly early age by his idol Johnny One Horn.

Johnny was missed very much as a leader at the Triple A, and Carl planned to go and visit him one day. When Johnny had left to help his people in the Mississippi swamp where he was born, he had left Carl his horse Coattail. The offspring of that elegant horse, Carl had named Corky, and Corky had soon become his ride. He was fast as the wind and, like Coattail, his trait was to bite someone who wasn't looking if they didn't know him. Sachi, the horse picked by Carl to be Charles' mount, was also an offspring of Coattail. Both were very elegant paints that had a strut to their walk, and both were amazingly fast.

In a minute or so Carl on Corky streaked up beside the schooner.

"I saw some tracks by the east hills – makes me think we're being watched by somebody. I thought at first it might be a Sioux scouting or hunting party, but then I looked closer at the tracks and realized they had shoes. Might have been just traveling settlers, or bandits; hard to say."

"Anybody seen Slick Harry? He was due back two days ago, wasn't he, Carl?" Charles looked worried.

Carl tipped his hat back. "I've been thinking the same thing myself. I think I'll send Pete to try and find him and Retha, or what happened to them. Something's not right about this."

Nate wheeled his horse around. "I'll ride over and talk to Pete, but he's probably already thinking the same thing."

## Two hours later

When Nate found Jose at the front of the herd, Jose informed him that Pete had already taken it upon himself to search for Retha and Slick Harry. Pete was already about four hours ahead of the herd.

"I wish somebody would tell me what's going on once in a while, Jose! Hell, I am the boss." Nate paused. "I think."

"Well, boss, I was going to come and tell you, but I was busy rounding up a few strays; besides, he's a boss too, as far as I've been told. I got my job to do, and he's got his. That's the way I look at it."

Nate smiled. "I know, Jose, and you're damn good at it. Never mind me. I was just blowing off steam."

"Nate, I heard some stories in Eula May's saloon that there was a crazy man that would take shots at anybody that passed the old Goat Head Rock. I sure hope they didn't go close to there. They called him Crazy Slim Dick, and he's as crazy as a bed bug, they said."

"Does Pete know about this crazy man, Jose? I sure don't want anything to happen to him. I won't ask how that ol' boy got his name."

"Yes, we talked about him this morning. He knows, and he will be watching for sure," Jose answered.

"Good," Nate nodded. "I know Pete can take good care of himself. Now let's get back to gathering up them strays."

## Searching

Pete was weary in the saddle when he saw some green trees ahead and thought there might be a chance for water and a campsite. Arriving there, he found a tribesman dressed in white man's clothing roasting a rabbit over a native-style fire pit. The man stood and gave the greeting sign from his chest.

Pete felt comfortable to ride on in and dismounted. "Howdy, my friend; seems like you got you a good supper there," he said. "I've been riding most of the day – do you mind if I make me a camp? I'll move farther down the creek if you like." Not receiving an answer, Pete mumbled some hard-to-find words dug from his limited knowledge of the native language, but he noticed the man started to laugh. "I'm not very good at this, but you can see that," he explained.

"No worry," the man laughed. "I speak your language very well. Sit, my friend, and share the rabbit," he smiled as he gestured toward a large rock. "They call me Sad Hank. I was a scout for the army until they decided to hang me. I escaped from their fort in the middle of the night. Don't worry, I didn't ever hurt anybody, but when they had no more use for me, they decided to hang me. It's been about nine seasons that I've been hiding, but I don't think they are looking for me anymore."

"Really?" Pete replied. "That's dirty. I never heard anything like that. That's really low down. By the way, name's Pete." After he had settled himself on the rock, Pete looked up. "Where did you scout, Sad Hank, and for how long?"

"I'm from the Oglala Sioux and our home was in the north. It was a little south of the Black Hills, but not anymore. The white leader Grant decided to take it from us because of the yellow iron that was there. I left and came here after our people went farther north. I stayed with them for a while, but a Crow scout told them where I was, and I left and came here only to find the Sioux that once were here had all gone farther north also."

"You can scout for the herd, Sad Hank, if you want to. We need a few people that know the land here. We will pay you good and you'll like the people."

"Well, you got a deal, Peter," Hank agreed.

"The name is Pete, Hank, not Peter. I can't stand the

name Peter."

"OK," laughed Sad Hank, "You got a deal, Pete."

"I see you've got a pack mule. We need a few of those around the Triple A, too" jested Pete.

"Oh, he is not mine. I believe he belongs to ol' Slim Dick. He lives across the valley by Goat Head Rock. That man has been possessed by evil spirits. I knew his brother – he took care of ol' Slim Dick for a long time, but I think he died. He got bit by one of those buzzing snakes. At certain times in the dry season the mice in the valley go after the water that comes from under the Goat Head Rock. That brings the snakes, then they are gone when the season is over. I was thinking something must have happened to ol' Slim Dick. He always kept that mule close to him."

"How far is this Goat Head Rock, Hank? If it's not too far, shouldn't we ride over and see? I'm looking for two scouts of ours and we may find some answers there."

"Was one of your scouts a woman, Pete? I saw a woman about a day's ride north of here. She camped by a burned-out cabin. She offered me a cup of coffee and we talked for a few minutes. She was very wary of me and sat cross-legged, with her rifle cocked and ready on her lap. I was there for just a few minutes, but I didn't see anybody else. Kind of a big woman, but I thought she was pretty, dressed like she was. She dresses like a Sioux woman, but with cowhide pants."

"Yep, that's the Coyote Woman for sure. I kind of feel sorry for her – she was kicked in the head by a buffalo bull and hasn't had any memory of who she is for years now."

## The morning

When sunrise arrived the two were up and drank some coffee Pete had in his poke. Then they saddled up and rode across the valley. After about four hours, they arrived at Goat Head Rock. They came to the wash and started climbing toward the peak. When they arrived at the campsite, they found Slim Dick lying face down in some cactus spurs. Most of his head was missing and it looked like coyotes had gorged on him as well.

"He was shot in the head with that same buffalo gun that's lying beside him," Pete said, shaking his head. "Damn, someone wanted him dead for sure."

They spent the next half hour covering up ol' Slim Dick in a makeshift grave in the hard rocky ground. Then Sad Hank went above the wash and found the mule tracks heading south.

"If we follow these tracks, Pete, I'm sure we'll find your other scout someplace between here and the herd."

They rode, leading the mule, for a couple of hours following the tracks. Then they saw a few buzzards circling and landing in a gulch ahead. When they got there, they found the body of Slick Harry decomposing in the hot sun. In horror, they looked at the swollen carcass, and could readily deduce what abuse he had endured.

"Look at that leg, Sad Hank. It's twice the size of his other one. And it looks like part of his scalp is missing. This man has been tortured for days! I bet it was him that killed ol' Slim Dick before he died."

"You're probably right, Pete. No Indian did that to his scalp. That's not our way. Slim Dick did this – his brother often talked about how Dick loved to inflict pain on people and loved to see them suffer."

They buried Slick Harry beside a small tree by the west hills. Before burying Harry, Pete had removed a leather string and a small wooden cross from Harry's neck. He draped it around the stick cross they used to mark his grave.

Then Pete decided they would return to the herd and he could introduce Nate and the boys to their new scout. Along the way Sad Hank told Pete to be wary of some bandits he had been watching. The murderous and notorious Rico gang had robbed travelers in the valley for several years.

## Back at the Herd

When they met up with the herd, Nate and Carl were riding point. The two galloped out to meet Pete and the stranger.

"Boys," Pete explained, "this is Sad Hank. I hired him to be our new scout. He knows the valley and we need that. He used to be a scout for the army, at least before they decided to hang him."

"Hang him?" laughed Carl. "Boy, that's really what we need now, don't you think?"

"Well," Pete chuckled, "it's a long story, and I'll tell it later. But for now, I've got some bad news about ol' Slick Harry. We found him dead south of Goat Head Rock. He suffered terrible days of torture from what we think was that crazy man they called Slim Dick. It was an awful sight."

Carl sat back in his saddle, wiping his brow in disbelief. "Well, let's find that Slim Dick and hang him from the nearest tree," scowled Carl.

"No need for that. We buried him too. We think Harry killed ol' Dick and escaped, but it looked like a rattler got Harry, and he didn't get very far. It was a bad deal all the way around. Sad Hank here said he ran into Retha about a half day's ride north of Goat Head Rock and she was fine. It's clear she knew nothing about what went on."

After the other men had taken a moment to digest this news, Pete exchanged looks with Hank, then took a deep breath. "That's not the only problem, boys. Hank here says there's a bad bunch of outlaws that's probably watching the herd right now."

Sad Hank nodded in affirmation. "They are called the Rico gang. I think there's six men. They probably already stole some of your cattle and you didn't even notice.

They're cunning and work in the dark. Their camp is over those hills," he gestured in the direction. "They have a smuggler's den with cabins and a big corral. I stumbled on it one time by accident." He shook his head. "They are very evil men. They kidnap women and take them there, and they'll kill at the drop of your hat."

Carl sucked in his breath. "I saw some tracks by those hills, and I knew they were suspicious. We better let all the men know that we've got some bandits on the prowl. Sounds like this is a pretty bad bunch."

Nate stared at the hills for a few seconds. "Pete, you and Sad Hank see what you can find out. Don't let them see you! You might not live if they do, from what we've heard."

~ ~ ~

Retha had decided to wait for Slick Harry's return and had kept a fire burning to mark her location. But now a few days had gone by without a sign of him, so she decided to backtrack. As she traveled back toward the herd, she passed the burned-out cabin and made her way to Goat Head Rock. There in the wash she found the grave of Slim Dick. She could tell the disturbed sand was recent and found the tracks of Sad Hank and Pete.

"I wonder if these are people from the Triple A," she wondered. "How strange."

She still had the strange feeling of *déjà vu* skipping through her mind and suspected something terrible must have happened. She followed the tracks for a couple of miles and found the grave of Slick Harry. When she saw the wooden cross hanging from the marker, she knew it was her old friend Harry. Slowly, she dismounted, gazing at the makeshift grave as she reminisced. At last, she mounted her horse and sadly rode away.

# CHAPTER 4

Later that afternoon Retha arrived back with the herd. Around the nightly campfire she told the hands what she'd seen. She had also seen some suspicious tracks from time to time in her travels. Carl informed her of what Sad Hank had said about the Rico gang and all their foul deeds.

Retha was disturbed by the thought that the gang had kidnapped young girls from wagons traveling through the valley. Sleep wouldn't come that night. So, in the middle of the night, she decided to investigate the whereabouts of the gang. She knew Pete, along with the new Sioux guide, was ahead somewhere, but she was determined to make sure this evil was stopped.

The following morning Nate went to the place she had camped, only to find her gone. Shaking his head, he thought, "Man, we've got an undisciplined bunch of hands." He went in search of Jose.

Jose had seen Retha ride off into the night, but he had assumed she was scouting the herd.

"Jose, you were on night watch – did you know Retha left?"

"Yes, Mr. Nate, I sure did. She rode northwest. I didn't talk to her, though. She rode right past me, but never said a word. Wherever she was going, she wanted to get there fast."

"Damn! Now I don't have a scout one! I was going to send her back north," Nate said, shaking his head.

"Another thing, boss," Jose continued. "I saw some tracks in the back of the herd, and they also led northwest. Some were cattle, but several of them were horses with shoes."

"Then they have already taken some of our cattle," Nate spat. "We can't put up with rustlers, but all of us can't leave in pursuit – we've got to take care of what's here. We all need to start watching the herd around the clock, and just getting our rest a couple of hours at a time. Hopefully we can catch some of these bastards."

He spurred his horse back to the main camp and shared the news with Carl. "Carl, you spread the men around the herd and at the first sight of trouble, fire a shot and the rest of us will come running. That goes for everybody, so when night falls, be on the watch. Remember, this is a bad bunch, so everybody has to be careful."

stay in the ranch's comfort zone.

~ ~ ~

Retha had ridden for several hours, scanning the hills to the northeast. The wind had picked up and she could hear the rumble of thunder to the west. Dry lightning was putting on a ghostly show in the western sky. This frequently happened when the clouds forming to the west built up in the mountains. They usually seemed to dissipate without leaving any rain, so she wasn't too concerned. But in the flashes of lightning, she noticed a lone rider awfully close to her on the hillside below her. Quickly, she dismounted and led her horse back below the hilltop. Then she watched as the rider passed by. She figured she would follow him without being seen. If he was one of the Rico gang, he would lead her straight to their camp.

It did not take long before she was on a hilltop

overlooking a small valley where she saw several cabins. The camp had a large corral with what looked like about twenty cattle inside. She rode as close to the camp as she dared and dismounted. Her horse was nervous from the sound of coyotes howling in the distance. From her vantage point, she could see four men standing around a campfire sharing a bottle of whisky. Beside them cowered what looked like a young girl who was only half-dressed, with her clothes torn on her knees. Her hands were bound behind her, and the men seemed to be mocking her. Retha had to turn away to keep from responding.

Before she reached her horse, though, the horse panicked, broke the tie, and fled into the darkness. Retha searched the hills as the lightning flickered, but could not locate her mount. What she didn't realize was that the wind had carried the sound of the whinnying horse and got the attention of one of the bandits at the camp. He slipped through the dark using the flickering lightning to light his way, and eased through the cover of brush until he was right behind her. Armed with a ten-gauge shotgun, he shouted for her to stand very still. He quickly disarmed her of her forty-four and buffalo gun. Tying her hands behind her, he poked her continuously with the barrel of his gun, marching her down into the camp.

## Green Tree Creek

Pete and Sad Hank had camped at what Sad Hank called Green Tree Creek. Pete had been there before, along with Retha and Slick Harry, but never knew what it was called. In the early hours of the morning, coyotes had also spooked their horses and the mule. They searched the area around the creek but did not find even as much as a track. At dawn hard winds and smothering dust filled the air. Sad Hank tried to scan the hills, but visibility was extremely limited.

"There is nothing we can do, Pete, but stay near the

water until this storm blows over. If we leave now, we will only get lost. We have to wait until it stops, then we can fill our canteens and walk south toward the herd. I smell smoke also. The lightning must have started a prairie fire. I sure hope this fire blows away from the herd."

Pete had to agree. By noon, the west winds had settled down, and Pete and Hank watched the prairie fire as the winds moved it slowly northwest across the valley. "Maybe we should get to the center of the valley and wait. The herd should show up by late afternoon."

Hank nodded, and the two set off on foot.

"Looks like those cattle won't have any grass for a day or two. I remember from the last drive, there was a creek with good water about five hours north of here. I'm hoping that prairie fire will burn out. I remember there's a dry lakebed that is barren of vegetation on this side of the creek and nothing can burn there," Pete speculated.

"Yes, I know the place well. It is called Cricket Creek – not too big and it always seems to have water. "Hank turned and gazed westward. "Moon Rock is among those mountains in the west."

"I've heard so much of this Moon Rock. Exactly what is it? Hank, have you ever been there?"

"Yes. One day there was a great storm, and I was looking for shelter. I came to a rocky draw and got under an overhang to escape from the lightning. I finally managed to build a fire as the sun was setting. I could see the overhang had been used for shelter for a long, long time. Somebody must have lived there once. They had made rock dwellings in the back of it. Rocks had been placed together to form shelters. My people called these cliff dwellers. But these people have been gone for many moons, or seasons. It is said the dwellings are haunted and that bad luck befalls anybody that disturbs them. I didn't sleep much that night with the storm and the wolves wailing. They were terrifying, with glowing red eyes. I had no gun but threw flaming pieces of sagebrush at them." He wiped his brow as he recalled the experience. "I have never seen such fierce looking animals. It seemed they were possessed by evil spirits."

"According to the stories ol' Earl Stockman used to tell; the place was loaded with gold. Did you see any gold?" Pete questioned eagerly.

"No, but I never look for gold, because the legends say it's cursed. This Stockman you talk about, I knew him from the old days. He was a shrewd ridge runner. Nobody would want to cross him. Tell me, is he still alive, my friend?"

"No, he's not, I'm sad to say, but he spent his final years entertaining all of us with his stories. He freed many of the girls that now live at the Triple A from Mexican bandits and Comancheros."

"This Rico gang is the same," frowned Hank. "It is said that Rico Garza and Earl got into a fight one time and Earl cut off his right ear and one of his fingers. He left Rico to die here in this same valley, but Rico survived."

"I don't doubt that for a second, Hank. Ol' Earl was one tough mountain man. He was as tough as anyone I ever saw." Pete paused a moment, thinking about Earl. But then he brought his thoughts back to the stories about riches that he'd heard. "Maybe you could show me where this place is, Sad Hank. I don't believe in spooks, and I could sure use some of that gold."

"Well, I can point to it, Pete, but I promised the spirits I would never return if they let me live. Maybe when we get there, I will point you in the right direction, but as for now I think we'd better find that herd."

"Yeah, I know you're right, Hank," smiled Pete, "even though I have to admit that the gold is mighty tempting!"

## A few hours later

Pete and Sad Hank joined the herd in late afternoon and

told everyone about their failed adventure.

"Well, we thought something bad might have happened when Jose found your horses and the mule a mile or so north of here," Nate said. "Did you see Retha anywhere? She left in the middle of the night – probably on some crazy mission to find the Rico gang. I swear I don't know how that woman has made it this long."

"Nope, sure didn't, but we had no idea. She never showed up at Green Tree Creek. But I know one thing – if she was still in the coyote skinning business, she could make a fortune by that creek," Pete answered, shaking his head.

"Well, you men go get your horses and put a few provisions on the mule. Carl and I are going to join you and Hank and go after those rustlers! If we're lucky, we might get Retha back, if she's still alive."

Nate placed the ranch hands on high alert, and a twenty-four-hour watch. The four men would leave at dusk, being careful they were not spotted in the half-moon light. Sad Hank knew the general vicinity of the Rico camp and would lead the way.

It was bright for a new moon, and fluffy clouds created large shadows that seemed to creep across the valley landscape. The sound of crickets and the wailing of coyotes filled the air as they approached the hill and Green Tree Creek. Hank led them above the creek and followed the ridge he knew well. In an hour or so they reached the hilltop overlooking the Rico camp.

In the dim light of a campfire, they could see Retha tied to a post in the center of the camp. It was clear that only a couple of the gang members were in the camp. They had stripped Retha of her clothing and were mauling her. Nate, using his buffalo gun, sighted in on the one closest to Retha. The gun rumbled down the small canyon like thunder as the bandit's head exploded. Pete also fired, and the other fell like a rock, stone dead.

"Damn, you boys never let me get a shot in, but I tell you one thing, that was some damn good shooting, boys! Hell, that must have been at least three hundred yards! Holy moly." Carl said in amazement.

Nate, tipping his hat back, rubbed his forehead. "I hate killing a man, but I don't mind killing a rat, so I'm not going to let myself feel bad about this. Damn, I hate this kind of thing." He adjusted his hat and kicked his horse. "Now let's get down there and cut Retha free. There is no telling what we'll find in those cabins."

When they arrived at the camp Carl removed the gag from Retha's mouth.

"Untie my damn hands," she yelled. "One of you get my clothes – they're probably on the ground somewhere around here."

"Yes, ma'am," Carl said, though he couldn't keep from staring.

"Carl, stop your gawking, for Pete's sake. Ain't you never saw a woman before?"

"Well, sorry, Miss Retha, not a real one," he replied as he gathered her clothing from the ground.

Pete and Nate turned their heads away in the dim moonlight to hide their smiles. Sad Hank just tipped his hat back and walked towards the cabins. Inside he found four young girls, with their hands tied behind them and staked to the ground. Some had been beaten and one was unconscious. He slowly turned and looked at Pete and Nate standing behind him in the doorway. "They're terrified," said Hank. "They think we're part of the Rico gang."

Retha had dressed and pushed the men out of her way as she untied the girls. "There are still four of those bastards, and I'm going to kill them all," she stormed.

"Where are they, Retha?" frowned Pete.

"I'm surprised you didn't run into them on your way here, Pete. They left about sunset to steal some more of your cattle. I've never saw such a slimy bunch – they all deserve to be dead."

Her voice grew suddenly tender as she turned back to the girls. "These babies have been here a long time. They have been beaten, raped, tortured and starved by those slimy bastards. We need to get them somewhere safe."

"What about this Rico Garza? Retha, did you see him?"

"I'm not sure. It was dark, and I didn't ever get a good look at him. They gagged me and most of the time they had a blindfold on me. But I heard one giving orders so I guess that must have been him."

"Well, they are going to get a hell of a surprise when they get back." Pete surveyed the camp, then continued with his plan. "Retha, we'll ready that wagon over there, and you take these girls and get as far away from here as you can. Go south and we will find you." Meanwhile, we are going to arrange a little homecoming party for those yahoos."

After the wagon was safely out of the camp, Nate continued to scan the moonlit hilltops as he watched Retha and the girls move slowly down the hill.

Nate suspected that there would be a large number of cattle spread out around the rustlers. He also figured they would be drinking whisky in celebration of their spoils. He stationed Sad Hank on the hilltop to watch for the approaching bandits and cattle. Hank would make the sound of the night hawk three times to alert the Triple A crew. Pete would be hiding in the cabin where the girls had been imprisoned, and Carl and Nate beside the corral. Sad Hank could fire from the hilltop. If all went well, it would all be over in a few minutes.

A few minutes after his crew was in place, Nate heard the screeching of three night hawks. He watched the first rider open the corral as two others herded what looked to be about ten cows. Nate and his men didn't make a sound, but as soon as the lead rider dismounted, he must have sensed something was different. He quickly drew his gun and walked toward the cabin. Then he stopped a few feet from the cabin door, turned back and mounted his horse. As he spurred his mount into a gallop, Nate fired his ten-gauge shotgun. The rider sank in the saddle but managed to keep riding. The three other gang members fired their guns blindly into the night. One ran into the cabin where Pete was silently waiting, and Pete quickly disposed of the outlaw with his forty-four.

Carl had quietly come up behind the two that were left and instructed them to throw their weapons to the ground. They quicky complied, begging for mercy.

Their pleas were not acknowledged by Nate as he threw two ropes over a lone oak tree that stood by one of the old cabins. The two bandits changed their humble attitudes and began spitting and cursing Carl and Nate. But Nate quickly tied them together and placed nooses around their necks. He motioned for Carl to ride to his side, and the two lifted the bandits' feet from the ground. Hanging about two feet off the ground, it wasn't too long before the struggling outlaws were dead. The sun was rising as Pete broke a couple of boards from one of the buildings and sketched the words, "Cattle Thieves and Child Killers," and tied the boards to the bodies.

After the ordeal was over, Pete and Carl rode in search of Retha and the young girls, while Sad Hank and Nate drove the cattle back to the Triple A herd.

Retha and the girls had made their way to Green Tree Creek, and she was trying to comfort them the best she could. Some could speak a little broken English, but the oldest, a yellow-haired girl that was in shock, was rocking back and forth and staring at the barren sand.

The sun was high by the time Carl and Pete arrived, and the morning air was quickly warming. The girls, still shaken from their imprisonment, panicked when they saw the men coming. It took a while for Retha and the gentle men to calm them down.

"Any of them hurt, Retha?" asked Carl.

"No, just beaten up mentally, as far as I can tell. But the blonde one must have had one hell of an ordeal. She won't talk and just keeps staring at the ground. There's no telling what she went through or for how long."

"Do any of them say where they came from?" Pete wondered.

"No, they can't speak much English. They're mostly Pawnee, except the blonde. If she ever talks, it will be one hell of a story."

Pete mounted his horse. "Carl, why don't you stay here, and I'll get another wagon from Jose. I should be back in a couple of hours. The herd's not too far in the distance – I can see the dust from here."

## Two hours later

Pete found the herd and instructed Jose to load a wagon with enough supplies to make the journey back to the Triple A. There would be plenty of help from Cindy and the other women to take care of the grief-stricken girls, and there was no way they could travel with the herd; it was just too rough.

After Jose turned to this task, Pete went to look for Charles so he could update him about what had happened.

Charles, riding the rear of the herd, saw Jose loading the wagon and had headed over to meet him when Pete rode up beside him. Pete explained that they were sending the girls they had rescued back to the Triple A.

Charles agreed that was a good call. "Send Carl with Retha. He can catch up to us later, and Retha can too, if she chooses. Carl's good with kids and he can be a lot of help to Retha."

"Yeah," Pete nodded. "It was good that Carl helped rescue them – they seemed to know he was one of the good guys right away."

"Send them from Green Tree Creek directly back to the Triple A, Pete. Have Jose take a horse for the trip back."

When Jose and Pete arrived back at Green Tree Creek with the wagon, they told Carl and Retha of Charles' decision to send them to the Triple A with the rescued girls. Retha agreed quickly, but Carl balked at the idea. Pete took a while to convince him that it was the right thing to do.

Carl, shaking his head in disappointment, finally agreed. "Well, give Uncle Charles a message that I'm coming back just as soon as I see they are safely there," he sighed.

Jose looked at Carl and smiled. "I think he already knows, Carl. It will be sunset in a few hours so we all better be on our way as soon as we can get these kids in the wagon."

"We might have to do some talking before we get that one in the wagon," Carl remarked, pointing at the blonde girl and shaking his head. "Her mind is a thousand miles away."

When they tried talking to the girl, she would not even look at them, but continued to sit on the ground, swaying back and forth.

Finally, Pete just picked up her frail body from the ground and carried her to the wagon. The girl looked at him and finally spoke. "Are you taking me home, Daddy?" she whimpered.

Pete, being a tough man, but with a tender heart, replied softly, "Yes I am, sweetheart." Tears running down his cheeks, he gently placed her in the wagon and covered her with a blanket. Then he pointed to Retha and said, "This nice lady is taking you home, honey, but don't worry, I'll be there soon."

Retha was watching sadly, wiping the tears from her eyes. She was almost overwhelmed by sorrow burning deep in her throat. Pete mounted his horse and noticed that Carl was walking his horse away from the group. He, too, was very touched by the scene he had just witnessed.

"Damn this country," Carl said as he gazed across the valley. "That hurt."

Jose pulled his sombrero down to cover his face. "Well, my friend, it's time. See you soon, Miss Retha. God will watch over you."

Pete and Jose returned to the herd to look for Charles. That wasn't hard because Charles, anxious for their return, was far ahead of the herd and watching for them.

"What about those cattle thieves, Pete?" Charles asked.

"Well, boss, they were bad men, and we hung the ones we didn't shoot. One got away but he had a load of buckshot in his ass. I don't know if he'll make it or not – we didn't find a body. I kind of think it was their leader, Rico Garza, by the way he acted."

"Damn, I wish we had got that cutthroat bastard! Damn," frowned Charles, shaking his head and beating his fist into his hand.

"We need to track him down, boss. If he heals, after this, he'll just continue to rob and kill," Pete asserted. "And if he figures out who we are, we'll probably be on the top of his list."

"Well, you're right about that. You and Sad Hank should see if you can pick up his tracks. We sure don't want this man to get away. Get the supplies you need from the supply wagon and keep looking until you find him," instructed Charles. "Anybody that would do something like this needs to be on the end of a rope."

# CHAPTER 5

## Rico Garza

Rico Garza was suffering from the shotgun blast in his shoulder. He was barely able to stay on his horse as he headed south. Eventually he came upon a lone prairie schooner with a family, also heading south. The couple in the wagon had three young children. Rico rode to the wagon and asked the man driving for a drink of water.

The man, seeing that Rico was hurt, was quick to oblige. "Mister, that shoulder looks bad. What happened to you?" he asked. When Rico didn't answer right away, he continued," I'm Jake Barrow, and this is my family. We're heading to the Triple A ranch a couple of days south of here. I hear they're good people, and they have a lot of jobs there right now. We've been told they even have a school for the kids, and there's plenty of land to build on. My wife Julie, here, has been schooled in St. Louis and she'd love to be a teacher one day." Still not getting an answer to his original question, he pressed, "You never told me what happened to you, mister."

"Bandits," Rico whined, "they robbed me and shot me. They left me for dead, but I managed to find my horse and ride here. I was coming from Denver to see my kinfolks in Abilene when they attacked me. My name is Franco Riaz."

With Rico slumping in the saddle for show, the sympathetic travelers quickly loaded him in the back of the schooner and comforted him. Julie Barrow cleaned and bandaged his wounds, while Rico, an expert in deception, pretended to be unconscious.

The Barrows pampered Rico for three days until they arrived at the gates of the Triple A. They were amazed to see workers everywhere. The small community was booming, filled with tents and people. Joe had acquired at least thirty hands from Garden City and Abilene. Men, eager to work, were busy in every direction. The construction of two buildings was already completed, and four or more foundations were being laid out.

Joe and Cindy had been watching as the prairie schooner made its way into the thriving community. Now Joe rode to the schooner. "What brings you here, mister?"

Jake Barrow climbed down from the wagon and walked a few steps toward Joe. "My name is Jake Barrow, and I'm looking for work. This here's my wife, and those are our three children." He took his hat in his hand as he greeted Joe with a friendly grin. "We're also looking for a place to settle. That road west is just too much for my family. We came all the way from Missouri but turned back just south of Denver when we heard of the work and jobs here."

"Well, I'm Joe Armstrong, and I do need help, Mr. Barrow, depending on what you can do. As for settling, there is open land a few miles south of here." He gestured in an expansive circle. "But this here is all Triple A land. You can live or build here, but the land will always be ours. We were burned out awhile back, and, as you can see, we're in the midst of building back. You can park your wagon here. Now what was it you can do for us?"

"Well, I was a blacksmith in St. Joe, but I'm good with horses and I can build. I guess I could do just about anything you need me to do, Mr. Armstrong." As an afterthought, he added, "I need to tell you we have an injured man in the back of the wagon. He was attacked by outlaws, and he's hurt pretty bad."

Joe wheeled his horse around to the back of the wagon, reached down and pulled the blanket off of Rico. Rico acted as if he were unconscious, and Joe pitched the blanket back.

"Sorry, but we can't trust everybody we see, especially when they come in with gunshot wounds. Pull your wagon up to the second large building, The girls there are particularly good at taking care of things like this." Joe reached out to shake his hand. "I think you and your family will fit in very well with the people here. By the way, the job pays twenty-five a month, but if you're worth more than that, you'll get more. For now, though, that's all you'll get. You can start tomorrow. By the way, we have a herd heading north – did you run into them?"

"I did see them, but mostly only the dust rising from the valley floor. We followed the foot of the eastern hills. There was game there, especially jackrabbits."

"Jackrabbits, huh? My old friend Earl Stockman used to make a jackrabbit stew – as I remember, it was damn good." Joe turned his horse back toward the office. "Ok, Jake, when you get your family settled, find Tex Luna; he's out riding fences now but he should be back by sundown. Tell him I said he should find you some work. We gave him the name 'Tex' because he brought his family up from Texas to work here. He's a good man, but he might come on a little strong, so bear with him."

## The Triple A

Retha, Carl, and the girls arrived three days later. Carl was surprised at the work that had been done on rebuilding the Triple A. He rode in before the wagon on his horse, Corky, and dismounted. He motioned for one of the ranch hands to unharness the team and tend to them.

Retha led the girls into the large schoolhouse that had been converted into what looked to be an army bunkhouse. Cindy Armstrong and the other women all helped to get them comfortable. Yolanda, who had married Shorty, a long-time hand of the Triple A, and now a ranch supervisor, was helping Cindy run the facility. She was especially sympathetic to the abused girls, and was able to communicate with them as they settled in to the welcoming place.

Cindy and Yolanda had also made a place for the bandit Rico when he arrived, had cleaned him up and dressed him with some clean clothes before moving him to one of the two bunk houses that housed the hired hands. They'd had to shave his hair and beard to clean the pellet wounds from the shotgun blast. He was getting better, and Cindy thought he would be up and around in a few days. He was at his best behavior around the women and children, trying to win their approval. He teased the girls and made them laugh. Unaware of his true nature, the ladies on the ranch had taken a liking to the outlaw. But when he realized that Retha and Carl were back at the Triple A and that the same young girls that he and his cutthroat gang had abused were now being cared for by his benefactors, his behavior changed. Fearing they would see him, he kept out of their sight and pulled his hat over his eyes even when he was in the bunkhouse bed.

After seeing that the rescued girls were safe and being cared for at the Triple A, Retha left within hours. She had always been a loner, so nobody was surprised. It touched her heart to leave the girls, but she displayed little emotion when she left.

Carl had decided to spend the night at the ranch before returning to the herd. He found his mother Cindy inside the school building and hugged her. When he asked how everything was going, she explained that his father, Joe, had been working along with the new hired hands day and night trying to rebuild the once-thriving community.

"It's coming along very quickly," said Cindy. "Lots of new people are here, and this place is going to be quite a bit bigger than it used to be. Why don't you stay here and help your father, Carl? He's been so tired at night that he goes to sleep sitting in the old wooden chair."

"Well, I'd like to, but it looks to me like Shorty and Tex have it figured out. I would just be in the way. Besides, everything I build comes tumbling down in a few days, remember?" laughed Carl. "I love the cattle drive, and besides, I want to see this new land in Cheyenne Wells. I'm riding out first thing in the morning."

Cindy slowly dropped her head and sighed. She knew his determination was coming from the bloodline of O.C. and Joe. "I know, son – I wish I didn't, but I know," she said, hugging him. "Don't forget to say goodbye to Earl and James before you go. Your little brothers have really missed you."

Carl spent the afternoon sitting on the riverbank telling his brothers about his adventures. They were full of questions about the drive and the stories Carl was sharing.

The boys loved sitting on the benches by the river. At night, the place seemed magical as the sounds of night birds and crickets filled the air. This night the full moon lit the sky. They all loved the river and believed, as Johnny One Horn had taught them, that all the spirits play when the full moon lights the water. Johnny had taught them a lot about life's purpose, and it had heavily influenced their lives. Many fond memories crossed Carl's mind as he soaked in the beauty of the full moon reflected on the flowing water. This year the drought had affected the Arkansas River in a lot of ways, but the snow from the Rocky Mountains kept the river flowing. Even so, the lack of rain had caused the grass to dry and disappear.

The boys sat for hours reminiscing about their childhood. Finally, when the moon was high in the night sky, Carl said goodnight and goodbye as he would be leaving to join the cattle drive at first light. Earl and James had decided to sleep by the river's edge and Carl was nostalgic as he looked back at them. He smiled as he remembered growing up in this beautiful, serene place.

Rico noticed Carl coming into the bunkhouse and turned his back to him. He wasn't sure whether Carl had seen his face at the outlaw's hideout or not. Carl walked on through to his old spot, a small room in the back, and spent the night without even realizing the outlaw was there.

The early morning came quickly, and Carl left the ranch to join the herd.

# CHAPTER 6

**One week later**

Rico Garza had mostly recovered from his wounds, and, since he seemed to get along with the other hands, Joe Armstrong offered him a job riding fence. He continued to shave his head and beard. He hoped that the girls wouldn't recognize him because he looked vastly different. He had decided to gain the confidence of the Triple A community so he could search for the gold he had heard about from some of the bunkhouse hands. No one noticed anything unusual about him, and everyone was unaware of what they were letting into their innocent community.

Cindy and the women of the Triple A were much too busy dealing with the abused girls and the influx of new people to be wary of the people they didn't know. Rico gradually blended into the hustle and bustle of the crowd.

~ ~ ~

Retha, still enraged about what had happened to the young girls, was deep into her quest to find Rico Garza. She made her way back to the abandoned cabin used by the outlaws. She never considered that the madman might be at the Triple A at the same time she was. As she looked down on the place from the hill above, it occurred to her that this would be a good place to start a small ranch and farm. She had always wanted a place of her own, and this place was definitely up for grabs.

She planned to hide and see if the outlaw would return, and then she planned to kill him. She would hide her camp in the trees by Green Tree Creek and frequently run spot checks on the place to see if Rico showed his evil face. She felt that the outlaw would return after he recruited new gang members. Many times, she told herself that he may have been killed by the shotgun blast, but something always told her he was still alive.

Coyotes and wolves had feasted on the bodies of the outlaws that had been hanged only two feet off the ground, and their foul stench permeated the air. It was a gruesome sight and she had look away as she walked her horse to them and cut the ropes. Most of the bodies were gone below the waist already, and now that they were on the ground, the night scavengers would devour the rest in no time.

The feeling of *déjà vu* kept returning. With everything she did, it seemed she was just reliving her past. Now, as she made her way down the hills to Green Tree Creek, she felt as if someone or something was watching her.

## The Herd

Nate was back to performing his duties with the herd and was glad to see Charles finally turning back into the cowboy he had once been. The herd had made its way, slowly grazing, through the valley and had arrived at Cricket Creek. The grass was lush, and the fast-running creek was cold and clear.

"Man, oh man," exclaimed Charles, "I'm going to find out if anybody has claim or owns this place! Damn, Nate, this is kind of pretty, don't you think?"

"Sure is, boss. We can't be that far from the land you bought, can we? Only trouble, I guess, is how will we know it when we see it?"

"Well, according to the owners, the place is marked by several posts and flags. It's close to, or on the boundaries of, this Cricket Creek. Why don't you send Sad Hank and a couple of hands out to search for the markers?"

Nate complied, then turned back to Charles. "Anybody seen Retha?"

"Carl said she left a day before he did and should have been here by now. I swear, that gal is wilder than the Kansas wind, meaner than a bobcat, and sometimes crazier than a Garden City bed bug." Charles couldn't help but smile.

"Nobody's seen her yet, boss. She's out there just being what she is and still trying to find out who she is, I reckon. I often think that if she ever does, she may not like what she finds. Of course, that's my opinion, I guess. She favors ol' Pete, but she's a might young for him. You know she's damn pretty when she lets that long hair down."

"Hell, Nate, you're starting to sound like ol' Slick Harry. I think these cows are finally starting to get the best of you," laughed Charles. "Tell me, Nate, why don't you have a woman? Have you ever been married? You're not getting any younger, and that grey hair will probably run all of them off before long." Charles lit a cigar and reached across old Sachi to hand one to Nate.

"Watch where you throw that damn match, Charles! Hell, man, we'll burn the whole prairie!"

After Charles made sure the fire was out, Nate tipped his hat back and shifted in his saddle. "Oh, I had a gal friend once, but she didn't like my ways, I guess. Damn if she didn't run off with some barber over in Abilene. I heard they got in a fight, and she shot him dead because he banged a saloon gal. Anyway, I got better things to do than discuss my love life. I've got a herd of cattle to watch."

Charles took a big puff of the cigar and laughed and choked at the same time. "Now, Nate, everybody knows you've been taking a shine to that big Comanche gal Beba, there at the ranch. Why, I've seen you talking to her myself, more than once. I heard she shot her last man for eating all the biscuits a while back," he teased.

"I swear, Charles, if you weren't my boss, I'd shoot you dead. Besides, I should ask you why you don't have a woman."

"It's because I never had the time, you know, always working and such," his boss drawled lazily.

"Working and such?" Nate laughed while wheeling his horse around. "Well, I actually DO have work to do. Don't you get that ass raw from working too hard."

Charles just grinned and shook his head.

## Three days later

Sad Hank found all the markers on the newly acquired land and, just like the owners had promised, he found that it bordered Cricket Creek. Post and fencing were not needed as the land had no neighboring ranches. The only thing that Charles found strange was a marker that read "Pacific Railroad." Hopefully, that meant that the land had once been purchased from the railroad. But, just in case, he dispatched Jose to carry a letter back to the ranch asking Joe to inquire about it from the former landowners. Also, Charles asked Joe to buy materials to build bunkhouses and a supply house, as well as other needed supplies.

One thing Charles and the hands noticed on the new land was an onslaught of coyotes and a few wolf packs. The hands guarding the herd were all warning him about them. Charles could tell that many new challenges were on the horizon for the Triple A, and he wondered if he might have made the wrong decision to expand this far north. This was raw land with many mysteries and legends, many things unseen, and many unknown dangers. Around the campfire that night and after everybody bedded down around the fire, Charles gazed at the ever-clear celestial light show. His mind drifted back to his younger days growing up in the unforgiving swamp, and he wondered what ever happened to Little Boy Horse and Johnny One Horn. Thoughts of those days danced through his mind as he watched the sparks rising from the fire.

## Green Tree Creek

Retha had been watching the outlaws' hideout for several days but had seen no sign of Rico Garza. She liked the outlaw camp with its two cabins and corral, and decided to claim it for her own – after all, it was deserted. The longer she stayed around it, the more comfortable she became. She set to work cleaning the place, which already had all the necessities she could wish for. There were bunk beds, kerosene lanterns, and a wood stove in each cabin. She thought she could make a deal with Charles to buy a few cattle, by working around the new ranch the Triple A had acquired. Since she would only be about ten miles away, she figured she could easily travel back and forth several times a week. Finding a place like this that was already built and available for the taking only happened once in a blue moon, so she named the place "Blue Moon Ranch." She smiled as she hung a sign she had made over the door of the large cabin. Then she spent several hours posting the hilltops around the place with "keep out or be shot" signs.

While posting her newly claimed ranch, Retha noticed a young boy mounted on a beautiful paint horse watching her. But every time she tried to approach him, he would disappear over the hilltops. This happened many times, but then while she was boiling the bedding from the cabins, he suddenly appeared, walking his horse slowly toward her, and gave a greeting sign from his chest. He spoke broken English and she wondered how he had learned it. He also had an intimidating wolf hide, complete with the face, sitting on his head. He wore nothing else except a leather breechcloth and moccasins. Retha could tell he wasn't very old by the sound of his voice.

"I am Little Cricket, but most call me Cricket. We live here before bad men kill my mother and father. I hunting and when I come, I find them dead. Bad men not know I come. I want kill them all! But cowboys you know kill some. Then I see bad boss Rico ride to valley. I no have rifle to kill him, just father's old pistol. I see him get in wagon with people who go south." He pointed. "He have much blood. I hope he die."

"Well, howdy, Little Cricket," Retha answered. "I've been trying to fix up the place, but if it's yours, I can leave."

"No, I not want that. I see you work hard. You good woman. I want you stay. You stay big cabin, I stay small one."

Retha rolled her eyes when she realized he had been watching her. She thought of all the times she had to use the brush to do personal things. "Oh," she said, "how close did you watch me, Cricket? Real close?"

"Not close," Cricket smiled, "Close enough."

"I'm not sure what that means, but how old are you anyway, Cricket? By the way, why do they call you Cricket?"

"Mother tell me I born by Cricket Creek. It near here. She say thirteen seasons ago." He looked wistfully in the direction of the creek, then toward the corral. "Mother and father buried behind corral. I like build markers so they rest in peace. They die two years."

"Well, you look older than you are," smiled Retha. "Don't be watching me anymore – I can take care of myself. What keeps you in this place now that your folks are gone?"

Cricket gazed at the corral where his family was buried. "I will kill Rico Garza – he will be back here one day if he still alive. Then I take body to Echo of Moon so spirit damned for eternity."

Retha, shocked, slowly turned his way. "Wait – does that place really exist? I always thought it was just a legend told in saloons and by old men at campfires. Do you know where this place is?"

"I know place called Moon Rock. It point to Echo of Moon. I go there many times, spend time with spirits there. Many people go there, not welcome by spirits. They soon die, never leave. I not know why I not die. I go there when family killed. Spirits save me. Spirits now welcome me. But many white men who seek yellow iron die. Many bones there."

"I always heard there was gold there, but all I've seen in this country so far is fools' gold. There is plenty of that across the valley and old Goat Head Rock," Retha remarked.

Cricket smiled as he picked up a small shovel by the cabin. "If you go there, you lucky you not die. Slim Dick once look for yellow iron at Echo of Moon. Spirits curse him. He believe fool's gold real. But they not let him leave Goat Head Rock. They send many rattlesnakes. He cursed to get much fool's gold and never leave. He crazy now. He kill many men there."

"Well, he's not there anymore. He's dead," Retha explained. "I guess you might say he was killed by his own greed, wasn't he? Of course, he had a little help from an old friend." Retha could imagine what her friend Harry had gone through in his last hours.

When Cricket heard of Slim Dick's death, he stood quietly for a few seconds. "I not so sure. I hear he cursed to never die." He slowly turned and walked to the corral.

## Days later

As the days went by, Retha and Cricket became a lot closer to each other. They shared their life stories of good and tough times. At times the *déjà vu* feeling would return stronger than ever. Retha felt this young man fit into her story somehow, but she still couldn't tie it together. She was amazed how smart he was and was learning a lot about the country from him. They worked a few long days repairing the corral and cabins, and Cricket finished marking his family's graves.

Retha's plan was to go to the new Cheyenne Wells ranch at Cricket Creek and make a deal with Charles to buy a few good cattle. She always fared well with the Armstrong boys and felt good about dealing with them. There was a lot Cricket knew about this land, and she was determined to learn more. She felt that Cricket was keeping something from her, but she suspected it would all come out in time. They had formed a close partnership and they needed each other.

# CHAPTER 7

## Triple A Headquarters

Joe and Cindy Armstrong were working together to oversee the rebuild of the ranch and were pleased that it was going according to plan. They had even added several more buildings to the small town. Workers were kept busy; yet some of the Triple A's usual music and gatherings had resumed. There were many fresh faces, and people were still getting to know each other. Some arguments broke out, mainly between the young singles and new ranch hands. But Joe refused to let it get out of control by creating a standing order that anybody caught fighting would be fired and banned from the ranch.

Cindy had managed to keep the school going. Lately this was needed mostly for teaching languages. A mixture of English, Spanish, and mixed Comanche, Kiowa and Pawnee was heard in town every day, and Cindy believed that everyone should be able to communicate. New ranch hand Jake Barrows' wife Julie was a welcome addition in this respect and turned out to be an exceptionally good helper and teacher.

Midsummer rains had returned, and along with them, grass was returning to the parched prairie. The cattle and horses were doing a lot better, and things were returning to normal at the sprawling Triple A Ranch. Rumors of hidden gold were starting to spread among the hands again. Joe talked it down and threatened to fire any man caught spreading the tale. Most of the men believed Joe, but there was still a lot of whispering between them. Shorty, Joe's right-hand man and long-time Triple A hand, ran the ranch with a strong hand. It was a changing ranch, not the small family-centered enterprise it once was. People were friendly, but not as close.

Shorty was assigned to the riders and herders taking care of the cattle. He took an interest in new hand Franco because Tex Luna, his fence rider and trusted friend, had expressed some concerns. He thought it might be time to get to know Franco and decided to work alongside him for a day or two.

Shorty rode to the highest hilltop and gazed over the open landscape before seeing Franco, a.k.a. Rico, riding the fence line. He was alone and Shorty decided the time was right to investigate Tex Luna's doubts about the man. He walked his horse in the direction of Franco until he came along side of the outlaw. "It's Franco, right?" he asked.

"That's what they call me, Mr. Shorty" the man answered sarcastically as he dismounted adjacent to a broken fence post.

Seeing right away that Franco was not the friendly type, Shorty remained in his saddle. "I make it a custom to get to know our new hands so I can better relate to them," he informed the man. "Tex told me your work was ok, but you seem to be asking a lot of questions about an old wives' tale of hidden gold. Just so you're clear on this, the Armstrongs did at one time find gold in an old Mississippi swamp. But it's been used up long ago. Make no mistake, talking about it will get you in a lot of trouble here at the Triple A. The Armstrongs are very strict about spreading rumors here. Take my advice and don't bring it up again."

Rico stared at Shorty for a minute, as if considering what to say and what not to say. "I'm just working here for a month and then I'm moving on," he finally mumbled. "I don't really like ranching, but if I run across a little gold once in a while, I do like that," he retorted defiantly.

Shorty tipped his hat back and suspiciously surveyed the man. "Well, I don't really think you were listening to me, Franco. Maybe you should just move on now."

Looking away from Shorty as a distraction, Rico moved his hand slowly down toward his pistol. Shorty was very aware of this and had already pointed his firearm to the middle of Rico's back. "You thinking about using that on me?" Shorty said, his eyes narrowed. "You're not working here as of now. Throw that pistol on the ground and walk to the bunk house. Get your belongings and I'll give you your pay for your work, but if that is not good enough, I'll bury you right where you stand. Something tells me you're not who you say you are."

Rico started walking toward the ranch bunk house. Shorty grabbed his horse's bridle and led it as he followed.

"I'll leave your damn ranch, Mr. Shorty!" Rico yelled as he stomped toward the bunkhouse. "Be glad to."

Shorty saw Tex Luna riding toward him with a shotgun across his saddle. When Tex came alongside Shorty and saw what was going on, Rico turned and grinned at him. "I see the little dog came running, huh, Mr. Shorty?"

Tex immediately poked Rico with the shotgun and backed the hammer. "You better get your gear and leave, and you better make it quick," he growled. "If you ever show your face here again you will be floating face down in that muddy river over there."

Shorty handed the reins to Tex. "March this fool to the bunkhouse Tex. I'll get his pay and be back in a few minutes."

After getting his pay and escorting Rico to his horse, the two held their guns on him as they sent him on his way.

~ ~ ~

After crossing a few hills, the outlaw turned and glared back toward the ranch. Hate and revenge clouded his thoughts. He decided to wait until nightfall and slip back into the ranch. He had his eyes on the oldest Barrow girl. She had smiled at him several times and he liked what he saw.

Rico rode a few miles out of sight of the ranch and made a camp in one of the small canyons. He would wait until after midnight when the half-moon would rise in the eastern sky. He knew the night guard's routine and exactly where Beth Barrow would be. Beth always chose to sleep in the family's prairie schooner parked beside the main bunkhouse where all the single women and young girls were temporarily housed. She was a shy young lady and spent much of her time to herself.

When the light was right, Rico walked his horse slowly toward the dimly lit ranch. He dismounted a few hundred yards from the schooner and crept through the darkness until he reached the schooner. He climbed the small ladder the hands had built for Beth, and wasted no time grabbing her and gagging her mouth with his dirty bandana. He tied her arms and legs with cut pieces of rope and wrestled her onto his horse. She tried to scream but was only able to make a few faint sounds due to the tightness of the gag. He threw her small body over the horse as she violently struggled. To keep her quiet, he began beating her in the back of her head until she lost consciousness.

Rico rode several miles to an abandoned mine shack that his gang had once used as a hideout. He tied her still-unconscious body to an old support beam inside the dusty cabin, then tried to revive her by pouring his canteen over her head, to no avail. It occurred to him that he might have hurt her much more than he meant to.

Nevertheless, he spent the last couple of hours before dawn drinking whisky. He untied the young girl and laid her on the cabin floor to make it easier to have his way with her, and the whisky dulled his conscience completely so that he rather enjoyed the experience.

As the morning sun heated the cabin, Rico woke from his drunken stupor. He staggered to Beth's still-inert body and kicked and cursed her for not waking. Then he spit on her, slammed the cabin door, and mounted his horse. He figured the ranch hands would be looking for her and rode west toward Goat Head Rock.

## The Triple A

It was breakfast call at the Triple A, and it didn't take long for Cindy and the women to realize Beth Barrow was gone. They called her father, and Jake Barrow frantically joined his wife Julie, who was running from place to place screaming her daughter's name.

Joe Armstrong was busy at the horse corrals when he heard the commotion. He hurried up the street and entered the large bunkhouse where Cindy was trying to calm the remaining Barrow girls. "What the hell is going on here, Cindy?" he asked nervously.

Cindy explained that one of the Barrow girls was missing. Joe ran back to the corral to saddle his mount. Shorty and Tex were already there, getting ready to ride the fence lines.

"Shorty, have you seen the oldest Barrow girl this morning?" he asked.

"No, but if she's gone, I smell that no good Franco. We fired him yesterday and I wouldn't be surprised if he doesn't have something to do with this. He's the kind to try to get some kind of revenge. Tex, you cover the fences, and I'll go with Joe to see if we can find that little lady before that scoundrel harms her any more than he already has." He shook his head. "I tell you, Joe, something stinks about that man. I know he's not who he says he is."

Jake Barrow came running to the corral, insisting on going with them on the search. As the three men mounted their horses, they decided to ride the perimeter and see if they could find any tracks leading close to the prairie schooner where Beth had been the night before.

"Shorty, send a rider to the herd and tell Charles to send Sad Hank as fast as he can. I've heard that man can track over solid rock," Joe ordered before setting out.

"I will, but boss, how will he find us?" questioned Shorty.

"Don't worry, he'll find us. From the stories I've heard, he is relentless."

Shorty picked one of his best riders and sent him to find the tracker Sad Hank. Then he, Joe, and Jake Barrow started the search. Within an hour they found the tracks that were closest to the Barrow wagon. Following the tracks was slow going, though, because the morning prairie winds were erasing them quickly. The tracks followed the river, and Franco, a.k.a. Rico, had used an old native trick of going in and out of the river sand and backtracking to throw off any pursuers that might follow. By late afternoon they had lost all trace of any tracks. The sun was setting, and there was no moon to help them. Any moon at all would rise only a couple of hours before dawn. Still, they fumbled through the darkness for several hours before Joe called it off for the night.

"If we're going to be in good enough shape tomorrow, we better get a little rest and continue after the late moon rises," Joe decided.

Jake Barrow refused to stop and left on his own to continue the search, even though Joe and Shorty both tried their best to talk him into getting a little rest.

Joe wiped the tears from his eyes as he watched Jake disappear into the night, calling out his daughter's name.

"Damn, man, can you imagine what's going through that man's head?" frowned Shorty. "You think that young girl is still alive, Joe?"

Joe just stopped and was still for a second as he removed the saddle from his exhausted horse. "Let's hope so, Shorty, let's hope so."

The next two days were spent riding the river and then the tracks disappeared. There was no sign of Jake Barrow either, and it concerned Joe and Shorty.

In the moonless night the wind grew strong, and the smell of rain permeated the warm air. Lightning and thunder in the west were sure signs of needed rain. They searched for shelter and found a small cave on the river's edge, gathered some dry sagebrush from their surroundings, and built a small fire.

"This cave has been used many times, my friend, probably by the Sioux and many others. I bet it can sure tell some stories. Too bad it can't talk," Joe said as he examined the cave walls. "You know, Shorty, time is probably running out for that poor little Barrow girl."

"Yeah. Damn it, Joe, we found nothing for three days now. It's just like they disappeared or something."

Joe began roasting a rabbit they had shot along the edge of the river and noticed the lightning getting very close. A light sprinkle of rain began to fall.

Looking out the small cave entrance, Shorty could see the eyes of coyotes glowing in the dark night. "Look at that, Joe. Eyes everywhere out there! Damn strange if you ask me."

"Yeah, it's reflecting from the fire. I don't think they will get too close. I'd shoot a couple, but if ol' Franco is anywhere close it might alert him. Keep an eye on the horses – they're getting kind of spooked."

The coyotes moved on after an hour or so and the night got quiet. The rain had moved through the valley and a slight rumble of distant thunder remained in the distance. Now, after getting some rest, they would be ready to resume their quest in the morning.

As the morning sun broke the horizon, Joe woke to see Sad Hank sitting cross legged beside the small fire next to him.

"If I were a Sioux warrior, I could have had your scalps swinging on my mule out there," said Hank, looking very concerned.

"Holy crap, how did you slip up on us like that?" yelled Shorty.

"I've been here for a couple of hours, my friend. You never moved or stopped snoring. This man we're after could have killed both of you easy."

"Well, you're right, but we were exhausted from our search and worry for Beth Barrow," said Joe. "It won't happen again."

"This young lady you're looking for, it's sad to say, is probably already dead. If I know Rico, the one you call Franco, he has killed her. At best we can find her body, or what's left of it and bury her."

"You think that guy is Rico Garza, Hank?" asked Joe.

"I know it is, from what the rider you sent told me. He said he had an ear missing. I know he's got a couple of fingers missing also. Your old mountain man friend Earl Stockman saw to that in a fight. Earl spared his life, but always regretted it. I think it was because Rico was such a young man at the time. He's out there somewhere – he's afraid to go into any town for fear of someone recognizing him. He's wanted everywhere and a lot of people know his face from the wanted posters. I'll find him and your missing girl. This time I'll make sure he never does this again."

"Do you have any idea where he might be taking her, Hank? We lost all trace of any tracks by the river," frowned Joe.

"I do, but there are several. For years now I have left him alone, because I knew his mother and made her a promise to watch over him. She was the wife of a dear friend. After he grew up, Rico became unruly and hateful. I saw him rob a prairie wagon and torture a young woman. Luckily, she didn't die. I told him then I was through with him and if I ever heard of this again, I would come after him and place his soul at the Echo of the Moon. I always keep my word."

"Do you know of this place, Sad Hank? This Echo of the Moon seems to come up a lot in this country."

"I do know it, Joe. It is a spiritual place. White men would say Hell or Heaven – both places exist at the Echo of the Moon."

Joe and Shorty looked at each other for a few seconds in disbelief as they mounted their horses to continue the search. Sad Hank was in the lead, and it wasn't long before he picked up the trail. He led them for several hours away from the river to the west hills of the valley.

"You see any tracks, Joe?" asked Shorty.

"Nothing," answered Joe, "but he does. He keeps staring at the brush and dismounting every so often."

Sad Hank mounted his horse and told Joe and Shorty he knew where Rico Garza was headed. He told them of an old mining shack that he knew Rico had used down through the years as a hideout. Now he stopped looking for tracks and continued leading the mule behind but hurried straight toward a distant bluff. A few miles and hours later they arrived at the old miner's cabin. Nothing was moving and the cabin looked deserted. Joe and Shorty, with guns drawn, opened the door. Blood was smeared everywhere on the floor. They looked in horror but there was no body.

Sad Hank took one look at the scene and said, "Your girl is dead, boys." A sad expression came over his face, and he continued, closing the door, "Let's see if we can find her body."

Behind the cabin Hank saw a newly dug grave with a carefully made cross from cabin wood that read "Beth Barrow." Sad Hank and the men stood looking at the grave, amazed of how carefully the grave and the cross had been constructed.

"Rico didn't make this – he would have just left her to rot. He always thinks of himself and doesn't care about people's feelings," Hank remarked.

Joe stood with tears streaming down his face, and Shorty choked up and walked away, kicking some brush in anger.

"I swear, Joe, it looks like someone butchered a steer in there. I've never seen anything like that before in my entire life. We've got to find that bastard and give him justice."

"Well, someone gave her a good burial. I wonder if, and I think it was, her father. Jake Barrow seems to be an honorable man. You know, Shorty, we don't know a lot about him. Either he was lucky, or he just stumbled on this place. If he's the one that found her, I feel hurt inside for that poor man."

"Can you imagine if that were your own daughter?"

Sad Hank sat on his horse looking in the direction of Goat Head Rock. "There is a cave in the bluff at Goat Head Rock and that's where Rico is headed. He can watch the valley there as usual for his next victims. There is only one way in, and he has water to drink and rabbits to eat. It will be very difficult to get to him."

"I heard that place was crawling with rattlesnakes. Why in the world would he go there?" Joe asked.

"I guess there are some, Joe, but the mating season is mostly over, and they seem to thin out this time of year. We can approach it through the wash leading up to it. We'll wait for nightfall."

The new moon gave very little light, so when they reached the wash where they could see the entrance to the cave, they decided to rest and take turns watching the entrance. Sad Hank pointed to a flicker of a fire in the cave and knew the murderous Rico was there.

As the sun rose red in the morning sky, Sad Hank had left the camp and was several hundred yards up the wash from Joe and Shorty. He knew Rico had a telescoping lens and had to move very carefully so he wouldn't be seen. Hank also had the same from an army issue. He watched Rico scanning the valley using his lens. As Sad Hank scanned the walls below the bluff, he noticed what looked to be a body lying on the rocks below. Several buzzards were picking at the lifeless form. He watched until Rico went back into the cave and then made his way very carefully back to Joe and Shorty.

"Rico is there for sure, Joe, and I'm afraid Jake Barrow is there also – I saw a body at the bottom of the bluffs. Now we will have to wait until Rico makes a mistake. He would pick us off now if he knew we were here."

Several hours went by with Sad Hank closely watching the cave entrance. A summer storm rumbled in the distance and a huge dust cloud crept up the valley. High winds and lightning moved in very quickly. With no shelter, they slipped back down the wash to Slim Dick's abandoned lean-to. Since they were already soaked to the bone, the rain seemed cold and forever, though the storm only took several minutes to pass. The lightning had spooked the horses and the pack mule, and they had run down the wash. When the storm passed through, Sad Hank quickly focused his lens back on the entrance of the cave. He watched for several minutes and turned slowly and told Joe and Shorty that Rico was gone.

"How do you know that, Hank? quizzed Shorty. "We haven't even looked in that cave yet."

"He probably heard the horses spook, or he was already aware of our presence. He used an old Pawnee trick and left with the cover of the storm, most likely following the storm. If my guess is right, he went up the hills into the high ground. If you and Shorty will bury Mr. Barrow, I will keep on this devil's trail. Go back to the Triple A, Joe. The people there will need you, and you, Shorty. No need for you boys to get yourselves killed over a devil like Rico. I will find him. It may take a while, but I will, and he will pay for his evils. You need to go now and get the horses and leave."

Joe had to agree. "He may be headed in that direction as we speak, so Hank, you go ahead and we will attend to Jake Barrow."

Hank sat on his mount and stared at the mountains he thought Rico would use as his escape route. He knew Rico's ways and hoped he was right. Now that he knew Sad Hank was tracking him, he would be extra cautious and dangerous.

After two hours of hard digging, Joe and Shorty had buried the body of Jake Barrow, who had been shot several times. The body was badly decomposed from the hot rocks, and Joe and Shorty used all the strength they had to complete the job.

Afterwards, they searched the cave to make sure Sad Hank was correct that Rico had departed. There were several skeletal remains scattered on the sandy floor.

"Damn, Joe," frowned Shorty, "looks like a burial ground in here, but I guess they're all victims of ol' Slim Dick or this slime bag Rico."

"Well, sure looks like he was alerted to our presence, doesn't it? He never touched that rabbit he was cooking. He left in a hell of a hurry. I sure hope he don't bushwhack Sad Hank, although I think that would be hard to do. Well, Shorty, let's get the hell out of here ourselves. I can't wait to ride away from this part of hell."

Shorty remarked as they rode away, "The worst part is yet to come – telling Mrs. Barrow about her daughter and husband. Damn, it's something all the time here. This land seems to be crawling with devils."

# CHAPTER 8

## Retha's Blue Moon Ranch

Charles and Carl were working on the corrals of the newly obtained Cheyenne Wells land. It seemed the drought had broken, and afternoon storms and rain showers were turning the valley into an ocean of prairie grass. Along with the rain, swarms of hated mosquitos plagued the men at night.

Charles' thoughts flashed back to the Mississippi swamp where he had been born. Sometimes he could still smell the kerosene thickening the air in the small wooden dwelling. He was amazed, when he thought about it, how long ago it had been, and how far they had come. Tears would fill his eyes as he remembered his small brother Carl, teasing and always making the best of things. His nephew Carl, Joe's son, was named after him and reminded him somewhat of him. Still, he always wondered what Carl would have been like if he had survived. Sometimes he would imagine, then just smile and shake his head.

He had just shaken off one of those nostalgic moments when he noticed Retha and her new friend Cricket riding into the busy new development. "Well. I'll be dammed if that isn't the Wild Coyote Woman coming, Carl. Looks like she's got a new friend. Isn't that something?"

As the pair got closer, Carl noticed the two knives at

Cricket's waist, and was amused at the sling over the young man's neck that haltered a Winchester rifle. The skinned wolf hide sitting on his head made the young warrior a fearsome sight.

"Hello, my friends," Retha greeted. "This is my new friend Cricket. Never mind his clothes – that's just his way. His parents were killed by Rico Garza and his butchers. He's sworn to get revenge one day, and he's always prepared."

"That Rico you mention, Retha – he kidnapped a young girl from the Triple A. They asked me to send Sad Hank back to help find the girl and deal with this Rico. I guess the guy's been right under their noses all along, hired by Joe as a fence rider. When they fired him, he slipped back at night and took the girl. We haven't heard anything more."

"Miss Retha, that girl probably dead now," Cricket intoned solemnly as he sadly contemplated the situation. "Very bad man. Sad Hank good tracker. He will find. But I not know if he can kill him – he disappear like ghost in night."

Looking very stressed by the news of the young Barrow girl, Retha was quiet for a few minutes. When she regained her composure, she explained why she was there. She discussed the purchase of ten cows and a young bull, explaining that she could start payment in the fall and work building corrals for the Triple A to help pay for them.

Charles agreed reluctantly, but he trusted her word and as a friend he would comply.

"Retha, you might want to be watchful of your new claim," Charles warned as Retha prepared to head back. "Rico may show up there again. It sounds like he's crazy, and it wouldn't surprise me at all. You and young Cricket better sleep with one eye open."

Retha just nodded. "I'll be back in a couple of weeks, Charles, to help build those corrals. We've got a little work to do to the place first, and Cricket will watch over it."

As Charles watched Retha cut her purchase from the herd, he let his thoughts drift to the stories he had been writing about his life and the incredible journey he had witnessed. Today's episode would continue the remarkable saga. "Someday people are going to read these stories," he thought, "and probably be amazed at how raw this country is in this time period."

## Keeping their Word

A light rainfall glistened in the new grass as Carl awoke the next morning. As he made a quick survey of the camp and herd, he noticed smoke coming from one of the canyons to the north and strained to get a clearer view. Finally, he decided to ride to investigate.

An hour later, up a rough draw, he was taken aback by the scene. A small band of Sioux, composed mostly of women and children, had set up a rag-tag camp near a small spring. Cautiously, he rode and then walked Corky toward the camp.

A small group of young boys were quick to pick up their spears and bows and surround him. One of them summoned an old man from one of the dwellings. The elder told the boys to stand down and they quickly lowered their weapons.

Carl noticed a young steer roasting over a wooden tripod in the center of the camp. He could see how poor the group was. It was no doubt that the steer was Triple A property.

"What brings you here?" the man asked. "We don't see many people anymore."

"You speak our language very well," smiled Carl. "How long have your people been camped here?"

"We came here at the end of the falling leaves to escape the armies of the north. We had nothing left. They hunted our people down. Most were killed, and some were rounded up like your cattle and placed in pens. This is some of our northern people that are still free, but still they hunt us."

Carl looked compassionately at the group. The people wore ragged clothes and the children seemed sickly – mostly skin and bones. He felt sick inside, and his heart ached.

"We are not like most white men you've seen," he explained. My grandmother was Chickasaw, and I have the blood of the tribesmen in my veins. Your women and children need things, and we will help you." He nodded toward the fire. "That steer you have roasting there, is one of ours. There might be trouble if one of our foremen sees it."

"It was a stray the young ones found, and it was dying anyway," the elder explained, "but even if it wasn't, we have the right to take it."

Carl was shocked at the words that came from the old man's mouth. Confused, he slowly looked around the small village sorrowfully. "I know your people are hungry, sir, and I'm certain, by looking around the village, that your people needed the food, but things have changed now, and the law says it's rustling to take or kill another man's cattle."

"Come sit in the shade with me, and I will explain to you, my friend," the man invited. "I see you know nothing of our agreement made years ago."

Two of the women of the tribe laid out blankets beneath a small tree at the edge of the village. Carl respectfully agreed to join him, dismounted, and sat cross-legged on the blankets with him. The old chief looked weary but was very alert and intelligent. Carl listened very closely to what he was saying.

"I am the brother of Running Bear. Years ago, I was with him when he met the white chief O.C. Armstrong. He was an honorable man of his word. At the time we were a strong people, but we have been hunted and killed by years of war and disease. We were visited many times by the great Johnny One Horn, and he told of huge cities to the east of the mighty river. He said our way of life was ending and nothing we could do would stop the many wagon trains of white people from taking over our land. At first, we laughed, but now we know he spoke the truth."

Carl was very interested in what he had to say. "I am amazed that you know Johnny One Horn, and you have much wisdom in your words, but tell me why you believe you have this right to take our cattle."

"I was second in power below Running Bear. They call me Standing Man. I was there when O.C. Armstrong gave his word to Running Bear to give us twenty cattle every fall. It has been years since we have been close enough to receive our payment."

"This land you stand on is very sacred to us – it is the land of the moon. We ask you not to kill any more of our people, and to let us stay in our home. If your leader O.C. were here, he would honor his word.

"This O.C. you speak of was my grandfather. I promise I will talk to my uncle Charles, and I'll be back and meet with you in a day or so."

As the meeting ended, Carl mounted his horse Corky and slowly left the village. When he passed the small creek he was approached by a lovely young girl, and she handed him a desert flower. He smiled back at her but had a hard time averting his eyes. He nodded in thanks, and as he walked his horse slowly away, he thought of how beautiful she was.

## The Triple A

Joe and Shorty had arrived back at the Triple A and had informed the ranch and Jake Barrow's family of the unthinkable events they had witnessed. At first, Julie

Barrow seemed to go into shock for an hour or so, but then she tried to take her own life using a buffalo gun that had been stashed in the Barrow's prairie schooner.

Cindy pleaded with her and reminded her of the importance of staying alive to comfort and be there for her remaining two girls. Julie eventually saw the truth in that, and Cindy was able to lead her back to the safety of the bunkhouse.

Cindy was very emotional, but she knew she must continue being the strong one, even as she choked back the tears. Occasionally she had to walk away by herself to grieve silently. But Amy, one of the older women who had been very close to O.C. Armstrong, was there, giving constant advice like a mother figure to Cindy, and was always able to help her maintain composure and order. This peaceful atmosphere had been doing wonders to help heal the young girls that had been rescued recently. Though they would never be the same since their ordeal, it was clear that they felt much more secure now.

Cindy often talked to Joe about the seclusion of the ranch. She wished they were closer to medical help and especially to law and order. Joe agreed, but he also knew they were not city people, and the chances of getting a doctor to isolate himself on the ranch and live this rugged lifestyle would be slim. Amy was about the closest thing to a doctor that the ranch could get, having a lot of knowledge and old remedies handed down from her Pawnee ancestors.

The ranch buildings were being rebuilt faster than Joe could have imagined, and the streets bustled with workers finishing the buildings. It was looking more like a small town than just a ranch.

Drifters came seeking work, but many were turned away. There were problems along the way. Many pleaded for jobs, but the ranch was overflowing with workers, some good, some not so good. Since Pete was in Cheyenne Wells, Joe had thought it necessary to appoint Tom Sheen as the new acting sheriff of the growing community. Tom had once been a deputy and had come to the ranch several years before to investigate the Bennis brothers. He had been so attracted to the ranch that he had stayed and had become a top hand with the horses and cattle. Now Tom had grown up a lot and had a firm way of handling himself. He was a big man and spoke with the utmost authority. He observed the new workers very closely, recommending some of the best be hired directly by the Triple A. Tom was a fair man. Originally, his reason for staying was Yolanda, but he had lost her to Shorty. Even though Tom was bothered by the loss, he had become a very close friend of Shorty's, and still loved the ranch enough to remain a part of it.

The legend of the swamp gold was forever growing, and rumors that Joe and Charles had cashed in a fortune in gold coins spread through the plains. Joe tried to dismiss the rumors, but doubters and squatters multiplied around the river and the perimeter of the vast Triple A holdings. Most were just old prospectors digging holes in the hills, but some were the worst types of profiteers in the land. Cutthroats, thieves, and the dishonest were a constant problem.

Tom Sheen had organized a small group of the toughest of the Triple A hands to watch for and deal with the untrustworthy fortune hunters. They would encounter them every couple of days, either digging holes or erecting makeshift camps by the river close to the Triple A. The women and children of the Triple A family were always watched with a careful eye and were warned not to roam outside the boundaries of the ranch. They were not to leave the township without an armed escort. Most of the long-time hands had dismissed the old Armstrong legend, and all believed the gold had been used long ago. However, old stories about the gold at Echo of the Moon remained, and most believed those to be true.

Tom's crew would warn the profiteers and prospectors not to cross the boundaries of the ranch, and most would comply, but a few were troublemakers and would create conflicts. On one occasion, a gun fight occurred when two brothers, Lee and Nat Cobb, refused to leave after crossing the boundaries. Lee was killed in the gunfire. No one seemed to know who really shot Lee Cobb, but Nat rode away without being pursued by the Triple A hands and never came back.

Joe was disturbed by the death of Lee Cobb, and worried about future consequences to the ranch hands. He was also concerned about the growing stories of gold, but he had a job rebuilding the Triple A, and that was his main goal. He knew the day was coming when he would have to lay off the excess workers. Some had families, and he cared about them. Every once in a while, when bad things happened, he'd remember the curse of the gold and what Johnny One Horn and Little Boy Horse had always warned him about. At times it seemed very real.

# CHAPTER 9

## The search for Rico Garza

Sad Hank was on the trail of Rico Garza even though he hadn't found a true trail. He did find traces here and there, but they always faded. Sad Hank was confused – the trail seemed to lead in circles. He knew Rico was taunting him and this only made him more determined to catch him, but the trail eventually disappeared completely. Days passed without a trace and Sad Hank decided to call off the hunt. It was hard for him to admit that he had failed to find him, but he also knew Rico was a master of deception and cunning as a fox. Three days later he returned to the Triple A and informed Joe and Shorty of his disappointment.

As Joe listened to Sad Hank, he could sense the frustration in his voice. "Well," Joe frowned, "maybe we will cross paths with this cutthroat again, Hank. He can't keep up his evil without getting caught. It's just too bad we don't get to hang him now and get it over with."

Sad Hank stayed the night camped by the river – it was not his way to sleep in a bunkhouse. The next morning at sunrise he headed back to Cheyenne Wells. He felt ashamed that he had failed.

When he arrived four days later at Cheyenne Wells, Charles was eager to get any news. Hank sadly told his story to Nate, Pete and Charles.

"Damn," Pete said, raising his voice. "You can track a man over solid rock, Hank! How did he shake you?"

"I don't know. It makes me feel soft," Hank replied sheepishly. "He just disappeared. I was on his trail and then it was simply gone."

Nate tried to reassure him. "He will show himself again and will probably kill and rob again like he always does. All we have to do is give it time. He'll ride the coach roads and that's where one day we will find him. He will prey on the weakest and most defenseless. He will never change."

"I agree," Charles said, shaking his head. "We can't let up our guard. But for now, we've got a ranch to run."

Late afternoon brought thunderstorms. Lightning lit up the darkening sky. The fencing of the corrals was only about half complete, and the hands had to surround the cattle and try to prevent a stampede. All, being soaked and dusted at the same time, struggled to keep the herd calm. The dust in front of the rain made it very difficult to breathe and visibility was low. The ranch hands cringed every time lightning struck ever closer to the herd. Sometimes hail accompanied by heavy winds battered their mounts, making them spook, and they would buck the riders no matter how close the relationship. Some were hurt, and since the Triple A had no doctor, they had to travel to Garden City.

As the storm passed, in the dimly lit plains Charles saw a rider. He was hoping it was Carl, and it was. The night was calm after the storm as the men gathered around the cook wagon. Carl began to tell them of his encounter with the small group of Sioux.

"The group is very poor and weak, with mostly women and children, and no animals except a few worn-out horses," he explained. "The chief is named Standing Man and he seems very wise. I guess they are hiding, but they are in no shape to make any kind of war on anybody. As I talked to Standing Man about the steer they were roasting, he said we owed it to him because of a deal Grandpa O.C. made with him long ago. He says it is a debt and he wasn't stealing."

Charles' eyes widened as he thought back to the days of the Bennis brothers and their breach of the agreement made between O.C. and Running Bear. "There was an agreement made with Running Bear, I remember. The Bennis brothers almost got us all killed. O.C. met with the chief and made a vow to pay a few cattle every fall to stay on the land without war. They were friends and I guess that agreement still stands. I would like to meet Standing Man and find out his needs. Most of you hands know that my brothers and I are half Chickasaw – for those who didn't know, you know now. If any of you, no matter what color your skin is, doesn't like that, you can pack up and go."

Pete smiled and poked Charles in a playful way. "Boss, I don't think anyone would guess that with your red hair and all. And look at your nephew Carl with a long blond ponytail!"

The group had quite a laugh from the statement Pete had slyly slid in. He had just been trying to change the atmosphere of the gathering. It worked and the whole group settled down.

"Uncle Charles, I would sure like to go with you when you go. I met someone there I would surely like to see again," Carl said quietly when they were away from the group.

But Pete heard the comment and smiled as he was stoking the fire. "That someone, no doubt, is a little Sioux girl, I would bet. Carl, you don't know ol' Standing Man all that well yet – he may like to have that blond hair hanging from his teepee as a trophy."

"Well," laughed Carl, "I guess I just might have to deal with short hair for a while. She was about the prettiest little critter I ever saw."

Did you get her name, Carl?" grinned Pete.

"No, she walked away before I could ask her, but I could tell she liked me. She gave me a flower," Carl said, smiling shyly.

Nate had been listening to what everyone had to say about the Sioux group before he spoke. "You know, guys, it's been a long time since we saw any Sioux, or even knew where to take the cattle to. Suddenly, we have people claiming our cows. Somehow, I don't know if we should honor this agreement or not. Besides that, it was made with Running Bear, not Standing Man."

"You know, boss, Nate's got a point," Pete agreed. "What if other groups pop up and also claim this debt?"

Charles, raising his eyebrows as if the thought had merit, just replied, "Well, let's find out tomorrow when we talk to Standing Man." Suddenly he had an idea and turned to Sad Hank. "Sad Hank, do you know this chief? Can he be trusted?"

"I do, and I would trust him very much, although I thought he and all his followers were killed to the north of here. He is a truthful man with honor. He rode once with Blue Feather and the other village leaders of the northern Sioux. I would trust what he says."

"There's one more thing, Charles," Carl suddenly remembered. "Standing Man said he knew and befriended Johnny One Horn."

"Sad Hank, in all your travels and friends you've known, it would seem that you would know Johnny too. Did you ever meet or hear from him?"

Sad Hank smiled and kept stoking the fire. "I knew him well. And I was there just a few days after he fought a great grizzly. It was north of the Platt River in a cave. I was scouting for the Sioux, giving them the locations of the Army so they could avoid them. I remember Little Boy Horse and his great quest to find and kill the devil Bo Jack. When I was an Army scout, I would mislead them and send them in the wrong direction, away from our villages. When they found out what I was doing, I went to a northern Sioux village and traveled with Chatah and your friend Little Boy Horse. We had escaped across the Canadian mountains when I got word that a Crow scout had told the Army where I was. I left and they captured me in the Dakotas. They were going to hang me, but I escaped from their stockade. As for your friend, he took a young girl named Miki for his wife and I think they have a son now. Wind, the girl they returned to her tribe, was teaching the young people of the tribe survival skills. She is a beautiful spirit and has a couple of wolves for pets. They went far north, and I doubt that you will ever see them again, my friends, for that is their home now."

Charles stood leaning on one of the prairie schooner's wheels with a surprised look on his face. He wished he had his pen and paper so he could document what he had just heard. Sad Hank had never talked this much before. "All this time, Sad Hank, and you never said a word about knowing Johnny One Horn and Little Boy Horse? What's up with that? We would all have liked to know this."

"It is my belief that the less you say is sometimes the better thing to do. One day I'll tell you more about your friend from the north. Time will tell," Sad Hank replied, a relaxed look on his face. "Let us go when the sun is early in the sky and visit my old friend Standing Man."

**The following morning**

Led by Sad Hank, Charles, Nate and Carl set out for the village of Standing Man. When they arrived, the village was in turmoil. It seemed that one of the younger women of the village had mysteriously disappeared during the night. Consequently, the young braves were quick to draw down on the four as they approached the village. Before Standing Man could control them, one had fired a shot that creased

Nate's shoulder. Nate countered with his forty-four, striking a young brave in the calf of his leg. Charles quicky defused the situation as Standing Man scolded the young Sioux. The women of the tribe quickly ran to the young brave and attended his wound. Nate was looked after by Sad Hank. Fortunately, his was a very light skin wound.

Standing Man approached the men from the Triple A, who were still behaving cautiously, weapons drawn and defenses ready. He gave the sign from his chest to Sad Hank, and the group slowly dismounted. "It's been a while, Sad Hank, my friend. I am surprised to see you here. I was told you were hanged."

"I almost was," smiled Sad Hank, "but I managed to escape like a mole in the ground."

"Look around, Sad Hank, and you can see the panic of the people. One of our young women was taken some time in the night. We have several small groups of warriors out looking for her but have found no trace so far. It pains me for she is such a pure little spirit and daughter of my daughter. She is about fourteen seasons."

Carl had been scanning the village people, hoping to see the young lady that had reached out to him with the flower. He finally spotted her attending the wounded warrior. He was relieved to know she was still ok. He walked over slowly and smiled, expecting to get a smile in return, but to his surprise she said a few words he could not understand, and she then spat at him as she helped the warrior into a teepee nearby. He stood there for a few minutes and then realized today's situation hadn't exactly been conducive to making an acquaintance. Finally, he walked back to the group.

The group sat at the meeting tree as Charles led the conversation. "I know this is a very bad time to discuss this, Standing Man, but as for the agreement of my father O.C., I want you to know our family's word is always good. You can receive your cattle any time you want, but we will have to oversee it. I know you are trustworthy, and we can trust you. Sad Hank also assured us we can trust you, and in time we can all work together to make things better between your people and ours. We will help you find your granddaughter if you want. We would be more than glad to."

Sad Hank had been scanning the hills around the village quietly, and after a few minutes, he pointed toward one side of the west hills. "There," he said. "She was taken in that direction. The small wash would hide his motion. This girl was taken by Rico Garza, a devil of a man. If we are to find the girl in time, it will have to be soon." He rose to his feet and mounted his horse. "With your permission, Standing Man, I would like to be the one to hunt this devil. I know his ways, and that gives me some advantage over your braves."

Standing Man rose to his feet, walked to Sad Hank's horse, and placed his hand on Sad Hank's hand. "May the spirits be with you, my friend." And then he gave the sign from his chest and walked away from the group. Two women met him at his teepee and escorted the aging chief inside.

"We can go with you, Hank, after Nate goes back to the ranch to tend to that shoulder," offered Charles.

"No, I need to do this alone. We don't need anybody else getting killed. I really thought we would find him on the wagon trails, but then I didn't know Standing Man and his people were here." He kicked his horse and wheeled around, parting with, "I must go quickly, so I will see you soon with the head of Rico Garza."

## The Trap

Sad Hank suspected that Rico Garza was setting a trap for him. He hadn't covered his tracks like usual, and Sad Hank became very conscious of his own surroundings. Late in the night, Hank saw a small fire in a distant wash. He approached very cautiously. Rico had taken the girl to a box canyon and strapped her to a lone tree in the center. The fire was several feet from the tree and the girl. Hank dismounted very carefully and moved quietly through the underbrush of the hillside. He thought that Rico would be hidden in the brush nearest to the tree and would shoot him if he saw him.

Hank waited until almost dawn before trying to get closer. He had left his horse several hundred yards from his present location. While scanning the skyline, he suddenly realized he had made a terrible mistake. He ran back through the brush and, just like he suspected, his horse was gone. He knew that he had been outwitted again by the sly Rico Garza. He shook his head, disgusted at himself. Rico had made a fool of him. There was no use hiding anymore because he knew Rico was just using him in some other kind of diversion.

As he approached the young girl, she shook her head and tried to talk through the gag. Sad Hank didn't realize she was trying to warn him. When he reached her, he felt the horrible pain of a bear trap dig into his right leg. As he dropped to the ground, he hit another trap buried in the sand. This one clamped into his right shoulder. As he lay on the ground in extreme pain, he saw Rico loom up beside him.

"I should just shoot you, old fool," Rico said, laughing derisively. "But that would be too easy. It's for sure you're not going anywhere with those bear traps chained to the rocks. One on one end, and one on the other. I think you taught me that, Sad Hank."

Sad Hank moved his left hand slowly to the knife on his side. Rico dismounted and kicked Hank several times in the midsection while he lay on the bloody ground. Sad Hank plunged the knife into the calf of Rico's leg. Rico screamed but smiled.

"I should have known better than to get too close to you," he moaned. "I should kill you and that squaw right now, but you will both die anyway."

Before he mounted his horse, Garza pinned a piece of dried rawhide to the young girl that said, "Joe, Shorty, you're next."

"Thanks for the horse and supplies, old man, and tell that Joe and Shorty they will be next – that is, if you don't die here. You know," he smiled again, "I found this place as a kid – it's real hard to find. Lot of snakes too. Farewell, my friend, it's been a lot of fun."

Sad Hank struggled on the ground for an hour or so trying to free himself from the teeth of the giant bear traps. The sun was high in the sky and its blistering heat seemed to be cooking his flesh. The young girl struggled to free herself from the grip of the rawhide straps. As the day steamed into the late afternoon, Hank's strength was going fast. The girl fought to stay conscious. Hank tried to talk to her, but she, too, was weak. As the sunset approached, a summer storm was developing to the south. Hank, lying on his back, kept struggling with the unforgiving bear traps until he became unconscious from the pain. He awoke to the smell of rain as small drops streamed from his face. He said a Sioux prayer as the rain increased.

As the rain increased, a trickle of needed water ran down the rocky wash. Sad Hank was able to drink the cool water as the creek rose, but another problem was developing. Since he was anchored to the ground, he was praying that the water wouldn't rise too high, or he would drown.

Standing Man's granddaughter had regained consciousness and she, too, was gaining strength from the cool rain. She was able to sip a little water from the bandana that was gagging her, to give her strength. She struggled until the small tree uprooted in the muddy ground and fell. Then she moved the rawhide up and down the bark until she was able to break it. When she was free, she lay on the ground for a few minutes, resting. Then she moved to Hank, and he used his one hand that was free to untie the gag from her mouth.

"They call me Tiny," she said as she tried with all her strength to spread the jaws of the bear trap from Hank's right shoulder. After a long period of time with no success, Hank told her she would have to go for help. He could only lie helplessly on the ground, bound by the powerful traps. Tiny agreed and would go for help, knowing the village was not too far.

"It's just a few hours to the north if you follow the hills. Go as swiftly as you can because I'm losing a lot of blood and it won't be long before the coyotes and wolves pick up the scent."

As Hank watched the small figure fade into the moonlit night, his hatred for Rico Garza grew ever stronger. Tiny knew the area and it didn't take long before she was on a direct route to the village. In the dark, the brush and yucca plants took their toll on her small body, and at times she felt like she couldn't go another step. The sharp needles of the yucca pierced her skin in several places, some breaking off beneath the skin and causing terrible pain. Her feet were bleeding, and she tore some of her clothing to make bandages to wrap her bare feet. She finally staggered into the village as the sun was rising, her clothes torn and shredded. She made her way toward Standing Man's teepee.

Standing Man was shocked to see his granddaughter in this condition. He quickly called for assistance as he held her in his shaking arms. As soon as the women were present, they calmed her down enough for her to tell them about Sad Hank.

The chief summoned his oldest brave, Sunnie, to his side and relayed instructions about where to find Sad Hank. Sunnie quickly appointed ten braves and trackers and they left hurriedly to find Sad Hank.

The search party arrived at the small wash an hour later to find Hank unconscious, still imprisoned by the traps. It was clear he had fought for his life by the shredded clothing and bite marks on almost every part of his body. Many coyotes could be seen in the surrounding area. He was very weak and not able to talk. The men quickly made a drag from tree limbs they found down the wash and removed the death grip hold of the traps. As soon as they arrived at the village, the women began attending to Hank's mangled, unconscious body.

Sunnie's first words to Standing Man were not favorable. He entered the teepee shaking his head as he spoke to the old chief. "I don't think Sad Hank can make it, my chief. He's very bad. It looks like he has the rot in that right leg that was caught in the bear trap. His shoulder is also broken from a bear trap."

Standing Man stared at the floor of the teepee. Finally, he spoke. "We will let it be in the hands of the Great Spirit. If he lives, he lives. There's nothing we can do except try." As Sunnie nodded in agreement, the chief sighed, cleared his throat, and once more took on his fatherly role as he instructed, "Now take five warriors with you, Sunnie, and track this devil down. Bring me this man, and if you can't, bring me his head."

"I will take the best warriors, and we will find him."

Before he left, Standing Man said, "Post extra braves around the women all the time until we have this devil. Let this not happen again. And send a message to the one called Charles at the cattle ranch. Tell him of this and tell him we all need to work together to find this killer."

## Cheyenne Wells

Sunnie's messenger arrived the following morning and gave Charles the news. Immediately, Charles sent Pete and three ranch hands to join the search for Garza. Carl argued that he should go, but Charles refused to listen.

Two days later, Carl decided to take out on his own to visit Retha and Cricket at the Blue Moon Ranch. Carl always made his own decisions within reason, and he knew if he asked Charles, he would say no. Retha had worked at the ranch as payment for the cattle she had purchased, but a couple of weeks had gone by since she had gone back to the Blue Moon Ranch. Carl had taken quite a liking to Retha, and even though she was a little rough, he thought she was pretty. Maybe he had more reason for the visit than neighborly concern.

He arrived at the Blue Moon to find many nice changes in the former hideout of the Rico gang. The corrals were completed, and the place even had a nice sign painted with the name Blue Moon Ranch. He found Retha busy building a cattle chute. Cricket was skinning a couple of jackrabbits. Neither stopped working as they watched Carl approach them.

"Well, well, well." Retha smiled, "if it isn't the baby Armstrong. So, what brings you up here, my friend? Did you get lost, or did you just miss my good company?"

Carl smiled as he looked down from his saddle. "A little of both, Retha," he laughed. "I came to ask you to marry me," he grinned as he swung his leg over the saddle and hopped to the ground.

"Well, that's flattering, but I may already be married – I can't remember. If I was sure I wasn't, I wouldn't mind having a good-looking man like you," she laughed.

Carl threw a neighborly arm around her shoulder and gave her a squeeze. "Truth is, ma'am, I was a might worried about you and Cricket. We got word that Rico Garza kidnapped a young Sioux girl and almost killed Sad Hank." At her look of shock, he reassured her, "Oh, he's still alive but in pretty bad condition. The girl got away, but she's pretty beat-up and I think a little in shock. It sounds like Garza just used her as bait to catch Sad Hank. It worked, too – Sad Hank fell for it and was caught by two bear traps. Garza left them both to die, but he didn't know the rain was coming and it probably saved Hank and the girl."

"Where did the girl come from?"

"She lived in a village of Sioux about two hours' ride north of here."

"Yes. Cricket told me he saw this village when he was hunting a few days ago. He ran into a hunting party, and said they weren't the friendliest bunch."

"Well, that's what I thought when I first met them, but then we met their chief. They came here from the north because many of their people were hunted and killed or thrown into stockades. They are very cautious for sure," explained Carl. "Their chief, Standing Man, is very old, but wise. He once knew Johnny One Horn and Little Boy Horse. He said they were trusted friends."

"Well, I need to get back to work on this chute," Retha said brusquely, wiping her hands on her pant legs. "You can tell Charles I'll be back to work off some more of my debt as soon as I finish a few things around here. I plan on spending about ten days here and ten there." She picked up her tools, then smiled and winked at Carl. "Thank you kindly for paying us a visit."

Carl reached out and gave her another hug before mounting his horse. "Just remember, my friend, not to let your guard down. We're dealing with a real cutthroat."

As Retha watched Carl ride away from the Blue Moon, she was thinking about how long it would take her to pay off the money she owed the Triple A. She turned to Cricket, who had begun roasting the rabbits, and asked, "Cricket, you've talked of gold in this area. Do you know where any is?

He pursed his lips as he looked up pensively. It was several moments before he answered. "I know gold is somewhere near Echo of Moon. But spirits see. We take it, we cursed. We die."

"Maybe that's just an old wives' tale, and maybe there is nothing to it," countered Retha. "I owe the Triple A so much for our cattle, it will take over a year to pay it off. I just need to come up with another way," she explained, pursing her lips. "You said you have been there, so you could show me and then I'll go myself. Besides, I don't believe in these curses and things like that."

Retha continued to plead with Cricket as they ate their rabbit roast, though it seemed to get her nowhere. He just shook his head. At last, she gave up, threw her piece of rabbit on the ground, stomped away, and leaned on the corral chute she was building. Wiping frustrated tears from her eyes, she contemplated her cattle and dreamed of having a prosperous ranch one day.

After a while, Cricket pitched his remaining bit of rabbit to a stray wolf pup that had been hanging around the corrals. He walked to Retha and took her hand. "I take you. It not easy find.

Go to Moon Rock easy. Must go to Echo to get gold. I take you to Moon Rock when you ready. Two-day ride." he gestured to the northwest.

Retha was confused but was also intrigued by the words she had just heard. That strange *déjà vu* feeling swept over her once more, until she felt Cricket shaking her shoulders, concerned if she was all right.

She shook her head to clear the cobwebs. "You mean you have to go to this place in two places? I don't understand this."

"Hard to tell, but I show you. Then you know. Many people try to find, but find only death. First we go Moon Rock – it very hard. But it show way to Echo. Need ropes – rocks very steep, and Moon at top. I know this place, but I not see Moon they talk of on top. I see many bones – many men die there. Medicine man show me when I small boy, eight, nine seasons. He say never go. Only pray to spirits there – never go Moon Rock."

"Well, if you show me, I will go alone. You can stay and pray to the spirits if you want to, but you don't need to come along."

Cricket looked concerned. "Who watch place here when we go?"

"Well, Carl couldn't be too far from here yet. I'll ride and try to catch him, and we'll try to figure out something. I'll be back as soon as I can get it figured out." Retha saddled her horse and rode down the trail and into the valley. Finally, she saw Carl a mile or so ahead. When she reached him, he looked very surprised.

"What in the world is going on, gal? Did something happen?"

"Well, sort of," she answered. "Let's ride a little toward Cricket Creek and I'll tell you." They continued to the creekside while Retha tried to explain what she had planned.

Carl dismounted and led his horse Corky to the creek. "Ok, Retha, I realize it's going to be hard for you to pay your debt, but going off on some wild goose chase that might get you killed is crazy. You know, come to think of it, I hope Cricket hasn't told anyone else this yarn – it could get him killed. Droves of prospectors have tried to find that gold and it has never been found."

"Yeah, but Earl Stockman told us the place really exists," insisted Retha. "Cricket said he was taken there as a child. He knows where the place is. You don't know him like I do; he never lies."

"OK, Retha, I'll make you a deal. I can send a couple of hands to the Blue Moon to watch over it for a few days, but the bad news is I'm going with you. If you're not good with that, then I'm out and there is no deal."

Retha smiled, hugged Carl, and then kissed him, before quickly mounting her horse.

Carl stood bewildered as he smiled. "Well, I don't think

I've ever been kissed like that before! I might just have to tell those other gals I've got to up the ante!"

Retha smiled, "I might up it myself if this all works out. I'll wait for you at the Blue Moon but bring me a couple of good men. I don't want all my work to go to waste."

Carl mounted Corky, promising he would be back in two days, and they would start their quest. He would tell Charles of his plans at the campfire circle in the evening.

# CHAPTER 10

### Cheyenne Wells later that evening

"That's about the craziest thing I ever heard, Carl!" blurted Charles. "That's just an old bar room tale used to entertain the drunks and children; the place doesn't exist, Carl. Sad Hank seems to think it's a place created in the minds of witch doctors and wizards. He says it was a place of spiritual worship for the tribes that used to live here. As for the gold, I've only seen fool's gold in these parts." Despite his commonsense advice, Charles knew he wouldn't be able to change Carl's mind. He turned and dashed his coffee on the fire before walking off, shaking his head in disbelief. His nephew had always had a mind of his own.

The following morning, Carl picked Jose, a ranch foreman, and Pedro, a fence rider, to accompany him. They had worked for many days straight and welcomed the days off looking after Retha's ranch. By late afternoon they arrived at the Blue Moon.

Carl, Retha, and Cricket planned to leave early the next morning and to be at Moon Rock the next night. They sat around the campfire at the Blue Moon and watched as the celestial light show seemed to be brighter than ever.

As Jose listened to their discussion, he expressed a lot of concern for the group. "I have heard this story many times by prospectors, and they all say they never found a trace of the Moon gold. But they told stories of wolves with red glowing eyes that guard the place. Not many that got close to it managed to stay alive," he warned. "It's the last place I would go to look for my friends! Be careful. Even ol' Earl Stockman said to avoid the Echo of the Moon, and he was just about as rugged as they come."

Carl lay back on his saddle and contemplated the star-filled night. He was wondering if he had made the right decision or not. It was a little bit late now – he was already committed. The night seemed to pass very fast, and the rising of the sun almost blinded him when he awoke.

The three said their farewells at sunrise and rode out to start their journey. Jose stood shaking his head as they rode out of sight.

The first few hours were easy riding, but the terrain began to worsen as the day passed. The higher they ascended on the steep trails once traveled by the Pawnee and Sioux, the more dangerous they became. The old trails were fraught with steep cliffs and loose rock. At times they dismounted and led their horses to keep from slipping on loose rocks and sliding over the edge. Rattlesnakes lay in hidden spots scattered along the incline, making the trail even more dangerous. Rain showers, along with some high winds, also hampered their movement. By late afternoon the trio and their horses were worn out from the steep body-draining climb. At last, just before sunset, they came upon a cliff dwelling that was a very welcome sight.

"Wow, what a day," sighed Carl, as he gratefully slid from his horse. "Cricket, you didn't tell us we had to be part mountain goat to find this place."

Cricket smiled. "We not at hard part yet. I get dry sage brush to make fire."

Carl and Retha looked at each other with concern. The valley down below looked quite small from this height, and Carl wondered why anyone would take so much time to build these dwellings in such a place. White, fluffy clouds moved across the valley floor, leaving giant shadows as they passed. The smell of new rain permeated the air. Carl and Retha were awed by the beauty of this magical place. After the sun set, a half-moon rose in the east and the rain and clouds diminished. The night air cooled so quickly, it almost felt like late fall.

Carl turned to Cricket. "How far are we from this place, Cricket? I'm worn out already!"

"We leave when sun rise, we get there by noonday. It be easy for little while. Then it be hard again." He gestured upward. "Near top now. Then go north three-four hour. Then go down to Moon Rock."

Carl took his hat off and shook out his hair. "Oh, goody, I'm having more fun all the time."

Retha laughed as she watched Carl dance around in the dwelling, mocking the situation. Cricket just watched and shook his head. He walked over to where Retha was brushing her horse and whispered, "Carl crazy, Retha?"

Retha laughed and patted Cricket on the head, saying, "Sometimes, I guess. Sometimes we all are. He's a jokester for sure, but make no mistake, he can change moods in a split second if the time calls for it. I've seen him draw that old forty-four and fire before you could blink an eye. Don't make him mad, Cricket – you surely would not like the change."

Cricket's expression changed as he stood and stared as Carl explored the ruins. He wondered what Carl stood staring at and walked up beside him.

Carl called for Retha to join them. "Look at this, Retha. It proves the story is true."

There, carved in the wall of the ruins, were the initials EWS.

"Do you know who that is?" he asked. "That's Earl Wayne Stockman. He said he had been here, and this proves it. I remember the night he told us all the story of the Echo of the Moon. It seems like only yesterday. I remember Charles sitting in the gazebo and writing the story as he told it." He turned and headed back to the campfire. "Well, we better get some sleep, if we're leaving at sunup. I can't wait to see this Moon Rock."

Carl was awakened by a crash of thunder as a morning storm rumbled across the mountains. He quickly secured and settled the horses and led them under the overhang of the giant sandstone dwelling. The storm settled into a soft but menacing rain, making the narrow trail slippery and even more dangerous.

Retha worried for their safety, suggesting they wait out the rain, but Carl wanted to continue, rain or not. As they ascended the last half-mile to the summit, they dismounted and led the horses by hand. When they reached the summit, the plateau leveled off, making the riding much easier, but the trail disappeared. Cricket led the way for a couple of miles until they reached a huge outcropping of granite. Beside the huge rock there were traces of a very old trail, grown up with brush, that led down the mountain. Parts of the old trail were impassable until the brush was removed. Making their way down became very slow and dangerous. They had to use small mining spades to clear the brush, which consumed most of the day.

Finally, they came upon another huge outcropping on the side of the mountain that dwarfed the one at the trail's beginning. It extended out of the mountain and hung over a tremendous cliff. Ancient native paintings were scattered throughout the area. The trio was awestruck as they stood at the foot of the mammoth promontory. A few cliff dwellings had been constructed on the rock faces thirty or more feet up from the base.

Ancient natives had carved stepping holes that led all the way to the top of the edifice. At the first step were two skulls, likely placed as a warning to trespassers. Scattered at the bottom were remains of natives placed on wooden pedestals, as well as several skeletons tied to old posts.

The trail had consumed the complete day, as the sun was now setting over the western mountain. The trio hurriedly gathered firewood to build a fire before the night engulfed the area. A strange howl of the wind surged from the canyon below. Inside a small native dwelling they made their camp.

As they sat around the fire, they used a small pot and tripod to boil some beans and eat the dried bread Retha had in her saddlebags. They were all exhausted from the day's ordeal.

"Looks like they tortured and killed the old prospectors that found this place," Carl commented. "Cricket, you never said anything, but I know this is the place. Why, nobody's been here in years. Probably very few in the last hundred years. The only thing is, I don't see any gold, just granite. I thought this place was supposed to be laden with gold."

"No, this spiritual place. No gold here. I say you come here first to find the Echo. Gold at Echo. Medicine say much gold. Top of Rock has answer."

The morning came with a sprinkle of rain, and the trio watched from the opening of the ancient dwelling.

"That rock is going to be slippery; I think we should wait awhile," jested Carl. "Who's going up and who's staying here?"

Cricket agreed to stay and watch the horses, and an hour later Carl and Retha started their climb using the ancient footholds. Some of the weather-beaten steps were partially filled with years of dirt that had washed down from above. Carl, in the lead, took his time and used his hunting knife to dig them out as they fought to climb the many steps. A strong wind again hampered the climb. It didn't take long for Retha to back off because of the falling debris from Carl's digging that continually blew into her mouth and eyes. But as the angle of the steps changed, the dirt fell in another direction and Retha could stay ten or more steps behind him.

"Hold tight," Carl yelled, as gusty winds whipped at his clothing. "Whatever you do, don't look down."

Retha, trembling from the thought of falling, had to stop for a minute and hold herself tightly against the rock. She yelled that she would have to stop moving for a while because her legs were giving out from the strain of the climb.

"Only twenty or so more steps, Retha," Carl reassured her as he fed some rope from his side. He had reached the top, exhausted, and told Retha to tie the rope around herself. He quicky secured the rope to a huge boulder and waited as she regained her strength. He pulled as she climbed, and several minutes later, she reached the top.

Carl grabbed and hugged her with great relief that she was ok. "Damn, I don't know why the natives would ever climb this place. I wonder how many were killed from falling. It must be six hundred feet or more up here."

He gazed with amazement upon the valley below. The small trail led around the colossal rock, and it hugged the edge very closely. It would be certain death if one were to fall. A strong updraft wind roared from the valley below. The trail led to a natural formation of round, flat granite, formed in a large circle with a huge sliver standing along the upper edge. The angle of the circle was very steep and looked slippery. There were etchings in the granite, but it was weather-beaten and unreadable. After they looked at it for a period of time, they both realized that, whatever the formation was meant to tell them, they couldn't understand.

"I wish we knew for sure what we're looking for," frowned Retha. "There's something here, but what is it?"

Suddenly, Carl lost his footing and his foot slipped down into the steep circle. As he slid downward, flat on his side, he scrambled to dig his boots into some kind of hold. Retha saw what had happened, and quickly tossed her rope to him. With her help, he was able to inch his way back up the steep incline. Out of breath and exhausted, he finally managed to climb back onto the rim of the circle.

"There's nothing here that we can see or understand, Retha," Carl gasped as he tried to catch his breath. "We need to get more information from somebody. If there is something here I damn sure can't see it." He slowly pulled himself to his feet, "Let's look around and try to remember what we've seen. Then we can get out of here. Maybe it will make sense one day."

Retha and Carl very carefully made their way back down the steep steps and arrived at the bottom in late afternoon, relieved to find Cricket where they had left him. Completely exhausted from the day's ordeal, they decided to stay the night there and head back to the Blue Moon ranch when morning came.

Sitting around the fire that night, they told Cricket all about their trying day. Thankfully, Cricket had managed to snare a couple of rabbits. At least the trio would have a decent meal.

As they told their story, Cricket pointed to the moon in the eastern sky. "Moon very bright. More than I ever see."

Marveling at the sight, the trio was amazed by a strange reflection that beamed across the valley. As the moon rose higher in the sky, the reflective beam grew even brighter. It slowly moved across the mountains to the east and suddenly faded from sight.

Carl and Retha stood gaping, amazed at the strange phenomenon.

"It's real! it does mean something," Carl said, in awe. "That beam was pointing to something, but where? The moon is forever changing in the sky, like from winter to summer it is in a different place. We don't have a clue as to what time of year it points to the Echo."

The next morning, they had a discussion, and all agreed they should stay another day and scour the area looking for clues that would give them any solution to the baffling puzzle. They set out separately and met at sunset to compare notes. But all they'd found were the ancient etchings that the wind and sand had all but erased down through the decades.

That evening, exhausted once more, they watched for the second night the spectacular light show as the three-quarter moon rose.

"You know, Carl, I wonder how bright it would be if it were a full moon. Even if we stayed, we would have no way of knowing if we are even close to the right time of year. I guess we just don't know enough about this yet. I think you were right – it's best to just keep seeking more information and try it again one day," Retha told him. "I'm disappointed, but I'm proud we tried, and of what we found out. We probably know more about this place than most of those prospectors that spent their lives looking for it."

"Well, one thing's for sure, Retha, a lot of them were killed here. I can't believe so many bones are here – they're everywhere you look," Carl said, shaking his head.

As the trio bedded down for the night, the sounds of wolves echoed from all around, and the three took turns watching the horses. Every so often they would have to fire a shot to scare the beasts away. As the sun began to tint the dawn sky, reddish clouds and sifting dust from the valley left an eerie red reflection in the eyes of the fearsome predators. Carl remembered that legend, and in his mind another piece of the story had proved to be true. When the sun rose above Moon Rock, the wolves disappeared.

## Three days later at the Blue Moon Ranch

It was midday, and as Retha, Cricket and Carl wearily rode onto the Blue Moon Ranch, they were greeted by Jose and Pedro, who had a pot of deer stew boiling over the fire.

As they ate hungrily, Jose told them about a big cat of

some kind who had been stalking the cattle at night. None of the cattle had been taken, but they were all spooked. He showed them the huge tracks around the corral. This make the already-exhausted Retha even more tired and worried.

Carl agreed to stay the night, but he sent Jose and Pedro back to the Triple A. "Tell Charles I'll be back sometime tomorrow," he told them as they saddled up. "And I'm sure you both want to know what we found. But the answer is, nothing. We did find another clue that might mean something, but we're not sure how to follow it."

"I was warned about that place by ol' Earl Stockman years ago," Jose replied as he mounted his horse. "You won't catch me chasing that rainbow – most that do, end up dead." He wheeled the horse around. "Remember, my friends, that cat is a big one, and hungry, so watch the cattle or some will be gone!"

Jose and Pedro departed, and Carl and Retha had a new quest – to rid the Blue Moon of the hungry beast. Carl planned to tie a young steer outside of the corral to use as bait. That night they would set their plan into action. The three-quarter moon would rise about two hours after sunset, and they would wait until it lit the corrals before putting the steer in place. They would place themselves in a triangle and shoot as the cat entered between the two corrals. Carl had scanned the area, and it seemed it would be the easiest way in for the large cat. As the sun set, the moon was already high in the sky, and the transition would take an hour or so.

Carl sat and wondered how long it would take the big cat to show up. Would it wait until the late moon set and the night would become completely dark, about two hours before sunrise? For some unknown reason, Cricket was smiling all the time as they made their plans. He knew from experience that these big cats were very cunning.

Since the trio was already exhausted from the previous days' journey, they drank coffee and positioned themselves. As the night passed, Retha and Cricket found themselves nodding off to sleep occasionally, and Carl found it very difficult to stay awake as well.

The moon set late in the night and the area became very dark. Carl knew they wouldn't have much of a chance at getting a clear shot. The steer started getting restless just before dawn, but the sly cat never showed up. Just before the morning sun rose over the hill to the east, Carl noticed the silhouette of the huge cat on the crest of the hill. It sat there for a few seconds, and just as he was getting ready to pull the trigger, it disappeared.

Carl came out of hiding and walked to where Retha and Cricket were, to find them both asleep. He leaned back against the cabin, knowing that the cat wouldn't come back, at least not until the cover of night. At last, he fell fast asleep too.

## Cheyenne Wells

Jose and Pedro had arrived late in the afternoon but decided not to tell Charles until the morning gathering at the chuck wagon.

Charles saw them at sunup and approached them as they were drinking their coffee. "Well, if it isn't the cow sitters from Blue Moon," he said as he tipped his hat. "What's going on with the fortune hunters? I bet they were laden with gold when they came back."

"No, no gold," smiled Jose, 'but they found some clues. They do have another problem though – a mountain lion has been stalking their place. I saw it several times, but never could get a shot off. It's a big female and she is very smart. I didn't see her attack any cattle, but I think she might have gotten a couple of their chickens. I don't really know. Carl said he would be back, but first he wanted to take care of that cat."

"Yeah, I'll bet the cat he wants to deal with wears leather and has a long blonde French braid," smiled Charles.

"Well, you have to admit, that coyote woman can look real nice, señor Charles."

"She can at that, and Carl knows that for sure," agreed Charles.

# CHAPTER 11

## The Marshal at the Triple A

Time had passed, and the shooting of Lee Cobb was almost forgotten, when a territorial marshal with three deputies from Dodge City showed up at the ranch asking questions about the incident. It turned out he had a warrant for Shorty's arrest. He began questioning Shorty in the main bunkhouse, and Tex Luna rode to inform Joe, who was riding fences, of the marshal's presence.

Joe returned to the ranch and went directly to the bunkhouse, but by the time Joe arrived, the marshal had Shorty in handcuffs and leg irons.

"What the hell is this?" Joe yelled after crashing through the door.

The three deputies drew down on Joe, and for a second it looked very dangerous. They were ordered to stand down by the tough-looking marshal, who then addressed Joe. "I'm Sam Tig, U.S. Territorial Marshal out of Dodge City, and I have a warrant for this man for the murder of Lee Cobb." His tone softened a bit. "I'm not saying I'm going to take him in. I just need the true story of what really happened here."

As he was focused on the marshal's explanation, Joe hadn't noticed Nat Cobb standing to his left side.

"Marshal, I'm Joe Armstrong. To tell you the truth, there was so much gunfire that day, no one actually knows who shot Lee Cobb," Joe explained. "They drew down on our security officer, Tom Sheen, and there were several shots fired. They were trespassing and refused to leave. Why are you putting the blame on Shorty? He was assisting our appointed security officer."

Nat Cobb stepped from behind Joe's left and began yelling and pointing his finger at Shorty.

Joe quickly recognized Cobb and pushed him away. "Don't breathe in my face, mister. You're just a damn liar, and you and your brother brought all of this on yourselves."

"Well, I hope all of you hang!" Cobb yelled. "We were just camping on the river fishing."

"Well, Marshal, he was trespassing. He's lying. They were looking for gold and listening to an old phony gold story from some of the disgruntled ranch hands. I'm glad to say those ranch hands aren't here anymore."

Marshal Tig walked to the window and stared out for a while, relighting a half-smoked cigar.

"Well, Joe, that story is no secret. I've heard it myself – how you Armstrong boys found gold somewhere in the swamps in Mississippi," said Marshal Tig. Seems to me a hell of a lot of banks spread from Abilene to Garden City have purchased gold from you boys. Old coins too – I heard they weighed about four ounces apiece." He took a slow drag on the cigar and then stubbed it on the windowsill. "I believe you Armstrongs know more than what you're telling me. But as for the dead man, Lee Cobb, I don't think he would have pushed everything that far if it was just an argument about a fishing spot."

Shorty, who had been tied to a chair, tried to explain to Marshal Tig that he'd had several encounters with those two mangy dogs before this incident, and they hated him already. "That's why he's pointing his finger at me. All I was doing was my job, and they couldn't stand it."

Joe motioned for Shorty to be quiet and addressed the marshal again. "We did find gold coins down in the swamp," explained Joe, "but we've used it all to get to where we are now, with the ranch and all. We haven't had any gold for a long time. I'll go get Tom Sheen from the north pasture; he can explain to you what happened also."

"Well, while you're fetching Tom Sheen, the boys and I are going to get a little rest," agreed Marshal Tig. "We'll meet you tonight over by the river where we plan to camp. When you see the fire burning, you can come over with Sheen and we will talk. Meantime, Mr. Shorty here is going to stay with us. I know this Sheen you talk of – he used to be a sheriff over in Abilene and Garden City for a while. As I remember, he had a real temper. Tell him we won't put up with any trouble," he warned.

As Joe rode to where Tom Sheen was mending fences he wondered if this Marshal Tig had some kind of motive for his behavior. Tom was walking the fence line back toward the Triple A, so Joe turned around and rode alongside him. They were able to talk as they slowly walked their horses. Joe explained the events and the strange-acting marshal.

"Yeah, I know Tig," Tom frowned. "From what you've told me it sounds like he's on the take. The only way we can get Shorty off is to see what Tig wants in return. Ol' Tig is a dishonest lawman and has most of the territorial judges in his pocket."

Joe and Tom waited around the newly rebuilt gazebo until they saw the flickering of a fire burning a little south on the river. They mounted their horses and walked the short distance down to the river. As they arrived, a couple of the deputies were already drunk from whisky and were shooting crazily across the river. Marshal Tig approached their horses as they dismounted.

"Well, if it isn't Tom Sheen, gone from lawman to cattle puncher," Tig laughed.

"Marshal Tig," Tom Sheen smiled, "I see you've got yourself some real dandies for deputies. I bet you had to look far and wide for that bunch." He and Joe dismounted as he spoke. "But let's get to the real reason you're here, shall we? I see you brought that mangy Nat Cobb with you." He led his horse away from Cobb and Tig followed. "You're such a delight as always, Tig. Now, tell us your real reason for coming here, or better yet, how much do you want?"

Tig surreptitiously glanced at the deputies staggering around by the river and saw they couldn't hear their conversation. "Well, I'd say ol' Shorty might be worth about fifty of them big gold coins you boys have stashed," smirked Tig. "Otherwise, I'll just take him back to Dodge City and have my friend Judge Simms stretch his neck. I'll give you til sunup tomorrow."

The man ambled back toward his campfire, twirling his cold cigar between his fingers as if he hadn't a care in the world. Tom snorted in disgust, while Joe just stared.

Joe felt like his hands were tied and he had no choice but to pay the ransom. He felt like just shooting Tig right on the spot, but his conscious told him not to. He also knew that retrieving those hidden coins was going to be impossible at this late notice, because they were hidden in plain sight and people were always around that area.

After a second of thought, Joe followed and offered Tig another way of paying the ransom. "How much cash would you take? Remember, I told you that gold from the swamp has been gone a long time."

Tig walked away, as if contemplating the river. Finally, he spoke. "Well, I don't believe you about the gold, but if you give me two thousand dollars, me and Cobb will forget the whole thing."

Joe and Tom were shocked that a man of the law would stoop to this level. They watched Nat Cobb's face light up with joy as he quickly downed a shot of whisky.

"Give me two days," Joe reluctantly responded. "I'll have to go to Garden City to get the money. That's the best I can do."

After arguing for a few minutes, Tig agreed to give him the two days to deliver the cash. "I'll give you until noon on the second day or I leave, and your man Shorty swings," he yelled after them as they mounted their horses. "We'll still be here by the river," Tig continued, "and throw in a few bottles of good whisky, just because I'm so good natured!" he laughed. "I'll even untie him once in a while and let that little wife of his visit him, if he stays tied to that chair."

"Well, that's damn right friendly of you, Tig. You always were a loving man," frowned Tom. Seeing that the longer they talked, the worse things got, Tom and Joe returned to the gathering park to discuss their plans. It was decided that Tom would stay and watch over the ranch and Tex Luna would accompany Joe to Garden City. They would need to leave right away to get back by the deadline the marshal had set. Joe and Tex packed a few supplies, and then Joe had to do a lot of explaining to Cindy before he left.

## The Betrayal

One day had passed, and on the second afternoon Tig decided to send the deputies back to Dodge City. They knew nothing about the deal he had made with Joe Armstrong, and he planned to split the money with Nat Cobb. Joe and Tex were due back from Garden City the next morning.

In reality, Joe and Tex had faked the trip to Garden City. Instead, they took the cash from the safe in Charles' office, and then stayed out of everybody's sight by hiding in Charles' office. Even Cindy was unaware of their cover. They were giving themselves some time to evaluate the situation and make sure the crooked Tig and so-called deputies left the rest of the ranch alone, especially the women and young girls. Only Tom Sheen knew of the plan. He and Joe had had a suspicion that Tig would send the deputies back to Dodge City. Now, only Tig and Cobb were left, and they hoped to release Shorty after overpowering Tig and Cobb.

Tig, being the sly devil that he was, had already suspected something was afoot, and planned to take Shorty as insurance for his actions. In the morning when Joe and Tex faked their arrival, Tex Luna stayed behind, and Tom Sheen accompanied Joe to the campsite by the river.

"Well, you're almost late," smiled Tig. "You got my money?"

"I got the money you're stealing from us, if that's what you mean," frowned Joe.

"Well, boys, that's good, because there has been a change of plan. You see, I'm taking ol' Shorty here to Dodge City, I'll let him go just outside of town. Let's say it's just to keep you boys honest."

Joe looked at Tom in disgust. It appeared their plan had failed.

"If you try to follow me, I'll shoot him on the spot, and just leave that gag in his mouth. It really bothers me to see a grown man beg." Tig laughed as he mounted his horse.

Tig and Cobb had tied Shorty's hands and feet and laid him across the saddle. Tig walked his horse beside Joe and grabbed the saddle bag holding the money. Joe knew there was nothing more to do except to let them go, and hope nothing would happen to their old friend Shorty.

As they watched Tig and Cobb lead the horse carrying Shorty away, Joe felt sick inside and helpless. Tom Sheen suggested they follow them and at some point, bushwhack them. Joe argued against the plan for fear Tig would spot them and kill Shorty. Shaking his head, Joe gave in to the fact that he would have to take Tig at his word that he would turn Shorty loose once they reached Dodge City.

~ ~ ~

One day's ride away from the ranch, Shorty was begging Tig to let him ride upright in the saddle, but Tig refused. Nat Cobb taunted Shorty the whole way and made the agonizing trip even more painful. When nightfall came, they found cover in a small wash in the barren landscape. Tig removed Shorty from the horse by lifting his feet, causing Shorty to fall headfirst into the hot sand. Shorty tried to speak but the gag was so tight it caused blood to appear in both sides of his mouth. Cobb laughed and slammed down a slug of rye whisky. Tig quickly grabbed the whisky from his hand and ordered Cobb to build a fire to roast a jackrabbit they had shot along the way. Cobb cursed Tig but did what he was told.

After the rabbit was roasted, Cobb and Tig sat cross-legged by the fire eating. Drinking a bottle of whisky, the two argued over the money from the ransom. Cobb demanded that Tig give him his half. Tig just stared at him, then drew his forty-four and shot Cobb in the head. He fell instantly backwards, dead. Tig laughed.

"Never did like anybody to cuss me," Tig joked. "Hey, Mr. Shorty, did you ever see anybody kick like that? I wonder how he ever got the idea I was really going to give him half of that money. The boy was just plain dumb."

Shorty struggled to free his hands because he knew Tig would leave no witnesses. Tig took another gulp of the whisky and staggered to where Shorty lay on the ground. He pulled back the hammer of his forty-four, pointed it towards Shorty's head, and fired, intentionally missing him. As he was laughing deliriously, he fired another shot that went into the ground close to Shorty, grazing his head. Blood covered Shorty's face as he lay perfectly still. He knew his only hope was to act dead.

As Tig took another gulp of whisky, a voice from behind him yelled, "Why look here, look here. If it isn't ol' Marshal Tig himself."

Tig froze in his tracks and his eyes widened because he recognized the voice of Rico Garza.

"Been watching you for a couple of hours, Tig. You know, you're kind of predictable. I overheard ol' Cobb there arguing about splitting that money – why, it's right here," he laughed as he grabbed the saddle bag from the horse. "Much obliged for shooting that no-account Shorty too. Seems like my lucky day. But unfortunately, not yours, Tig."

Tig dropped to his knees and begged for his life, but to no avail. Rico had recruited a traveling partner, a Comanchero called Chico Blue, who came from behind Tig, grabbed his hair, and slit his throat. As Rico laughed, Chico sawed Tig's scalp from him while Tig was still gurgling, trying to scream. Rico laughed as he watched the horror unfold.

The two sat down by the fire and finished the rest of the roasted rabbit. After they fumbled through the belongings and saddlebags and counted the money, they mounted and walked their horses and the other three they had just acquired off into the desert night.

Shorty lay very still for a long time. When he was sure they were gone, he struggled to free himself. He knew he was very lucky indeed to be alive. He tore some of the clothing from Nat Cobb's body and used it to wrap his head wound. Knowing that the pitch-black darkness would hinder his travel, he made it a mile to a small stand of brush, and pulled the weeds and brush over him to hide as best he could. There he lay on his back in the sand with a blinding headache, his mind racing to his wife Yolanda and small child.

The morning sun reddened the sky as he regained some of his bearings. His eyes scanned the hills until he recognized the bluffs by the ranch. He found he could walk but struggled to keep his balance. He decided to cut directly across and not use any trail, for fear of being spotted by Rico and his cutthroat Chico Blue. Across the wasteland, the way was rugged with yucca thorns and brush. Even the dried tumbleweeds had sharp tiny thorns. By late afternoon he was parched by the sun and exhausted. His bare feet bled from the sharp rocks and rugged terrain. It seemed that the farther he traveled, the farther the ranch appeared to be. Thirsty and exhausted, he finally sat by an outcropping of rocks to rest.

Shorty was a strong, determined man, and knew how to survive. He gathered a few cacti around the rocks and quickly ate them, giving him a small bit of water and energy. The sun set on the first day and the wind howled of a coming dust storm. But he knew summer winds sometimes brought summer storms, and that gave him hope of some real water. He wondered if he would survive long enough to see his wife and child again. As the darkness filled the night, he could see the lanterns of the ranch in the distance. He moved forward and paced himself. As the night passed, he finally reached the fence line of the ranch. He felt relieved as he knew a fence rider from the ranch would show sometime that day. He leaned against a fence post and fell fast asleep.

The following morning, Shorty awoke to a wet cloth being rubbed on his forehead. As he regained his senses, he recognized Tex Luna at his side.

"My God, Señor Shorty, what have they done to you?" he asked.

"It's a long story, my friend. Please, just get me home, Tex."

"I will, my friend. Your woman is missing you. She will be overjoyed to see you back."

## The Triple A

When Tex arrived with Shorty at the ranch, everybody gathered around wanting to help. They carried him to his cabin with his loving Yolanda by his side. She, Joe, and Tom Sheen listened as Shorty told his bizarre story. None of it seemed to surprise Tom Sheen; he had heard many stories about Marshal Tig when he himself had been a lawman. Tom explained to Joe and the others that when Tig did not return to his job, there would be a day that some other lawmen would come is search of him. It might take a few months because a territorial marshal has to cover a lot of country, and it's not uncommon for them to be away for months at a time going from town to town. For now, Shorty would be safe for a while. But it might not be safe for too long. The deputies Tig had hired would probably tell their story when they returned to Dodge City.

## Abilene, Kansas

After killing Marshal Tig and Nat Cobb, Rico Garza had shaved his beard and cut his hair. He, with Chico Blue, wanted to exploit their newfound wealth, and drifted into Abilene, excited to live like the rich. The first stop was the Merchants' Hotel for a room and a bath. Then they both drifted to the mercantile store to pick up new duds and expensive cigars. Many gamblers exploited the booming cattle town of Abilene, and they would hardly be noticed. That, at least, was their way of thinking. Across the street was the wild Cactus Jim's Saloon full of girls eager to take the patrons' money any way they could get it.

The place was perfect for Rico, who planned to play the son of a wealthy railroad man from the St. Louis area with Chico Blue as his assistant and bodyguard. Rico was a sly man and would be able to play the part very well. He would blend in and have the women at his beck and call because of the money. Staying out of trouble was his goal and he would try to control his murderous temper.

Running the brothel at Cactus Jim's was a feisty young blonde woman they called Cat Brink. She ran the saloon with an iron hand, and the place was a boom every day. She had purchased the place from a gold miner who had found a fortune of gold in Colorado. No one really ever knew how or where Cat got the money to buy the saloon, but the pretty Cat Brink would, it was said, do anything for enough money. Rico had a strong interest in Cat Brink and was determined to make a play for her.

Chico Blue had a bad drinking problem and usually when he drank, he ran his mouth and gambled recklessly. Consequently, he was being carefully watched by Rico. Acting Sheriff Swartz had also heard of Chico's boasting and bragging and was starting to take notice of it.

As the days went by, Rico realized Chico was losing a lot more than he was winning. Rico liked his new lifestyle and figured he needed to get rid of Chico. He devised a plan to buy Chico a new horse and invite him to join him for a ride, and then shoot the outlaw and bury him somewhere in the plains south of Abilene.

~ ~ ~

Two days later, Rico purchased a horse from the local livery stable. He found Chico at his usual table at Cactus Jim's and walked him outside and surprised him with it. The drunken Chico was thrilled with the gift and hugged Rico and thanked him for being such a good friend. He agreed to take a ride in the moonlit night and share a bottle of whisky so they could talk about future dealings.

Several miles south of Abilene they were laughing and talking about their newly found lifestyle when Rico dismounted his horse and said he had to relieve himself. He had come to the spot earlier in the day and dug a shallow hole in the soft sand. When Chico got off his mount to join him, Rico came from behind and shot him twice in the back of his head. He dragged the body to the grave and, using a shovel he had planted there, covered the grave. As he kicked the last of the dirt over the grave, he smiled and poured the remaining whisky over it. "Have a good drink, my friend," he laughed. "I once told you I never leave any witnesses."

Rico assumed nobody would miss Chico because of his intimidating ways. He rode back into town full of confidence, to continue his quest for Cat Brink's affections and his new lifestyle. He took a new name for the part: Ray King.

# CHAPTER 12

## The Herd at Cheyenne Wells

Several of the hands were busy building a bunkhouse and a couple of cabins to accommodate the women that would soon be coming from the Triple A. The hands were all getting lonely for feminine companionship after being stuck so far away for so long.

The Cheyenne Wells project was developing as planned, and wagons were arriving almost daily with lumber and supplies ordered by Charles. Charles was an excellent business manager, and it seemed he had toughened up and was enjoying the challenge of expanding the ranch. He also kept writing down true stories as they happened. Several of his manuscripts had reached the east and people loved to read of the "wild west."

This morning, Charles watched the sun rise and wondered why his nephew Carl had not returned from Retha's Blue Moon Ranch. He was a little worried about Carl, but then he knew Carl had a fancy for Retha and that amused him. Still, he decided to take a ride to the Blue Moon to check on him. He packed a small amount of supplies in his saddle bags and informed Nate of his plan.

"Charles, you should take Pete with you. That Rico Garza could be anywhere in this valley," Nate warned.

"Yeah, but it's a big valley and we can't just run scared

all the time. Besides, I think ol' Rico has probably left by now, or else he's dead. I'll be fine," he smiled. "Anyway, I'll see you in a couple of days. If you need me, it's only a few hours' ride from here."

Charles knew the ranch was in good hands with Nate and Pete running the show and didn't worry about leaving for a few days. But Pete and Nate exchanged glances as their boss rode away.

Pete shook his head. "You know, Nate, these Armstrong boys have got more grit than anybody I've ever seen. They seem to love living on the edge all the time."

Nate smiled as he rolled a cigarette. "Yup. That's what makes them succeed, don't you think?"

"Maybe, Nate, but we're probably all crazy for being here in the middle of nowhere."

By midday Charles had arrived at the Blue Moon to find Carl and Cricket working on the corral. Carl didn't seem surprised to see Charles; he just looked at him and smiled. "I wondered how long it would take you to show up, Uncle Charles. Was it because you miss my smiling face or my outstanding personality?"

"Well, a little of both I guess," his uncle answered as he turned in the saddle to look around. "I don't see Miss Retha anywhere. Is she in the cabin?"

"Yeah, making a pot of beans and fried quail, I think. Get on down and we'll go see – she would probably be glad to see you."

"This place is really starting to look good, Carl, but tell me about that wild goose chase you all went on. I don't see any gold stacked up around here."

The men entered the cabin to see Retha stoking the wood stove with a big pot of beans steaming and quail frying on the top. When she saw her guest, Retha stopped what she was doing and ran to hug Charles.

"What in the world brings the big commander in chief of the giant Triple A way up here to the tiny Blue Moon?" she laughed.

"Well, I just wanted to make sure I got my share of the gold," he smiled. "You see, I don't trust that Carl." He winked.

Carl and Charles were still joking around as they sat down at the old wooden table. Retha soon joined them.

"We found the Moon Rock all right, but there was no gold there. It was a dangerous place and not for the faint hearted," she explained. "It was obvious that many people have died there – there were bones all around it. A native tribe lived or visited there long ago, and had some kind of rituals, I guess. We climbed to the top of it and about got killed. There is a huge round circle of solid granite and that's all we could see. It was at a steep angle and faced the west toward the bigger mountains. The only other thing we saw was a tall steeple of granite sticking out of it. It was about fifteen feet tall and only about five feet wide."

Charles sobered, staring at the table. "The sun dial. Well, I'll be damned – it's really true."

Retha sat up in her seat, her eyes narrowed. "Sun dial? What are you talking about, Charles?"

"The story according to old Earl Stockman. He said he left because the sun was a long way from the mark, and it would take eleven months or so before it reached the mark again."

Carl tipped back the old wooden chair and propped it with his feet. "We saw no mark, that I know of; yet again, we weren't looking for one. The moon those two nights cast an eerie reflection across the valley, so my guess is that it moves as the days get shorter or longer."

"Well, there's another thing I remember from my writing. Earl said he was there in October, and the phase of the moon had already passed the mark. That means the cycle wouldn't repeat itself until September of the next year. It also means that it would be the first full moon of September, judging from the drawings he found. He said he found two circles on the sundial; one was clearly marked."

Retha and Carl's excitement grew with every word. They asked many questions, including the most obvious: why hadn't Charles told them this before?

Charles shrugged, shaking his head. "I really thought it was just one of Earl's yarns he would spin to entertain everyone; I had no idea it was true. He said he never went back for fear of the curse the Pawnee warned him about. Besides, he felt it was guarded too heavily by several tribes including the Comanche. Now that they are mostly all gone from the area, our best bet is to wait until the first full moon in September, and damned if I won't go with you."

"Go with us?" Carl laughed. "I thought you said this was a wild goose chase."

"Well, now I don't know. I like adventures, Carl. Hell, if I didn't, I wouldn't be here! I'd still be down in that swamp in Mississippi, don't you think?"

"Yeah, I suppose we all would, Charles," smiled Carl. "Well, this is the first part of August. I guess we can plan to go back to Moon Rock in about six weeks or so, don't you think, Retha?"

"Yep, and it won't hurt to have some help."

Charles settled it. "I'm all in, and we'll plan on it. Another thing we need to talk about is, did you ever deal with that mountain lion that's been hanging around? There have been sightings around the herd at Cheyenne Wells, too. I'm wondering if maybe it's the same one. Sad Hank said there are a lot of them that show up in certain years."

As night fell on the Blue Moon, Charles helped watch for the big cat, but again there was no trace. He decided that he would leave the following morning but promised that he would definitely be back in September to help in the quest for the Echo of the Moon.

It was obvious that Carl and Retha had become very close, and it didn't look like Carl would be leaving any time soon. Charles planned to get a few things in order at

Cheyenne Wells and then return to the Triple A to finish some business arrangements he had planned.

Charles returned to Cheyenne Wells the following day and met with Nate and Pete to give them instructions to carry out while he was away. Then he started his journey south. After two long, dusty days of traveling, he arrived at the Triple A.

Within minutes after crossing the property line, Charles was greeted by several armed ranch hands. Tex Luna and his crew were always on the watch for thieves and predators. Tex didn't recognize him at first and fired a couple of warning shots in front of Charles' horse Sachi, causing him to buck Charles from the saddle. Thankfully, he landed in the soft sand. But as he was brushing himself off, he realized several rifle barrels were pointing down at him.

"Whoa! Whoa!" Tex yelled "It's Señor Charles!"

Realizing what they had done, several of the ranch hands jumped from their mounts to Charles' side, with everyone trying to dust him off at once.

"I'm all right," Charles laughed, scrambling to his feet. "I'm glad to know the Triple A is in good hands."

Tex, still sitting in his saddle, had to turn his head away to keep Charles from seeing him laugh. "Sorry, boss, to scare ol' Sachi like that. We just never know anymore who we're going to find out here."

Charles had trained Sachi well – he just had to whistle and Sachi walked back to him.

"A lot of things have happened since you've been gone, Señor Charles. We can fill you in when we get back into town."

Charles was pretty curious, but he didn't ask many questions riding the next mile or so back to the bustling ranch. As he rode down the street, he was amazed at all the work that had been accomplished. The place was almost completely restored. He was impressed by a barrier several hundred yards from the beginning of the main street made from timbers crossed in X-shapes that stood up to ten feet tall. He saw that it was constructed to keep burning tumbleweeds from ever repeating the chaos they had once inflicted on the Triple A. The timbers, laced with barbed wire in front, would, in theory, cause the tumbleweeds to stack there and burn out. Tumbleweeds burn out very quickly, and it was doubtful they would ever burn long enough to burn through the wire and the debarked timber.

Impressed by all he had seen, Charles looked forward to seeing Joe and Cindy and the two boys. As he neared the schoolhouse, Earl and James came running down the street to meet him. He dismounted in front of the school, and Joe's wife Cindy joined the two boys to greet him with joy. He was thrilled to have such a wonderful greeting from family, and quickly accepted their offer of fresh-baked apple pie and coffee. It was great to be home.

~ ~ ~

The next morning Charles and Joe sat in the office and discussed their plans for the coming months. It was agreed the two of them, accompanied by Tom Sheen, would go to Abilene to order coal from the railroad to be shipped in from Kentucky.

Joe remembered the experience with the depot manager and shook his head with dismay. "That depot manager was the rudest man I ever saw," he reminded Charles. "I don't look forward to seeing that old goat again."

"Well, we don't have to go there this time – just to the telegraph office to order the coal. The shipping company will take care of the rest," his brother said. "If we order now, it should be here by the winter, and we'll sure need it. At least we can hope it gets here before winter sets in!"

Charles spent the next two days at the Triple A checking on the construction. The ranch personnel were amazed at

Charles' transformation from a refined man in a business suit into a rough-looking seasoned cowboy. "Uncle" Charles also made sure to take time to go fishing with his nephews Earl and James. He was proud that both were good at riding and were helping around the ranch doing odd jobs and learning the ranching duties.

One afternoon, Joe came to join them at the riverbank as the three were fishing. "By the way, where's Carl?" Joe asked. "I thought he would be riding at your side when you got here. But you haven't even mentioned him since you came!"

Sitting on the riverbank on a wooden bench, Charles was enjoying watching Earl and James fish. Slowly he tipped his hat back and turned to Joe. "You sure you want to know, brother?"

Joe looked alarmed.

"Oh, he's all right, Joe, but he's just grown up some. He's not a little boy anymore. He's been living at a place the Coyote Woman named the Blue Moon Ranch. She found a young man named Cricket, a good boy and about as rugged as they come for his age. She's kind of raising him like a mother would."

Joe was confused. He just looked at Charles and opened his hands as if to say, "Well, you still didn't answer my question, Charles."

"Well, Joe, it seems to me your boy's hormones are getting to him, and he's taken quite a shine to Retha. They've got a real nice place up there; I visited them right before I came here. They been raising cattle, chickens, and a few horses I sold them – why, they've even got a couple of goats. By the looks of things, I don't think he will be leaving there any time soon."

"That's the darndest thing I've ever heard! His mother's not going to like that very much, I can tell you that! Why, Retha's a real pretty woman, but she's about nine years older than Carl, isn't she?"

"Well, Joe, love is blind. That's what they say," laughed Charles.

"Well, how would you know? Have you ever been in love?" Joe relaxed as he teased.

Charles returned his smile and stared across the swirling river for a second. "Yeah, I was, but she never knew it. I'll just leave it at that. If ever the right one comes along, that might be a different story. Now let's walk down to the river and see how those boys are doing with their fishing."

Joe couldn't seem to grasp the new rough-looking Charles – he almost seemed to be a different person. He had even grown a beard, which gave him a much more intimidating look than the clean-cut businessman he'd always been.

## Abilene, Kansas

Upon arriving in the bustling town of Abilene, Joe, Charles and Tom Sheen were eager to rest from the long ride. They rode down the dusty streets and were amazed at how the town had grown. The price of a room and bath had doubled since the last time they were there. After settling into their room at the Merchant Hotel, they were eager to have a meal and a few drinks. They walked across the street to the busy Cactus Jim's Saloon, where they were greeted at the bar by the pretty Cat Brink, who introduced herself to them.

Every card table in the huge saloon was full of people and noise. A piano player pounded out the songs continuously. Some people that recognized Tom as a former deputy in town came up to say hello.

Cat Brink overheard some of the conversation and took an interest in them. She came over to ask why they were in town. "So, you're the Armstrongs that own that huge Triple A?" she asked.

"Well, you might say that," smiled Joe.

Cat was known for gold digging, and she started pushing herself on Joe and Charles. It wasn't long before they attracted several more of the saloon girls. The smell of money was in the air and the girls of the trade sensed it.

Charles leaned toward Joe and Tom and whispered, "Joe, you shouldn't have told them who we are. I can smell trouble and we better be ready for it."

It wasn't long before Charles noticed a few dusty-looking cowhands whispering and staring in their direction. He was sure the rumors of gold were known to many.

Tom Sheen noticed a gambler at one of the tables that he thought looked familiar. The man was keeping his head down as if he was looking at his cards, but something was very familiar about him. He leaned across the bar and asked Cat Brink who the man was.

"Oh, that's my friend Ray King. He's a railroad man from St. Louis. Do you want to meet him? He's a real nice guy; besides that, he's got a lot of money."

"No, I thought he was somebody else, but looking at the way he's dressed, I'm probably wrong," said Tom as he took another glance at the man. "The man I know wouldn't be dressed like that."

"Anyway," said Tom as he put his hand on Charles' shoulder, "it's about time we go, don't you think, boys? Cat, can you send us three of those steaks on your menu over to the Merchant Hotel? We've got a real busy day tomorrow. Just have your girl leave them at the front desk and they'll bring them to us." As he turned back to the Armstrong brothers, he said in a low voice, "I don't want to give anybody our room number."

When they walked out of the saloon, they realized they had drawn a lot of attention. A couple of the saloon girls walked out after them, offering to spend the night, but were quickly turned down by Joe. The girls laughingly walked back into the saloon.

"That gambler in there, boys," said Tom as soon as they

were away from the saloon, "sure as hell looked like Rico Garza. He looked different in that fancy suit and hat, but I've seen Garza up close, and I'd almost swear it was him."

"You think it is? If it is, we need to deal with him," frowned Joe. "He's as low as they come, and I would enjoy putting a bullet right between his eyes."

"Well, we don't know for sure, Joe. Besides, we can't get into a fracas the first day we're in town. Let's bide our time and make sure we know."

~ ~ ~

The following morning Charles sent his telegram to order the much-needed coal. He had noticed Tom Sheen still seemed a little nervous, and the three kept thinking about the gambler. They inspected some horses at the local corral that were for sale and bought needed supplies at the dry goods store.

Before leaving town, Charles and Joe noticed Tom Sheen heading to Cactus Jim's saloon. They knew right away that Tom was going to confront the outlaw. They followed a little distance behind, just in case they were needed.

Tom walked into the saloon and, just as he thought, the man the town knew as Ray King was sitting at his usual table. Tom walked to the same card table and took a seat. He asked to be dealt in and started talking to Ray King, a.k.a. Rico Garza.

As he sat studying Ray King, he noticed he had a couple of fingers missing on his left hand. As the game was going on, he tried to act as calm as he could, and talked a little about what Cat Brink had told him about Ray being attached to some kind of railroad business. Joe and Charles had walked into the saloon and stood at the bar casually watching Tom and expecting anything.

After Tom had sat there a while observing, he noticed

part of Rico's right ear was also missing. His mind flashed back to the story he had heard years before. Rico Garza had had an altercation with the rugged mountain man Earl Stockman. Tom pulled his forty-four and pointed it dead at Rico's head. "You know, mister, an old mountain man once told me he encountered a young man that he had a fight with. He said he cut off two of the young man's fingers and part of one ear. That man was a cold-blooded killer named Rico Garza."

Rico just sat and glanced around the room. The other patrons had heard the conversation and were shocked at what they heard. Several of the men drew down on Rico and he had no choice but to raise his hands above his head. Joe and Charles quickly came to Tom's aid, and Charles stripped the guns and derringer from Rico. Rico cursed the men, and they marched him out of the saloon in front of a crowd of people who were shocked at what they had just seen. Cat Brink stood motionless with her hands over her face as she watched.

They marched him across the street to the Abilene marshal's office. Marshal Swartz opened the door to one of the cells and locked the still-cursing Rico in the cell.

"Well," Swartz declared, "you boys just done me a favor. I suspected this man was Rico Garza, but I was just waiting for the right time to get him. How you been, Tom? You ever want to come back here, I got your job saved."

"Well, I kind of like what I'm doing now, but maybe one of these days," Tom smiled as he shook his head.

Marshal Swartz stood in front of the cell bars staring at Rico and smiled. "I thought that was you all the time, Rico. You've already been sentenced to hang, Rico – remember that? As soon as I can, with permission from the territorial judge, I'm going to string that sorry ass of yours to the old oak tree in the square."

Rico just sat and cursed the marshal, saying anything that came into his evil mind. Joe and Charles shook their heads with disgust as they listened. Swartz laughed as he reached for a buggy whip coiled on the wall. There were two deputies playing cards at a small table in the jail. Swartz ordered the deputies to strip the outlaw and tie him to the inside of the bars.

Joe and Charles both agreed it was time for them to leave. As they walked from the saloon, they could hear the cracking of the whip and Rico still cursing.

"That ol' Swartz didn't take sassing very well, did he, brother?" Joe commented as he stopped and looked back.

"No – that's one place I wouldn't ever want to be, especially with him holding the reins. Ol' Rico has it coming and a lot more, though. Hell, we all know that. There's no telling how many people he's killed. I wanted to shoot him so bad, just thinking about what he did to that young Barrow girl. Whatever he gets, he deserves it."

"Yeah, well, looking back won't solve anything now, or bring anything back. I'm just glad we were the ones, along with Tom Sheen, that brought him to justice. I'm sure Sad Hank will be pleased. By the way, I really don't know how he's getting along; I heard he was sure in bad shape."

Charles reassured him, "He's in good hands with Standing Man. I intend on riding up there when I get back to Cheyenne Wells."

"You intend to go back to Cheyenne Wells, Charles? I really thought you would have had enough of the rough life by now. I'm looking at a rugged-looking cowboy instead of the brother I'm used to seeing in a fancy suit. It almost seems like I'm seeing a different man."

"Well," smiled Charles, "you are! Now, if you boys will excuse me, I made a date tonight with that cute little Cat Brink."

Joe and Tom watched in amazement as Charles walked away toward the saloon. Joe just shook his head, and Tom smiled.

"Did you hear what I just heard, Tom?"

"Yeah, I've been watching her come on to him. I bet he has a hell of a time with that little filly. Why, she's a handful and a half. Sure is pretty, though. You know, since this is our last night here, Joe, I think I'll go to the hotel and get a bath. There's a couple of little gals in that saloon that I'd like to get to know a little better too."

As Joe watched Tom walk away, he smiled. He thought how lucky he was to have his wife, Cindy. He didn't envy the bachelors at all. As he walked down the dusty street, a sign that read "Horses for Sale" caught his eye, and since he was by himself, he thought, "why not look at some horses?"

~ ~ ~

The next morning, Joe and Tom met at the Abilene House to have breakfast, as they had previously agreed. They sat drinking coffee, but Charles never showed. To their amazement, though, Cat Brink walked to their table. She sat down and smiled as she observed the two bewildered men.

"Here's a note from your brother, Joe. He's going to be tied up for a while doing business and wants you two to head on back to the ranch."

"Business?" Joe blurted. "What kind of business? It's funny he didn't mention that to us."

"Well, he said to tell you it's personal, boys," Cat laughed. "And Tom, that little Jena sure took a liking to you – says she's going to come see you at the Triple A one of these days."

Tom laughed and took a sip of his coffee. "You know, I'd kind of like that. Tell her she's welcome anytime, anytime at all."

Seeing the look on Tom's face, Joe stood and looked around the room for a second. "You know, I guess I won't be able to bring anyone from the ranch here anymore," he smiled. "They seem to go crazy here. But if that's what Charles wants, I guess I won't be able to talk him out of it. Tom, we'd better get out of here. Remember, we've got to stop over at that livery stable. I bought two horses. They said they came from Arabia or somewhere like that."

"Arabia?" Tom remarked. "I got to see this!"

When they walked into the livery stable, Tom stared at the two Arabian horses and smiled. "What did these set you back, Joe? They sure don't look like regular horses. I thought only camels came from that part of the world."

Tom watched as Joe counted out four hundred dollars to the man. "You know, Joe, it's a good thing Charles doesn't know about this. He would probably skin you."

"Well, you know, Tom, I'm still half owner of the Triple A, whether Charles likes it or not. I kind of look at this as a business venture."

Tom just grinned as he readied the two Arabian horses for the trip back to the Triple A.

~ ~ ~

When Joe and Tom got back to the Triple A they sat at the gazebo in the gathering park and told the story about their encounter with Rico. Shorty was elated that the murderous outlaw had been captured. The two Arabian horses got plenty of attention from everyone too. Joe's sons, Earl and James, laid claim to the offspring of the pair, and it seemed they would have it no other way.

The ranch rebuilding project was almost complete, and some of the workers were loading their belongings in wagons, ready to leave within days. Tex Luna had decided to keep several of the workers as permanent employees, especially the ones that had both building and ranching skills. Most of the men he kept on were married. Tex believed there would be fewer problems that way, since there were so many young ladies already living there.

Things were returning to normal around the ranch and the people had resumed the nighttime musical gatherings at the gazebo park.

Joe's wife Cindy was proud to see her small township come back to life. Although the rules were still strict, almost everybody would join in, and things were going well. Music was important, as guitars, banjos, rub boards and a few Mexican trumpets filled the afternoons and early evenings with melody. Earl and James loved the guitars and were learning fast to be a part of the festivities. Sometimes wagons heading west would stop by the newly-built dry goods store to buy supplies and essentials. Some would stay for a few days and were welcomed by the Triple A residents, while others chose to carry on with their journeys. Everyone was welcome except a few troublemakers that were immediately asked to leave.

Tom had advised Joe that he thought Shorty and his wife Yolanda should resettle in Cheyenne Wells, as he felt the search for Marshal Tig would continue when Tig didn't return to Dodge City. They met with Shorty and discussed their reasoning. Shorty agreed and would plan the trip. Not too many people knew of the Cheyenne Wells settlement, and it would be a safer place for him and his growing family.

Three days later, Charles arrived from the "business" he supposedly had in Dodge City. He spent the day fishing with Earl and James and planned to leave the following morning for Cheyenne Wells. He was amazed to see the Arabian horses that Joe had purchased, but never asked what the purchase price was.

"So, brother, how did everything work out with Cat Brink?" Joe teased as he walked up behind Charles.

"Good, very good," grinned Charles as he inspected the new rebuild of the ranch. "She's quite a little handful. She plans to visit me soon; that is, to see the ranch."

"None of my business, brother, but there are stories that

she's a little gold digger," Joe said, punching Charles playfully in the ribs.

"Yeah, I reckon, but she would fit right in with the Armstrong family. You may have forgotten, brother, that we once dug for gold ourselves. Anyway, she's doing what she thinks is best, and that's all right with me. When she shows up, I want some of the hands to escort her and a few of the saloon gals to Cheyenne Wells. I think they will have some fun there, at least for a little while."

"Saloon gals?" Joe laughed. "How many will there be?"

"Not many – I suppose four or five. It will be good for the hands there because most of them aren't married. Anyway, I'm going to ride out tomorrow. I've got some new plans for Cheyenne Wells." He adjusted his hat on his head and turned. "Well, I'm going back down to the river. Those boys of yours are waiting for me! You know, those boys have become damn good fishermen."

Joe just shook his head, grinning. "Well, I got things to do with Cindy. We're planning a get together at the gazebo tonight. I don't want to know how she's going to react to the thought of those brothel girls coming here."

"Well, I'll talk to her and tell her that they'll be going to Cheyenne Wells anyway and won't be a problem for her. She might not ever let you come visit me, though," Charles teased.

~ ~ ~

The late summer sun grew red in the sky as evening fell, and the Triple A gathering was beginning. There were a lot more people than before the devastating fire, and some were there for their own going-away party. The ranch had returned to true form and stature. Music filled the air as the people celebrated the completion of the rebuild. Charles was there to thank all the workers involved, some of whom he had never seen before. He invited anyone who was leaving to go to Cheyenne Wells to work because he had plans to expand the ranch there next.

As he sat at the table with family members, he couldn't help thinking that he missed seeing Cha-cha the wolf sitting out front of the cave where Johnny One Horn had once lived.

"Anybody use that cave now that Johnny's gone?" he asked.

"No," Cindy replied. "The boys – Earl and James – boarded it up and put a door and a lock on it. It's a place for them to remember their great friend – a special place, you might say."

Charles stared at the cave for a moment and shook his head. "You know, I sure miss that man – he was bigger than life, almost too great to be real. I wonder how he's doing with his people. I bet they are a lot better off now, with him there to guide them. Our scout Sad Hank said Little Boy Horse was in Canada with a wife and a small Sioux tribe that really loves him. I don't know if we will ever see either one again." He sighed wistfully. "Anyway, they were special to us, and I sure miss them."

Charles spent the night down by the river with Earl and James. The catfishing was good, and they camped out in the star-bright night. Charles caught himself gazing at the river as his thoughts drifted back to memories of his father O.C. and the incredible days of his youth in the Mississippi swamp. Many years had come and gone, but strong memories were implanted in his psyche. He – and the Triple A, too – was a product of those experiences, with those men and that swamp, and they would always be a part of him. Charles finally turned over in his bedroll. He needed to get some sleep. He would leave early the following morning, accompanying Shorty and his family to Cheyenne Wells.

# CHAPTER 13

## The Village of Standing Man

Three of the tribeswomen from Standing Man's village had been vital in nursing Sad Hank back to health. He was recovering now and had plans to resume his search for Rico Garza. Chief Standing Man advised him against it, but Sad Hank was determined to continue his search for the killer. Not knowing that Garza was in the Abilene jail and scheduled to hang, Hank said he would leave the following morning. His wounds were healed, but the emotional scars were still etched deep in his mind.

Hank had become very close to Tiny, the young girl he had rescued from Rico Garza. Tiny had no parents; she had lost them to the wars in the north. Everybody loved Tiny, and she loved Sad Hank like a father. She was very alarmed to think that he would resume his quest for the outlaw. She cried as she hugged him and begged him not to go, telling him that Rico was probably dead at the hands of someone else. But her pleas were not effective this time.

The next morning as he prepared to leave, Sad Hank leaned down from his horse and rubbed her hair, trying to comfort the sensitive girl. She continued to cry and cling to him as the tribe watched and felt her pain. At last, she loosened her grip on him, and Sad Hank assured her he would return. The village watched as he walked his horse down the canyon and out of their sight. Feeling the emotional stress of the moment, even Chief Standing Man dropped his head and walked away with tears streaming down his cheeks. Several village women approached him to check on his well-being, but he motioned them away.

As he turned to his people, the chief looked very concerned. "My pain is not just for Sad Hank, but for Tiny and all she has lost. We have all seen our people disappear through the years. Wars among our people's tribes are the saddest. Many lives were lost. War with the white man when our numbers were overwhelmed. Diseases have taken our children and fathers. Our way of life must go on in peace, or the rest of us will soon be killed. We must change our way of life if we as a people are to survive. The buffalo is disappearing and very few are left. We must change the way we live, or we will surely perish from Mother Earth like the buffalo. The cattle we have from the brothers called Armstrong are a start. They can teach us how to raise them and make our herds grow. They are good men and have our native blood in their veins. The answer is simple: we must make it here. There is nowhere else to run. So start today – our lives depend on it."

Standing Man turned and climbed to the hilltop, where he observed the valley below. He remembered when it was covered with thousands of buffalo. Now, in the distance he could see stacks of bones scattered throughout the valley floor. Again, tears streamed down his face. He dropped to his knees and prayed to the Great Spirit.

~ ~ ~

Four days later, Sad Hank approached a wagon accompanied by a lone rider. When he grew near them, to his surprise he saw that it was Charles riding alongside Shorty and his family. They agreed to camp for the night, and as they ate supper, Charles shared the news that Rico was locked up in jail, waiting to be hanged, in Abilene.

Sad Hank was amazed that anyone could capture Rico, so Charles explained what had happened. Intrigued by the story, Sad Hank decided that he was going to attend the hanging.

"Hell, Hank," Charles warned him, "they may have hanged him already. Why don't you just go back to Cheyenne Wells with us? You know you'll always have a job there."

"I know that, Charles, but I must see this for myself. It's very personal to me. I hope he sees all the faces of the people he's killed, and they haunt him forever. It sounds bad, but I want to see him die."

As the night grew late, Charles tried for a long time to convince Hank not to go, but he finally had to give up. Hank was a determined man.

The following morning the group said goodbye and Sad Hank continued to Abilene. He knew he would have to keep a low profile, as Abilene was full of rough cowboys that had experienced terrifying encounters with the Comanches on the cattle drives from Texas. Many of them had lost friends in those skirmishes and harbored a fierce hatred for people from all tribes after that.

## Abilene

Rico Garza sat in his jail cell, stripped of his clothing except some blood-stained trousers that had been cut off at the knees. He had said nothing for days – he figured he would be beaten for making as much as a gesture. He watched for the deputies to make any slight mistake that he could utilize. Most of the time they left Rico in a cell by himself for fear of the other inmates' safety.

Eventually, the day came when one of the deputies opened the cell door to throw in a town drunk. It was not intended, but the other three cells were overfilled. The drunk man was hanging all over the lawman. Rico watched and pretended to be asleep, waiting for a chance to make his move.

While the deputy scuffled with the drunk, his gun fell to the floor. In a split second, it was in Rico's hand. The shocked young deputy begged for his life. Rico demanded his clothing and then knocked the deputy unconscious with the butt of his gun. The drunk started yelling, but Rico strangled him with the coach whip that hung on the wall. Then, fully dressed, he carefully peeked through the jail door.

A lone horse, fully saddled, was tied a few feet from the opening. Rico walked very casually and mounted the horse, then walked it down the main street of Abilene, his hat pulled low to cover his face, so as not to attract any attention. At the edge of town, he kicked the horse to a fast pace, and was free.

The owner of the horse returned in twenty minutes or so to find his horse gone. He quickly entered the jail to report the theft to Marshal Swartz. He found the local drunk dead on the floor and the deputy unconscious in the jail cell. Running back outside the jail, he fired several shots in the air to draw attention. In minutes the townspeople were gathering in front.

Marshal Swartz was just returning from his daily rounds and was shocked at what had happened. He tried to organize a posse but could only get three people to join him and go after the murderous outlaw. He finally decided to let the territorial marshals handle it, because, in his words, he had a town to look after. Most people thought he was scared and wanted to stay in the safety of the town. When asked about it, he just said, "They'll find him somewhere on the western coach roads. That's the only thing he knows." With hands shaking, he rolled a cigarette and shook his head in disbelief that such a thing could have happened on his watch.

~ ~ ~

Sad Hank, still suffering from his wounds, became very weary from the hours of riding on his journey to Abilene. Finally, he dismounted to make camp for the night. As always, he made camp in the cover of a wash from the nearby hills.

Before bedding down for the night, Hank noticed a lone rider approaching, a man he recognized as an old prospector he had known for several years as Dusty Dan. Ol' Dan had searched the area for years seeking gold. He had a claim somewhere north of Cheyenne Wells and appeared to be heading home.

Dusty Dan was known throughout the territory for his drinking and funny ways. Many wild stories were told about him, and they were mostly true. After he spent about six weeks prospecting, he would have just enough gold to buy a few needed supplies and spend the rest drinking and having fun with the saloon girls. He loved to gamble and chase the girls at Cactus Jim's saloon. Sugarfoot, his old mule, would wait patiently for Dan outside the saloon. People were amused by the way the saloon girls would load him onto his mule and send him home after a wild night at the saloon. Sugarfoot knew the way home and would carry the old prospector out of town and northwest towards his claim. Somehow, ol' Dan would stay in the saddle as Sugarfoot would lead the other pack mule.

Sad Hank yelled to get Dan's attention, as it was clear to him that Dan was sleeping in the saddle. Dan was startled and grabbed for his buffalo gun before recognizing Sad Hank.

"What the hell," he laughed, "if it isn't ol' Sad Hank."

"I thought you might want to join me for a little rabbit," Hank grinned. "It's been quite a while since I've seen you."

"Yeah, that's for damn sure, Hank. My old claim is playing out on me. It takes me twice as long to get the same amount of gold as it used to. The creek dried up for a while. Dang! Makes it rough without water." He slid off Sugarfoot. "Want some whisky, buddy? I got some here in my poke."

"No thanks," laughed Sad Hank. "Me and that crazy water don't get along."

"Well, it gets along with me, just fine," mumbled Dan, taking a swig and holding out the bottle.

"Oh, I tried it a few times," Hank explained. "One time I woke up with a wild woman about the size of a buffalo! That was a bad deal all the way around – it turned out it was Chief Black Feather's sister. I barely got out of that village alive!"

"Mercy! Black Feathers sister? My friend, you are lucky," laughed Dan. "Besides all your dealings with whisky, what in tarnation are you doing out here?"

"Well, some friends told me they captured that snake Rico Garza, and I'm headed over to Abilene to watch him hang."

Dusty Dan tipped his hat back and replied, "Well, I don't think that's gonna happen. I heard he's out of jail already after he killed a drunk, pistol whipped a deputy, stole a horse and just rode out of town."

"Just rode out of town?" Hank asked. "What kind of law do they have there? You can't just let a murderer ride out of town."

"Well, all the townspeople were scared, and the marshal had no help to go after him. He said he couldn't just leave the town, so no one went after him," explained Dan, shrugging his shoulders. "Rico has hidden out in this valley for years, and knows every hole there is to hide in. I suspect he's right back here where he has been for years."

"Well, I intend to find him," frowned Hank. "He's got to be stopped. His lust for young girls is burned deep within his soul. He is evil. I pray to the Great Spirit that I find him before he takes another life."

"He used to stop by my claim once in a while and we would have coffee together. I always kept an eye on him, even though he never threatened me. He always laughed at me because I never found much gold on the claim. He thought it would be a waste of time to rob me – he even told me that."

"It's a wonder he didn't kill you for the fun of it, Dan; that's the way he is." Hank prepared to bed down. "When it becomes first light, I intend to try to pick up his trail. He will probably rob one of the wagons that's using the coach road, and maybe kill somebody. They're usually his main target. I feel so sorry for those people, but they never stop coming."

~ ~ ~

The sun was covered with clouds as it rose the next morning and Sad Hank mounted his horse and bid Dusty Dan farewell. Though Dan pleaded with Hank not to take on such a dangerous mission, he failed to convince him. He just watched as Hank rode off into the distance.

Soon after, Dan broke his camp and continued north with his mules toward his claim. It wasn't long before he spotted two skeletons drying in the desert sun and wind. One skeleton was wearing a U.S. Marshal badge. He took the badge and pinned it on his own vest. Then, being a man with strong beliefs, he was determined to give the two men a decent burial. It occurred to him that maybe he should return to Abilene to report what he had found. But, after much speculation, he figured he might be blamed for the killings, so he decided against it. A couple of hours later, he continued on his way, not knowing who the two men he had buried were. He had remembered hearing of a Marshal Tig being missing. He guessed it might have been him, but he wondered who the second man might be.

"Well, Sugarfoot, we've done all we can do. Let's get on home." Tired from the task of burying the two men, and still nursing a hangover, Dan mounted Sugarfoot and fell fast asleep in the saddle. Sugarfoot knew the way, and a few hours later they arrived at Dusty Dan's mining site. The site was far away from the beaten path and was hidden in a remote part of the valley's west hills.

When Dan arrived at his desert shack, before he dismounted, he noticed the door to the old cabin was open. He cocked the hammer on his old Hawkins rifle and eased through the front door. Behind the door stood Rico Garza.

"Mr. Dan," he said as he held his pistol to the back of Dan's head, "it's been a while, old friend."

Dan calmly replied by saying, "Rico, my son, how have you been?"

Rico had visited Dan at the mine site many times before and thought Dan was an old friend. Dan, knowing how dangerous he was, played along, fearing that Rico would kill him if he ever showed otherwise.

"I need a place to lay low for a while, old man. You can help me, or I'll just bury you under those sage brush and stay here anyway. But we've always been friends, haven't we?"

"Why, sure we have, Rico. You know I'd never turn down a friend. I just got back from hunting. Didn't get a thing, but there are plenty of jackrabbits around here. Can't believe I never saw a one this time."

Dan in no way wanted Rico to know he had returned from Abilene.

"You always take an extra pack mule with you just to go rabbit hunting, old man?" Rico asked. "Sounds strange to me. Where did you get that marshal's badge you're wearing? You know I hate lawmen."

"Well, I thought I might run into a deer or two. It's pretty hard for an old man to drag a deer all the way home,"

Dan laughed. "Tell me, Rico, what brings you out this way? I haven't seen you in a while. Oh, I found the badge on a dead man. There were two of 'em in a gulch not too far from here."

"You know me," said Rico, "I like to travel around, you know, to meet new people. Old man, I need a little money. How much gold have you mined lately?"

"Well," gasped Dan, "after my last trip to sell the gold, which wasn't much, I got sick for a long time. The doctor over in Abilene said it was called an ulcer, or something like that. By the time I paid him and bought some whisky, all my money was gone. I'm just now starting back mining again. Maybe this time I'll find something better. He said this ulcer thing was caused by the whisky, but damn, I got to have a drink now and then."

"Yeah, old man, as far as those two bodies you found, they tried to rob me, so I enjoyed killing them both. There was another one lying in the brush, but he was already dead. I guess the marshal had already killed him."

"I didn't see no other body, Rico, just the two. But there's lots of coyotes out there – they probably ate him or something else did."

Rico's eyes narrowed as it crossed his mind that maybe Shorty from the Triple A was still alive, and he'd been tricked. But he shook off the feeling – it was too late to worry about that now. He wasn't convinced Dan was telling the truth, anyway, but he trusted no one. He sat back on one of the old wood benches in the small cabin and popped a bottle of rye whisky. "Go get me something to eat, old man! And don't come back without it, or we'll just have to shoot ol' Sugarfoot here," he demanded.

Dan quickly responded and said he could make some biscuits and had some dried deer meat. For the moment Rico was satisfied, but Dan knew it was going to be a long time before Rico left.

Rico knew he would have to stay off the coach roads for

a while. The law would surely be looking for him there. He planned to stay at the claim until Dusty Dan mined enough gold to get him to Mexico. The valley was getting too populated with the Triple A expansion, and now more lawmen and bounty hunters were looking for him. Dusty Dan's claim was his only hope. Little did he know that Sad Hank, one of the best trackers in the land, had survived his ordeal and had also resumed his quest to find him.

Rico knew nothing about mining, and he would work ol' Dan into the ground to get the gold as fast as possible. His plan was to head south and watch for opportunities along the way so he could arrive in Old Mexico a rich man again. He daydreamed of young señoritas and cantinas that were very far from any kind of law. He could speak the language and would fit in very well.

Dusty Dan meant nothing to Rico, and he would probably dispose of the old miner after collecting as much gold as he could, but Dan also knew this and would be watching for a way to get out of the situation. He would go along with anything Rico said and act like he really cared, but at the same time he would be watching for a way to escape or kill the outlaw.

## Three days later

Rico sat in the old mine with his rifle and was working the old miner from dusk until dawn until he could barely move about. Dan watched Rico hit the whisky a little harder each day. Late each evening, Rico would be drunk and sometimes could barely walk. Dan hoped to wait until Rico was so drunk that he could make his escape. The fifth day, Rico barely made it back to the cabin and passed out on the bench sitting up. Dan saw his opportunity and took both mules and the horse that Rico had stolen in Abilene and rode off in the night.

Rico awoke a couple of hours later. After a few minutes

of trying to clear his head, he realized what had happened. Dazed and still under the influence, he sat down on the old cabin steps and watched as the early morning sun rose in the sky. Eventually, it dawned on him that old Dan would probably go to the nearest town and tell of his whereabouts. He had to get out of this place. He filled his canteen and began walking toward the high mountains to the west. He knew Goat Head Rock was close to his location, and not many people traveled there. The presence of rattlesnakes kept them away. Not many people knew that ol' Slim Dick was dead either, and they were afraid of being shot.

Being a creature of habit, Rico would always return to hideouts he knew. He knew there was water there, and caves – but he guessed even Sad Hank would never think he would return there.

Dusty Dan had taken all the guns and Rico's boots with him, and Rico had nothing to fight with. After several hours, he struggled into a small cave not too far from Goat Head Rock. With his feet wrapped in rags, the jagged rocks had severely damaged them. His mind was steaming with hate for Dan, and he swore he would kill him one day.

The next morning, he made his way to ol' Slim Dick's camp and found some flint to assist him in building a fire. He fought the pain from his feet, though it was almost more than he could bear. He turned over rocks to find lizards and a few mice that he quickly ate alive and raw. He managed to build a fire and would have to survive until he found his next unsuspecting victim.

## Cheyenne Wells

After Charles arrived back at Cheyenne Wells, he informed the hands, along with their foremen, Nate and Pete, of his plans to build more buildings. Sitting at the homemade table in Charles' cabin, Nate questioned his actions. "We barely have enough hands to take care of the business at hand, boss!"

"The construction work at the Triple A is finishing up, and before I left, I told Joe to send the workers here. They'll arrive in a few days with wagons and building materials. After that, I have a real surprise for you," smiled Charles.

Nate and Pete looked at each other, shaking their heads. Nate rolled a cigarette and laughed. "A surprise?" he snickered. "Why, hell, every day we have a surprise around here. It's just business as usual, don't you think?"

Pete stood up smiling. "Well, boys, this water is getting a little deep for me, and I've got work to do. I'm glad to see Shorty and his family here – we can really use a top hand right now! Tell me, how's that pretty little wife of his? I hear she had a child. I always thought she was one of the prettiest gals I ever saw."

"Yolanda's fine, and pretty as ever, and yeah, they had a little girl. Yolanda is good with native medicine and will be a big help around here. I'm going to give them my cabin and build another small one for me," answered Charles.

In the following days the wagons and supplies started showing up, and Charles appointed Pete to oversee the building process. Shorty and his family were settled into Charles' cabin. The Cheyenne Wells land was developing fast into the bustling ranch that he had hoped for.

Living in a tent was something no one thought Charles would ever do. The people that had known him for years could hardly believe the way Charles had changed. He refused to sleep in the bunkhouse now, and just loved the open air.

Charles was excited at the thought of Cat Brink and the girls that he expected to arrive in a few weeks. The living quarters for Cat and the girls were first on his agenda. The ranch hands lived in tents and were stationed around the herd since there were many predators in the area, as well as bandits traveling the coach roads. The cattle were doing well with plenty of water from Cricket Creek and plentiful green healthy grass. Pink eye had affected the herd several times, but no serious disease had shown. He loved to ride to the hilltops overlooking the vast landscape. Looking down at the campfires at night reminded him of the Triple A when it was first developing. Sometimes he would throw his bedroll down on his favorite hill and build a small fire.

As he lay there one night, his thoughts drifted back to the Mississippi swamp where he had grown up. Memories of people and days gone by stirred his emotions. Sometimes tears streamed down his face and other times, memories of incidents would make him laugh out loud. Although everything was peaceful now, he also knew this was a country where things could change in a heartbeat. The weather was good so far as they entered the fall. In a few weeks it would be time to return with Retha and Carl to the quest for the Echo of the Moon.

One of the supply wagon drivers arriving from the ranch informed Charles of Rico Garza's escape. He could hardly believe that the devil was on the loose again. That day, he rode Sachi to the outer fence line where Pete and Nate were mending fences. Pete saw him coming, and they met on a nearby hill. Charles gave them the news. "We can't let down our guard!" he warned.

Pete shook his head in disbelief as Charles explained the circumstances.

"Damn," exclaimed Nate, "that bastard is probably heading our direction! He knows this valley like the back of his hand."

"That may be so, Nate," reminded Pete, "but almost everybody here, except the wagons on the coach roads, knows what he looks like. Do you really think he would come this direction?

If I were him, I would find somewhere else to hide other than this valley. And it worries me that the Coyote Woman and Carl are living in his old hideout. Have they ever thought he might come back?"

"Oh, yeah, Carl is very aware of that," said Charles, "but he's not afraid of anything, and I've never seen anybody better with a handgun than he is. Also, if he hurls that knife at you, you're a dead man. Ol' Sad Hank probably knows about Rico's escape by now too and is probably on his trail. He's got a hatred for the man like no other and swears he will kill him. That's a man you would not want to have on your tail."

"That's not the only problem we have, boss," said Pete. "The other night the cattle were restless. While I was lying there staring at the full moon, the silhouette of a large cat was as clear as day as the moon rose above the hills. It's as big a cat as I've ever seen. It just stood there staring down on the herd. I suspect he's getting his nerve up to take a calf. Every time I get a bead on him, he quickly disappears as if he knows. It's almost like he's taunting me."

"Maybe that's the same cat Retha and Carl are having problems with. Alert all the hands to be watchful. I've heard lots of stories of those big cats attacking people if they are hungry. I swear, this country is as wild as the wind and will turn on you in a heartbeat. If it's not crazy people, it's a damn snake, scorpion, or now a big cat, that will have you for dinner. Be careful, boys – we've got some women on their way here, too. I'll be going to Retha's ranch in a few weeks, so keep on your toes. Don't become bear crap before I see you tomorrow!" Charles laughed as he turned Sachi in the direction of the herd.

"Damn, he sure makes you feel good about being here, don't he? I swear, sometimes I wish I was somewhere else, but I guess this is all I know. Damned if you do and damned if you don't!" Pete said as he watched Charles' retreating figure. Then he shrugged and, looking across the valley floor, commented, "Looks like we might get a little rain from those black clouds in the west."

"Yep," Nate drawled wryly as he rolled a cigarette, "I

hope that's all we get." After he lit up, he teased, "By the way, Pete, why don't you snatch up one of those saloon gals and settle down, old friend? You've been looking a might lonesome lately."

"Looking lonesome? Now, how in the hell does a man look lonesome? The trouble with you, Nate, is that you're the one who's lonesome. Maybe you should ride into Garden City and hook up with big Ula May. I think she would be just the woman for you. She's got money, too, now that she owns about everything in town," Pete grinned. "You know she's always had a fancy for you."

"Well, you forget that when she was young, she was a beautiful woman, and she bested Johnny One Horn. Your problem is, Pete, you just look on the outer layer and not the rest of the pie. Ol' Johnny bested a grizzly up north, but couldn't best ol' Ula," Nate retorted, chuckling.

"Well, there comes the rain. I better get back to them boys building Charles' saloon. He put me in charge of that." Pete wheeled his horse around, then turned back with a sly wink. "Next time I'm in Garden City I'll tell ol' Ula that you want to see her."

"You do, and I'll shoot you dead," laughed Nate. "Now get out of here."

The rain moved slowly through the valley, continuing most of the afternoon and night, and turning the landscape into a muddy bog. The construction came to a stop – the building supplies got bogged down with the wagons. Wind whipped the newly built structures, causing severe damage, and lightning flashed, spooking the cattle. The men were kept busy trying to round up all the strays. Most of the cattle were all right, though a few were killed underneath trees when lightning struck.

The next morning, Charles surveyed the muddy mess in disbelief. He had planned for this to be a main street in a thriving settlement, but now he could only think, "this sure is a muddy place to build a settlement when the rain falls."

He noticed Pete and his horse slopping through the mud toward him.

"Boss," Pete explained, "I pulled most of the workers off the construction and sent the ones that could ride to help round up the strays. We lost a few underneath the trees by the creek. Damn, this place gets muddy in a hurry."

Charles nodded, then spent a few seconds staring at the havoc the storm had caused.

"Pete, when this mess dries up a little, let's have some men and a few wagons haul some gravel up from Cricket Creek and spread it on this part of the street. It's a lot of work, I know, but we can't let this keep on happening. If it's this bad now, just imagine how bad it will get when the snow flies!"

"Will do, boss. Say, I was just wondering when those gals are planning to get here? I hope they don't get caught in this; that is, if they haven't already."

"Well, I asked Joe to have a good escort of men ride with them when they reached the Triple A. He's supposed to send a rider here to tell us when they're on their way. I think we have a couple of weeks, but knowing Cat Brink like I think I do, she could show up any day. We'd better put that building up first, Pete. I don't want them to try to live in a mess like this. If you have to, put all the workers on it. After that, use your own judgement as to which project is most important."

Pete sat in the saddle staring at the muddy mess and shaking his head. "Damn," he thought, "he doesn't ask for much, does he?"

~ ~ ~

After a day or two passed, the street was navigable again. Pete put every available hand on the building that would house Cat Brink and the girls. Summer days were now transitioning to the cool days of fall. Some of the wagons loaded with coal had been damaged when they bogged down in the mud between the Triple A and Cheyenne Wells, so a crew of the ranch hands was sent to assist in recovering the much-needed commodity.

# CHAPTER 14

C harles lay contemplating the new moon that would show them the way to the Echo of the Moon. It would be full in a few days, and he planned to be at Retha's Blue Moon Ranch when it was. He had picked out two of the mules from the ranch to carry supplies. He was also thinking that he may not be here when Cat Brink and the girls arrived. This didn't please him, but he was going to keep his word. Charles didn't care about the gold, but the story had intrigued him since the first time he heard Earl Stockman tell it. Besides, he did like the idea of Retha having a better life, and he would try to help her accomplish that. It seemed that his nephew Carl, even though there was a nine-year age difference, loved Retha. Sometimes he would smile as he thought of them as blond hair and buckskin. They seemed perfect together, wild as a Kansas tornado and determined to make it in the unforgiving land.

Often now, his mind drifted back to his childhood and the trying times in the lower Mississippi swamp where the family had once struggled to survive. Dreams were vivid of the fields and hard work, the small room where all the brothers shared the nights with the dreaded night mosquitoes, the smothering smell of kerosene that permeated the stuffy air. Fond memories of his late younger brother Carl raced through his mind, and he reflected how his nephew Carl was so much like him.

Hard work was something all the brothers were used to, and even though they had a new, better life now because of the gold they had found, they never forgot how hard it once was. Charles rubbed the big scar on his arm, and it reminded him of the day they had buried their sweet mother, and the pain the boys had endured. The scar from the tornado that day reminded Charles of how bad things could turn in just a day. He would never forget.

~ ~ ~

Sad Hank was circling the valley floor, alert for any trace of Rico Garza. With no sign of the outlaw, he expanded his search area to the foothills, using all his tracking skills to pick up any sign. Unfortunately, it seemed the recent rains had erased any signs the outlaw may have left behind. At the southern end of the valley, Hank finally spotted some recent tracks of horses and mules. Not knowing these were Dusty Dan's, he decided to follow them. The trail led him in the direction of the Triple A. He decided to follow the tracks even though he knew Rico would never return there. He figured that whoever this might be may have seen Rico or run into him somewhere.

When Hank arrived at the Triple A, several armed guards intercepted him. Some realized who he was, and they explained to him that ol' Dan had arrived there a few days earlier, told everyone his horrific story, and warned the ranch of Rico's presence back in the valley. Dusty Dan had told those at the ranch that he left the outlaw at his claim and escaped. Tom Sheen informed Sad Hank that Dan had sold a horse and a mule to Joe for whisky money and left the day before for Garden City. As usual, he figured ol' Dan would probably use the money to gamble and drink until it was all gone.

Sad Hank didn't bother to go on to the ranch; instead, he

left quickly and headed back towards Dan's shack and mining claim. It was a couple of days away and the terrain was rugged and dangerous. As he made his way to the claim, his loathing for the merciless murderer grew, and his mind churned with scenarios of ways he could kill the vile creature. From what he had heard, Dan had left the outlaw with no horse, boots, or guns. Hank didn't hurry because Rico would have no way of escaping this time. He hoped he would find him still trying to survive at the old shack.

On the second day, Hank's horse became lame from a sharp stone in his front foot. Hank removed the stone, but the horse continued to limp. Hank walked and led the horse the rest of the way until he was on the hilltop overlooking the old cabin. He used the army's expanding scope to watch for any sign of the movement in the camp.

Several hours went by and Hank saw nothing stirring. He thought it would be best to go to the cabin under the cover of darkness. If Rico was still there, he would be very cautious, and Hank knew he could never again underestimate the cunning of the outlaw. He hoped that by waiting a few hours after sunset, the outlaw would be tapping ol' Dan's whisky.

When it was very dark, Hank left his horse tied to a small tree at the top of the hill and slipped through the darkness to the cabin. As he circled to the door, nothing was moving, and he saw nothing. He searched the wash for any evidence of a fire, but there was nothing. After several hours of searching, he returned to the top of the hill and spent the night. The night was black with only a sliver of a new moon to the east. He realized that Rico had left the cabin, knowing that Dan would probably report his whereabouts to someone. The night was quiet with only the sound of an occasional night owl or coyote in the distance.

When morning came, Hank made his way back to the shack very cautiously and searched the surrounding area. Gradually, he expanded the circle to hunt for clues. At last, underneath some cliffs where the rain could not obliterate them, he found tracks and blood in the sand. It was exactly what he had been looking for. The tracks led in the direction of Goat Head Rock, a place he was very familiar with. It occurred to him that the cunning outlaw would probably think he would never return there.

It took several hours to reach the foot of the mountain. Hank dismounted and scanned the area. Coming out of one of the small caves was a tell-tale curl of smoke. He proceeded very cautiously to the entrance of the cave.

This time Rico had made a mistake that might be his undoing. He had drunk a lot of whisky and was fast asleep by a small fire. Hank noticed his bloody feet. This time there would be no escape. He stuck his rifle to Rico's head, and it was apparent the man was unconscious. He quickly tied Rico's hands behind his back and hobbled his legs. He then stripped him of all his clothing and attached a hangman's noose around his neck. Then he sat down beside him and waited.

Three hours later, Rico started regaining consciousness. Hank sat very still. Rico began to sense something was wrong and started moving around. When he discovered his clothing was gone, he panicked and jumped to his feet.

"Hello, Rico. Are you surprised to see me? I burned your clothes. You won't need them where you're going. Standing Man didn't think what you did to little Tiny was very funny."

Rico started cursing Hank and threatening him. Hank just smiled calmly.

"You're not in a very good position, boy, to start threatening me. You will be begging me before this day is over."

Rico just spit and cursed Hank again. This time Hank knocked him to the ground and stuffed a hard rock inside his mouth and secured it with a bandana.

"This should stop that dirty mouth of yours. You really

are an idiot, aren't you? You really know how to make things better, don't you, boy?" Hank motioned him toward the opening of the cave, mounted his horse, and instructed Rico to start walking. He released about twenty feet of rope and motioned for Rico to walk.

The day passed with Rico's feet and legs getting ripped and bloody. Hank showed no mercy as Rico started to change his tone of voice from threats to begging. Hank said nothing and kept motioning with his rifle for Rico to proceed. By late in the afternoon, Rico could barely walk on his mangled feet from the thorns and yucca plants. He finally collapsed in the dry sand.

When Hank saw that Rico could go no farther, he dismounted and prepared his camp for the night. He staked the outlaw to the ground about twenty feet from the campfire. At first, he felt some compassion for the man, but then he would remember all the terrible things Rico had done to so many innocent people with no remorse. Hank's heart would harden, and hate would build. He sat and roasted a rabbit he had shot along the way.

Rico became conscious and started motioning to his mouth. Hank walked over and poured a little water on the bandana that held the rock inside of Rico's mouth. As he looked down on the struggling man, he squared his jaw to hold back any emotions. Rico kept mumbling for a while and then became unconscious again.

Hank spent most of the night praying to the Great Spirit for guidance. Late in the night, the sound of wolves echoed in the distance. There was very little light from the moon and seeing them was impossible. Straining his eyes, he at last made out a single black wolf in the darkness. Hank sat still as the campfire flickered with just enough light to outline the majestic creature. Its eyes glowed from the firelight as it stood at Rico's feet. Several minutes went by, and just like it came, it disappeared into the darkness.

Hank knew this was a sign that he was doing the right

thing. He fell fast asleep in a sitting position and passed the night in peace.

There was a chill in the air as the morning sun rose, and again Hank had to fight his emotions. He rustled the shaking outlaw to his feet and forced the man to move. He walked his horse slowly behind as the man struggled for every step.

Sad Hank fought his compassionate feelings as the day passed until Rico finally collapsed. Then Hank searched the area for two strong limbs from the sparse landscape and made a drag sled. He loaded the unconscious Rico onto the sled and proceeded.

The camp that night was quiet, and Rico never moved; just a few moans and groans came from him. Hank removed the bandana and rock from Rico's mouth and trickled water to him. The night passed quietly with just a coyote howling from the distant hills.

The following morning Hank arrived with his captive at Standing Man's village. The young warriors went into a frenzy as they watched Sad Hank pulling the drag toward the chief's teepee. Standing Man looked at Rico with loathing in his eyes. One warrior grabbed Rico's hair and partially scalped the outlaw before he was ordered to stand down by the chief. Sad Hank untied the screaming Rico and rolled him on the skid into the sand. As he looked down on the man, he still felt strong mixed emotions.

"There's your demon, as I promised. If you don't mind, I will be moving on. Do with him as you like, but I need the skull to take to the Echo of the Moon. I will be back for it when the moon is full and meet you at our sacred meeting place at Moon Rock. Then I will return here to my people where I belong."

Standing Man agreed and slowly walked into his teepee.

As Sad Hank walked his horse away from the village, he could hear the screams of Rico echoing through the hills. His emotions overwhelmed him, but then he thought of all the crimes the man had committed. It made him stronger to know that was over as he made his way back to the ranch. He planned to talk to Charles about future relations between the ranch and the tribe.

~ ~ ~

Charles smiled as he noticed one of the arriving wagons contained a piano. He knew right away Cat Brink had sent it.

Pete walked his horse to where Charles was standing. "Would you look at that, boss? There is a damn piano in one of those wagons!" Pete laughed as he rolled a cigarette. "I didn't know you played the piano."

"I don't," smiled Charles. "You know I'm going to shoot you one of these days."

"Well, I think that little Cat is going to make you build her a saloon before this is over," Pete countered, before taking on a more serious tone. "The building is going up faster than I thought, and I believe it will be finished in a couple of days. The water tank came yesterday, and it's almost up already. The boys are building a tank shed for bathing, and then they'll run a trough to the buildings."

Jose rode out to meet them. "Boss, there are three prairie schooners and about a half dozen riders a couple of miles south of here. I think it must be those women you talked about."

"My Lord, I didn't think they would be here this quick! Anyway, Pete, we might as well ride out to meet them."

When they met the wagons, Cat saw Charles and came running toward them. She didn't look like the finely dressed lady he had met at Cactus Jim's saloon, but was dressed like a cowboy, gun and all. The other girls were also clad in cowboy clothing. They were covered with mud and didn't seem too happy about the situation.

Charles dismounted from Sachi, and Cat quickly jumped

into his arms. Pete just sat back in the saddle rolling a cigarette and looking on with amusement. He tipped his hat to the other ladies, but there was no reaction to his kind gesture.

One of the girls asked Pete, "How far away is this place we are going to, mister?"

"About a couple of miles that way," Pete answered, as he pointed north.

Charles remounted Sachi and reached to swing Cat up behind him. He greeted and thanked the six Triple A ranch hands, and had a warm handshake for old friend Tex Luna, his foreman from the Triple A. Tex motioned for the hands to head back to the Triple A.

Pete bid farewell to Tex as well and began helping the girls with the wagons.

Charles waved to him as he wheeled his horse around. "Pete, can you make sure they get to the ranch? We're going on ahead." He explained to Cat, as they walked Sachi toward their small community, that things had been held up by the storm and weren't quite finished.

"Good," she said to his amazement. "The girls and I will put our own ideas into it. By the way, I sold Cactus Jim's Saloon for quite a bit of money, and I have three more wagons coming with things we need for the business."

"Business?" Charles asked, astonished. "What business?"

"Well, you know – a combination of dry goods, maybe a small bar, and – you know," she laughed as she began tickling Charles.

Charles was so ticklish he almost fell from the saddle. "Damn you, Cat! Quit that! What if some of the hands see you?"

"Who cares?" she laughed as Charles settled down. "There are a lot of wagons traveling this valley on their way to Denver. I heard they discovered gold there and the boom is on. I'll be the only trail stop going this route between Kansas and Denver."

"Well, that sounds good, Cat, but will it work?"

"It will work. I've never failed at anything yet. I know a business opportunity when I see one. The other five girls are all in on this – I gave them all a share."

"Just want to remind you that this little settlement is just getting off the ground. I gave my cabin to one of my hands, so I'm sleeping on the ground until I can build another one. He has a wife and baby, so he needs it more than I do. I've been sleeping in a tent on a little hill, and sometimes I just sleep out under the stars."

"Well, that sounds just fine for you," laughed Cat. "I'll just bunk with the girls for now, but you need to start building a house for us."

"House for us?" Charles gasped. "You mean, like being married?" Charles was at a loss for words for a few seconds as he realized Cat's intentions. In some ways it made him feel happy, but it scared him at the same time.

"Well, kind of, but you know, it could be just on a trial basis," she reassured him. "And then, in about ten years, that is, if it works out, maybe then," she smiled.

"Good Lord, Cat, I'll probably be dead by then," Charles laughed.

Even though Charles was shocked by what Cat had said, he was also thinking about how pretty she was, and he felt proud that someone at least twenty years younger might want him for a husband. As they arrived at the ranch, they dismounted in front of what would be Cat's Place. She had picked the name even before she arrived there.

"This place needs to be bigger," she instructed. "I also intend to rent rooms to our customers. The girls and I will help build it because we know what we want."

Charles watched very closely as Cat inspected the building. He was bewildered by what he was hearing. He had always been the boss, but now it seemed Cat was going to take that job away from him. Every time he started to express his opinion, Cat would change the subject.

In a few minutes, the prairie schooners arrived in front of the building. Charles was amazed to see they contained nice furniture, as well as several beds and modern bedsprings and such.

Leading the girls was a lady they called Big Sally, who immediately demanded of Charles, "Where's the bath house?"

He quickly pointed to the water tank. "Sorry, with the flooding rain we've had, that's as far as we've got, Miss."

"Damn!" she retorted. "What kind of a mess have we got ourselves into? Come on, girls, let's get some of this dreadful mud off us! You can tell those men over there gawking that if they watch it will be a dollar apiece and no free peeks."

To Charles' surprise, Big Sally produced a shotgun, and all the girls walked to the newly built water tower. As the girls undressed, they just jumped in the lower tank on the ground level and, like a bunch of young children, started playing and dashing each other with the cool water.

The ranch hands across the road started cheering and laughing at the spectacle. Charles quickly ordered them back to work, but it took a while for them to settle down.

"Damn, Cat, what are we going to be running here? A cat house?" Then he realized what he had just said.

Cat just laughed and said, "Well, something like that."

"Well, Cat, you girls go ahead and do what you must do. I've got to go and check the north fence," Charles stammered, not knowing what else to say.

He mounted Sachi and rode to the fence line where Nate was being entertained listening to the ranch hands talking about what they had just witnessed. "I thought I told you men to get back to work! This is no picnic day," he scolded crossly.

Nate sat in the saddle smiling at Charles. "Well, good afternoon, boss. You in a bad mood?"

"Why do you ask that? It's a great day." Then, realizing he and Nate were alone, he confided, "Well, I guess I'm kind of confused as to what it is or what it's not."

"Well, boss, you'll feel better tonight when that little wild Cat gets you in her paws," Nate laughed. "Why, you'll be henpecked in no time." Unlike Charles, he pulled a pocket flask of whisky from his poke and took a big gulp.

"I don't know which one of you yahoos, you or Pete, I'm going to shoot first. Maybe both of you at the same time."

Nate laughed and walked his horse back to where the men were working.

Charles yelled after him, "I'll be leaving in a week for Retha's little Blue Moon Ranch, and I don't want any shenanigans going on while I'm gone!"

Nate saluted. "You got it, boss! I'll keep the herd in check." He hesitated. "Um, both of them."

Charles took a deep breath and shook his head. He was thinking of what a mess he had got himself into. His mind was coming up with ways to get out of the whole deal, but he was hooked on the pretty Cat Brink. "What is it?" he asked himself, "that makes me so crazy about this woman?" Still shaking his head, he rode to his favorite hill and surveyed the valley.

~ ~ ~

The following morning, Charles woke at the crack of dawn to the sound of hammering. He looked down at the buildings below and was amazed to see the women and several of the hands busily working on Cat's Place. "I didn't assign that many men to work on that building," he thought.

He quickly gathered his bedroll and rode into what now was looking like a small town. He saw that Cat was scrambling around the building giving orders like an army general. The girls were all dressed in their cowboy clothing and working alongside the men.

As he rode up in front of the building, Cat came to meet him. "Where in the hell were you last night? I thought you would be glad I was here, but it seems obvious that you're not."

Charles, not being used to being addressed in that fashion, lost his train of thought and couldn't quite get the words out. As he looked down from Sachi, he could see her mouth moving, but he heard nothing. All he could do was stare at this beautiful little hellion glowing in the morning sun. When he came out of his trance, he had to think for a minute to find the words to say.

"I was looking for strays from the storm," he finally stuttered. "Ranching is tough, Cat, and you've gotta take the good with the bad. Besides, I didn't know you wanted me here."

"You didn't know? Damn, you may not be as smart as I thought you were! You think I went through all the trouble to get here just so I could smell three thousand cow butts and work in this awful-smelling mud?"

Charles, looking bewildered, just looked at her. She finally broke into a laugh, and he sighed with relief as he took a deep breath.

"Make no mistake, mister," she smiled, "if you chase cows tonight, I'm going with you."

"Well, that may not be too good an idea, Cat. There's a big mountain lion that's been stealing some of our calves. It may be dangerous. That's the main reason I go alone. Besides, the weather can change here in a heartbeat."

"Well, if that's the truth, then it's ok," said Cat, frowning. But if it's not, I may have to rethink our little twosome."

Charles had to think fast about what he'd just said, so he dismounted and hugged Cat. "There is a big cat out there, but I'll fight a grizzly before I'll stay away from you tonight."

Cat looked up at the big man and smiled. "That's better. Now go on and let us work. I'll see you at the cookhouse about sundown."

Charles didn't really know how to tell her about the trip to Retha's Blue Moon Ranch coming up, so for now he decided to keep it to himself. "I'll tell her tonight," he thought as he mounted Sachi and headed out.

~ ~ ~

Sad Hank arrived at the ranch in the afternoon and met with Nate, Pete, and Charles and filled them in on the capture and demise of Rico Garza. He told the men that he planned to return to the camp of Standing Man and rejoin his people. He would be leaving the employment of the ranch.

"What did Standing Man do with Rico?" Pete wanted to know. "I sure would have liked to put a bullet in that bastard."

"I don't really know, my friend," answered Hank. "I left before I saw anything, but I told Standing Man I would return for his head in a few days. I plan to take it to the Echo."

Charles was intrigued by that. He asked Sad Hank if he knew where the Echo of the Moon was.

Hank was quiet for a second and then looked across the valley to the mountain peaks to the west. He turned slowly and met Charles' eyes. "I do know where it is, my friend, but the spirits say no other men can go there – only my tribespeople; for others, it is forbidden."

"Well, Hank, my question is, how can you go there if it is forbidden? The spirits shouldn't bother me as I have the same blood as many tribesmen."

Hank looked down before responding. "You may be right, my friend. I don't know. You are not Sioux, and that is all I can say."

"But my nephew Carl has been to Moon Rock, we know of the Sun Dial, and when the reflection will point to the Echo. The shadow of the sun tells the month, and the first full moon of that month points the way to the Echo."

"At this time of year," explained Hank, "many Sioux come from far away and they meet at Moon Rock. It is a spiritual time for us. I will tell you this, if you go there when the Echo appears, it will be very dangerous for you. You may be killed and sacrificed to the valley below."

"I had plans to go there with my nephew Carl and Retha in a few days when the moon is full. But I will tell them of this sacred meeting and maybe I can convince them not to go."

"Take my advice, my friend," Hank said soberly, "and stay away from there. There are many remains in the sand below Moon Rock of white men that searched for gold. There is no gold at Moon Rock. There also will be other men that arrive there that know the legend and search for gold. They will surely die. It happens almost every year. If the curse of the Rock doesn't kill them, they will be killed by the Sacred Clowns."

"What? Who are these Sacred Clowns, Hank?"

" I hope you never find out, my friend. It will be the last thing you ever see. Take my advice and stay away from there."

Hank mounted his horse. "I am going to the high country. Maybe I can get one of those great deer you call elk. My people need the meat, and I need to get away from people for a while." He gave the sign from his chest and slowly walked his horse toward the mountains.

"Well, boss, that was one hell of a tale, if you ask me," Pete commented. He looked at Charles curiously. "You still plan on going there?"

"Maybe. I don't know, but I bet I can't convince Carl not to. Personally, I don't like the idea of all those boogers."

Nate shook his head and started walking toward the fence lines. "Damn, flies, snakes, scorpions, mountain lions, coyotes and now we got some damn boogers to go along with it. It's a great day here in purgatory – damn."

Pete and Charles listened to Nate jabbering and laughed.

~ ~ ~

As the sun set, all the hands gathered at the partially finished cook house. Shorty's wife Yolanda had put together a Pawnee stew. The tantalizing aroma drifted in the light wind, beckoning everyone to the building. The men came quickly to the water tower to wash up. Big Sally sat at the back of Cat's Place flaunting her ten-gauge shotgun. Jose, the ranch foreman, yelled to her and asked if she was going to pay them a damn dollar. Sally just stood up and stomped inside the building. The men all had a good laugh.

Pete heard the comment and joined them at the tower. "Jose, I'd be careful joshing ol' Sally – you might get an ass full of buckshot. She's one mean-looking ol' gal."

When everyone arrived at the large bench they had constructed, they sat and Yolanda served the stew to everyone. She explained that it might be a little spicy.

Cat Brink was the last to enter and quickly moved one of the girls away from Charles and squeezed onto the bench beside him.

Big Sally was the first to dig in. Her face turned a bright red as the hot peppers took their toll. The men were already used to the native stew and loved it, but some of the other girls couldn't bear the burning stew. They picked out the beef and took it to the tower to wash it. All the hands laughed as Big Sally got up and ran to the outhouse.

Jose laughed as he told the hands about the curse of the Pawnee stew. "I guess nobody told her that it comes out the other end twice as hot as it goes in," Jose quipped.

Charles couldn't hold back the laughter, but he tried to turn away from Cat. To his surprise, Cat laughed also but explained to the crew that Sally wasn't near as gruff as they thought, and they might like her when they got to know her.

Yolanda and Shorty smiled at each other as she spoke. "Just so you all know, I'm not the camp cook. I did it this time as a favor. I make the Pawnee stew one way, and one way only. You can like it, or you can cook yourself a jackrabbit – I don't care."

"Miss Yolanda," said Jose, "please don't stop making the boys and I the stew! We love it."

"I know you do, Jose, but you know, it's not for these city girls," Yolanda pointed out.

"Yolanda, I had no problem with the stew! I loved it," Cat told her. "The hotter, the better."

After everyone got their fill of the Pawnee stew, Charles told Cat about his upcoming trip to Retha's Blue Moon Ranch. He was surprised that Cat knew Retha, and smiled when she heard the name.

"Charles," she said surprisingly, "I would like to go. You got a horse I can ride? I'd sure like to see that hellcat again. I got to know her once in Abilene, but other stories I've heard about her always make me laugh and respect her."

"What about the place you're building? I might be gone several days."

"Well, Sally knows what I want, and the girls will be in good hands."

Charles again got that look of wonderment on his face. "Well, we've got plenty of horses. Just go down to the corrals and ask Jose to show them to you. But, Cat, the place we are going to may be very dangerous. Our scout, Sad Hank, warned us not to make the trip to Moon Rock this time of year."

"Oh, don't tell me you're trying to find The Echo of the Moon?" she laughed. "Nobody ever comes back from there; at least that's what I've always heard. But if you go, I still want to go, just for the hell of it."

"Yeah," Charles smiled, "something told me you were going to say that very thing. The truth is, I'm going up there to try to talk them out of going there. I just feel that may be harder than I think."

# CHAPTER 15

C arl sat atop the hill overlooking the Blue Moon Ranch, cautiously scanning the horizon for the mountain lion that usually showed up around sundown. He suspected the big cat had been taking a few of the chickens he had acquired from the Triple A.

Cricket was doing his part helping to guard the livestock. The three had become very close as they worked to make a go of the ranch. Carl often smiled as he looked in amazement at the way Cricket dressed. He often wore buckskin trousers and no shirt. He was getting big for his age, and the wolf head garment would intimidate most anybody. He was an experienced hunter and kept the smokehouse they had built supplied with rabbits and deer meat.

As for Retha, she stayed busy building things, and the three had accomplished a lot with long days of work and hunting for materials to build with. Most of the added corrals had been built from evergreen trees brought down with great difficulty from the higher peaks.

Retha had become very fond of Carl – maybe she would even say they loved each other. But she was still haunted by the recurring feelings of *déjà vu*, almost on a daily basis now.

It worried Carl, as he would catch her staring across the plains with that far-away look on her face. When the episodes occurred, it seemed that everything else was blocked from her mind. Sometimes when he talked to her, he felt she wasn't listening to him.

Retha saw Carl on the hilltop and decided to join him. It had been a nice afternoon, and now a stunning orange sun was sinking in the west, tinting the clouds with color. He watched her walking up the hillside and thought how beautiful she was. She sat down beside him and put her hand on his knee as they watched the sun set.

"Have any more of those visions?" Carl asked.

"A lot lately," she answered. "It's starting to bother me. You know, I have them more when I'm around Cricket than at any other time. I wonder why that is. Things he says and does bring it on. You know Cricket says his Ma and Pa lived here and were killed by Rico Garza. I have no reason to disbelieve him, but things just don't add up. He makes me think that he's hiding something. He's such a kind and sweet young man, but he seems content to just to stay by himself a lot."

"Oh, he's just young, Retha. He'll change as he gets a little older. Nobody knows what he went through before he found you. I can tell he loves you a lot."

"Well, these visions seem very strong when he's around, and there must be a reason. One day I'll know, but until then I just feel lost sometimes." She sighed wistfully.

"Retha, Johnny One Horn once told me that when you have the feeling you said or did things before, it means your life is on the right track. Maybe it will all come to you one day."

"Well, it may be better if it doesn't. What if it's all bad?" She rubbed her forehead. "Makes my damn head hurt sometimes, just thinking about it."

As the sun set, they saw Cricket ride from behind the corral. He had been hunting as he rode the perimeter of the canyon that served as a natural barrier for the cattle. The canyon walls were steep, and the canyon floor ran a mile or so, gradually going uphill. The cattle drank their water from a small spring on the side of the hill. There was plenty of green grass for the number of cattle they owned. For now, the mountain lion seemed to be more interested in the chickens than in the cattle, and that seemed strange to Carl.

"No luck hunting, Cricket?" Retha asked. "We were getting a little worried about you running into that big cat."

"I not worry about Cass; she my pet before. She scared of people now."

Retha and Carl were shocked at that and just looked at each other in amazement. "You mean that mountain lion was your pet, Cricket?"

"I not sure at first when she come back, but she come to me when I hunt. She gone long time. I think Rico kill her. He shoot at her, and she run. Now she come back."

"How did you tame her?" Retha asked incredulously.

"Father find baby lion. We teach her not harm cattle. Not harm people. Now she afraid of people."

"Damn, that explains it all," Carl said, shaking his head. "I wondered why she had not bothered the herd, but damned if I ever heard of anybody having a mountain lion for a pet before."

"I wonder if the shot injured her in some way," said Retha.

"Why didn't you say something before, Cricket? I've been waiting to get a shot at her." Carl was glad he never had the chance.

"She move north, I think she hunt. Now come back to old home. She know me, let me touch her, but no one else can come close."

"Well, it's a relief to know we have a damn mountain lion as a family dog," smiled Carl. "What next?"

Cricket smiled. "Her name Puma Cass. My mother give name. You see her, say name. She know it."

"Then what?" Carl laughed. "Beg for mercy?"

Retha couldn't hold back the laughing. She turned and

headed toward the cabin, followed by Carl and Cricket. "You know, Charles is going to be here in a few days, and I was thinking I'd ask him if we could buy a few goats from him. They would be able to clean all that brush out in the upper canyon."

"No goats," said Cricket as he dipped into the pot of stew waiting on the stove. "That Puma Cass favorite food."

"Well, what if Puma Cass was taught to change her appetite?" smiled Carl.

Cricket thought for a minute. "No, it not work. We try once. Father buy five goats. They not last long."

Carl sat shaking his head with disbelief at what he was hearing. After a long discussion about the future of Puma Cass, he gave in to the fact that he would just have to deal with having the big cat around.

~ ~ ~

Back at Cheyenne Wells, Charles and Cat were busy loading some pack mules with supplies from the ranch – mostly salt, flour, and corn meal and things he thought Carl and his newfound family could use. When they were ready to leave, Cat said she had to change her clothing and would be back in a few minutes. When she returned, she had dressed in what looked like Comanchero clothing.

Charles stared for a minute at the transformation. "Damn, girl, you look like a west Texas bandit."

"Well, you thought I was going into no man's land dressed like a school marm, didn't you? Yeah, I came from Texas – how did you know?" she laughed. "Are we going to leave or are we going to sit here and talk about how the wind blows in Texas?"

Charles thought they would spend the night after about a half day's ride, at Cricket Creek. They walked their horses, leading the mules. Cat had chosen to ride a buckskin Jose had shown her. It fit her attire very well.

When they arrived at Cricket Creek, Cat fell in love with the beautiful blue water creek. Charles explained to her that the young boy that Retha had found as a friend was named after Cricket Creek, because that was where he was born. Cat was impressed by the story, and she marveled at the white sands and native artifacts and paintings on the rocks around it.

As she meandered up the creek admiring all the beauty of the surroundings and wildlife, she walked up on three of Standing Man's tribesmen. They had a small hunting camp set up. She turned and ran back down the creek toward Charles, went straight to her horse, and reached for the rifle. The hunting party stayed in place and one yelled to her in their native language.

Charles was gathering some dry wood to build a fire when he saw Cat frantically loading the rifle. He ran to her. "Cat," he panted, trying to catch his breath. "What the hell is going on?"

"There's three Indians a little way up the creek, and they all have weapons!" she said nervously.

Charles smiled, trying to calm her fears. "Just put the rifle back. They are from the village of Standing Man, and I know them. It's a small village not too far from here at the foot of those rolling hills." He gestured. "You stay here, and I'll go see how they are doing." As he headed away, he turned to say, "Oh, and they don't like to be called Indians. You can call them tribesmen and they don't mind. They say people of different lands called them Indians, but they are not from the land of India."

Cat watched in amazement as Charles slowly strolled up the creek. She was thinking to herself there was much she didn't know about this remarkable man.

Charles greeted the hunters, and they were very friendly. They knew him from the times he had visited Chief Standing Man.

"That woman of yours runs fast. Has she never seen a

Sioux before? She ran so fast her heels were kicking up sand," the leader laughed. "I am called Sunnie, and I am the son of Standing Man. My father talks highly of you and your brother. We didn't mean to frighten your woman; we didn't see her coming and we were startled at first."

"She's fine," Charles smiled. "She's just not used to this country. Tell your father we will be delivering more cattle to him before the winter snows. I'm looking forward to seeing him."

"We will tell him of your coming, and we know that your words are true, my brother," Sunnie said as he gave a sign from his chest. "Until then."

Charles walked back down the creek and found Cat sitting, staring into the rippling water.

"You know, Charles," she mused, "I'm never going back to a town to live. I never knew until now how beautiful the world can be. Even those tribesmen and the way they were dressed, it's all amazing. I heard you talking their language. How on earth did you ever learn that?"

"Well, I guess from being around them all my life. I've grown up around them and consider them family. And my mother, even though she was Chickasaw, knew several native languages. They are my people, as all races are, and that's just the way I believe."

"I didn't know any of my family, except for a drunk uncle," Cat sighed. "I ran away from him when I was twelve. I helped cook on cattle drives with an ol' gal nicknamed Bouncing Betty for about five years. Then I got a job at Cactus Jim's in Abilene and ended up owning that place. I never married Jim, and never had any kind of relationship with him, but he still gave me the place."

"I never thought you would sell or ever leave the place. You looked happy there, and everybody loved you," smiled Charles. "But I, for one, am glad you came here. I really don't know what you see in me, but I'm glad you do. Anyway, you will be meeting my nephew Carl tomorrow –

he's a handful."

~ ~ ~

Charles and Cat arrived at Retha's Blue Moon ranch in the early afternoon. Retha and Cat hugged each other like long-lost family members. Carl looked surprised at the reception, and Charles introduced Cat to Carl. He tipped his hat, still with a dazed look on his face. Cricket was riding the perimeter of the small valley's walls and usually would not come home until almost sunset.

Cat was impressed at how beautiful the small ranch was. The rustic log cabins and the setting between the hills pleased her very much. Retha walked her around the place, showing her all the work she and Carl had accomplished.

As Charles and Carl sat down by the old pump well, Charles began to tell Carl about Sad Hank's warnings, and the extreme dangers of traveling to Moon Rock during the native rituals this time of year. It was the first time Carl had heard of any such ritual, and he listened very closely. Charles explained that other prospectors who also knew of the legend of the Moon phase would show up there every year, and it seemed that almost every year most would be killed or blinded and left behind to die.

"I really think we need to heed this warning. Especially being of native blood, we should honor this, and stay away from their forbidden ceremonies," Charles urged. "We don't even know what the ceremony is about. It's surely not about gold, because Sad Hank says there is no gold at Moon Rock. The gold you seek is across the valley that is shown in the reflection."

Charles continued, "Sad Hank knows where the Echo is. He wouldn't tell me, but he said he was going to take the head of Rico Garza there. If there is a way we could get him to tell us we could avoid the risk of being killed – or worse for Cat and Retha. We don't want to take that chance! Hell, I just met Cat, and I'm liking the hell out of it."

"I never thought any woman could hog-tie you, you old goat," Carl laughed. "I agree there's too much danger involved, but I'd still have to convince Retha. She sees the gold as the key to a prosperous way of life she's never known."

"But, Carl, you're forgetting that just your part of the gold we already have would make ten men rich. If you're going to have a life with this gal, tell her about that. She would never have to want again. You can forget what she owes the Triple A – I'll give that to both of you as a gift."

"You know, Charles, sometimes I do forget we have money. It seems like we've worked for everything we've got. We live no better than the people that work for us, and that's all right with me."

"Well, it gave us a start. Before you were born, we were poor as the mud in Mississippi. We used that gold to give our family a chance for a better life by moving west and buying the ranch. I haven't touched any of that gold for a long time now. Johnny One Horn and Little Boy Horse told me the gold was evil, so your father Joe and I have tried to leave it alone. We've adapted to ranching and doing a fair job of it if you ask me," Charles smiled. "Tell Retha about this and try to persuade her to stay away from that place."

"If you can't change her mind, you could try to convince Sad Hank to show you the way. You probably already know what I've decided. I just got Cat in my life, and I'm damn sure not going to risk her life chasing gold when we don't need it. Before she came along, I would have done it just for fun, but not now."

Before Carl could leave to talk to Retha, he saw her with Cat walking down the hillside toward the cabin. He wasn't at all sure how she would react to the idea of giving up on her dream. He turned back as Charles changed the subject.

"Have you had any more trouble with that mountain

lion?" Charles asked.

"Mountain lion?" Carl chuckled. "As it turns out, she's a pet."

"Pet!" Charles blurted. "The hell he is."

"Yeah, it seems Cricket and his Ma and Pa found the cat when it was just a cub. The damn thing thinks this is her home, and she was actually trained to leave the cattle alone. Darndest thing I ever saw."

"Yeah, around here, just when you think you've seen everything, something else jumps out of the brush and bites you on the ass." Charles chuckled, then looked Carl in the eye. "Seriously, I want to stay for a good visit, but we won't be going to Moon Rock, and I really think you should give up on the idea too. If you want, we can try to catch up to Sad Hank. But I'm convinced it's too dangerous. Should I try to talk to Retha?"

"No," Carl said as he glanced toward Retha. I'd better talk to her myself. I don't think she will listen to anybody else – you know how hardheaded she can be sometimes."

"Yeah, I know and that's what I'm worried about." Charles shook his head.

Retha and Cat stood leaning against the eastern fence talking about old times and Retha's plans to somehow find the Echo. Cat, intrigued by the story of huge amounts of gold being there, listened very intently. In turn, Retha was confused about Cat selling Cactus Jim's saloon, and asked many questions about Cat's reasoning.

"I really don't know," Cat explained. "When I met Charles, there was just something about the guy that was different than anybody I've ever known. After he left Abilene, I started making plans to join him here. There was something there that I can't explain."

"You know, Cat," Retha cautioned, "this country is full of danger. It can take your life in seconds. Don't ever let your guard down here."

"Yeah, I know," Cat admitted. "It's crazy, I know, but

that's what I like about it." Then she looked pointedly at Retha. "Why do you like it, Retha?"

"Well, have you ever got the feeling that you're reliving things that happened before, or being someplace you've been before? I get what they call *déjà vu* when I hear people say things or go places I've never been. I'm still trying to find my past. It seems I'm searching for something all the time; it never ends. That feeling is strong here, stronger here than any place I've been. I think I might find the answer here. It's funny, but when I'm around Cricket, it's stronger than ever. There's got to be something to that."

"I've had that feeling before, but not often," answered Cat. "I can't imagine going through life and not remembering what happened in the past. I really do hope it comes back to you, Retha, but maybe there's a reason you can't remember it. Maybe it's better that you don't."

"Yeah, I've thought about that too. It seems I've been running for several years now. Every time I think I'm going to settle down, I always find the back door open, then I'm gone. Crazy, isn't it? Imagine your life skinning coyotes for a living. Those girls, I mean your friends building that saloon back at the ranch, making a living rolling in the sack. That's something I could never do."

"Well, maybe they feel the same way about skinning coyotes," smiled Cat. "Charles tells me you want to search for the Echo of the Moon, and that might be a hell of a lot more dangerous than hunting coyotes. I think you've got a pretty nice setup here. Besides, Carl's family is rich – you don't need to put yourself in danger that way."

"Yeah, but what he's got is what he's got – it's not mine. I intend to find the Echo and when I do, I'm going to have my own dynasty, not belonging to anyone else," Retha declared.

Cat, seeing that there was no changing Retha's mind, cut off the conversation. Retha could tell by the way Cat was talking that Charles was going to try to talk Carl out of the quest. She suddenly got quiet as they approached the corrals where the men were leaning against the corral fence.

Around the firepit that night there were a lot of discussion about the quest and the reasons why it was a bad and dangerous idea. Retha said almost nothing as she stared at the flickering fire pit. In her mind she already knew the outcome was inevitable. Charles and Cat were planning to leave sometime the following morning, and after a few drinks of ranch-made moonshine to celebrate their friendship, they prepared to turn in for the night. Charles, as always, chose to sleep underneath the stars and the nearly full moon. As the moon rose over the hills, they were amazed to see the silhouette of the big Puma Cass walk slowly across the hilltop followed by Cricket, passing in front of the rising moon.

"Does that boy ever come around?" Cat asked. "That's the most amazing thing I ever saw. That mountain lion really is Cricket's pet! I would have never believed it."

Carl answered, "Yeah, he's not too sociable. He likes to stay by himself, and he's different from anyone I've ever known. Kind of spooky, if you ask me."

The following morning Charles and Cat said their goodbyes, and Carl and Retha watched as they descended the winding trail to the valley.

"You know, Retha," Carl began, "Sad Hank begged us not to go to Moon Rock. I know this is not what you want to hear, but I think he's right. Charles says you don't have to pay for those cattle you bought, and there are plenty more where that came from."

"Well, I'm still going to pay for them, Carl. It's not my way to accept charity from anyone."

Carl was a little shocked at hearing this and realized that he wasn't as close to Retha as he thought. After they argued for a few minutes, Retha suddenly turned and walked back toward the corrals. Though Carl pleaded with her to be reasonable, she never said another word about it. There were two more days until the moon was full. Carl thought for sure he could still change her mind.

~ ~ ~

The next morning Carl awoke to find Retha missing. She had instructed Cricket to tell him she was out riding the perimeter. He was a little confused but wanted to believe the story. An hour or so later he was mending a corral gate when he noticed one of the pack mules was missing. He scanned the area for Cricket, but there was no trace of him either. After an hour he realized she was gone. He remembered waking shortly after they had turned in for the night and noticing her bed was empty, but he had just thought she was taking a moonlight walk, as she often did. This meant she had been gone for several hours. He knew Cricket was holding the answer, but now he was gone too. Carl hurriedly readied his horse Corky and rode in the direction of Moon Rock.

~ ~ ~

By the end of the day, Cricket had followed Retha's tracks, and met her at the sandstone overhead bluffs. Today there were many tracks on the seldom-used trail. They knew not to camp at the bluffs, because prospectors and several members of different tribes would no doubt be using the trail. Warnings left by tribesmen were scattered along the brushy trail in an eerie display to deter the gold seekers. Retha decided to camp off the path so they wouldn't be seen. The next night would be the complete full moon, and she was determined to be at Moon Rock. As she lay on her bedroll, the moon was a bright bluish color, and huge puffy clouds shadowed the mountainside.

In the early morning Retha woke to see Cricket watching over the winding trail. The night had been full of murmured voices, some talking in English and some in native tongues. Now Cricket turned to Retha, holding three fingers in the air. She kept low to the ground as she slowly slipped down to the brush where he was sitting. Coming up the trail were three men who looked like prospectors, each leading a pack mule. Retha was amazed that the three totally ignored the warning signs of the tribesmen.

As Retha and Cricket scanned the mountainside, they were startled by a snapping sound behind them. Turning in surprise, they realized Sad Hank was standing within a few feet.

"I snapped the twig to show you just how easy it was to slip up on you. If I were of a mind to, I could have killed you both." He sat down beside them in the thick underbrush. Cricket hugged Sad Hank. It seemed they were delighted to see each other. This amazed Retha since Cricket hadn't told her he knew Hank.

"I am saddened that you did not heed the warning I told Charles to give you. If you continue on to Moon Rock, you will most likely die. It is not a place for you. You need to turn back now, before you are found. These marked warnings are real."

Retha listened, her eyes focused somewhere across the horizon. "Then why are you here, Hank, if it's so dangerous? I'd like to know."

"I came here to pick up something. My people will not harm me. You are not of my people, and it is forbidden that you be here. But if you feel you must go there, go to the bluff above the west wall, and you can see the Echo when the moon rises. Watch from there but be cautious of your surroundings. There will be scouts watching the area." Slowly and carefully, Hank stood. "I must go from you now but heed my warnings. I cannot help you if you go there." He was looking directly at Retha. "Cricket can go.

We know him. He can tell you what he saw. Miss Retha, I sure wish you would listen. This is a very dangerous place for you to be."

Retha shook her head decisively. "No, I'm keeping Cricket with me. I have to see for myself what all this means. It's something I have to do."

Hank stood for a few seconds before mounting his horse. Finally, he sighed. "I can't be seen with you. Good luck, and may the spirits be with you, my friends. Don't let yourselves be seen, for they will come after you."

As they watched Sad Hank ride up the steep trail, Retha turned to Cricket and asked him to explain how he knew the tribesmen that participated in the ritual.

He turned to her and asked, "Did I not tell you I have been here?"

"I do remember you saying you were here once before, but I just thought you were in this place, not at the ritual."

"Yes, I about ten seasons then. I tied to post. Men dance around me. They want to burn me – stack brush around me. I see strange moon reflect across valley. Storm come then. Lightning strike near me – sign from Great Spirit. Men take off ropes and bow to me. Man with painted face put me on horse and take me away from Moon Rock. He say never tell anyone what I see."

Retha, shaking her head with amazement, slowly reached and took Cricket's hand. "Can you remember where the light from the rock shined?"

The boy nodded. "Yes. Three peaks across valley. It shine on first peak." He motioned to the south side. "It shine quick, then gone." He paused, contemplating what he would say next. "You want watch? I know safe place. I come each year. There is place in canyon walls they not see me. I see many times – five seasons. I hide in place marked by spirits. We hide horses in valley above. I know they be safe."

Retha listened very intently while Cricket was

explaining the plan. She was sure she could trust him. But as she made a move to leave, he stopped her.

"We wait here till dark. Moon not rise for three hours after all dark."

After the sun set, the two made their way up the canyon to the upper valley and hid their horses. From there they crept down the brushy trail until they reached the small ancient dwelling Cricket had described. As they approached, they could easily see the reflection of a large bonfire on the three granite walls of Moon Rock. Retha was nervous as she realized there was only one way in, and one way out. That was something she hadn't noticed the first time she had been there.

Near the bonfire were five men tied to posts, and one tied upside down. They could see Sad Hank sitting with what looked to be several chiefs. Retha was surprised to see Standing Man and wondered how the old chief even made the grueling journey to this strange place. Several tribesmen with painted faces danced slowly around the suffering captives.

Several scouts were stationed around the area, all dressed in ceremonial clothing. Sometimes they would look up at where the pair was hidden, but never made an effort to approach.

Retha's mind was troubled, knowing that Carl would likely be following her. To her surprise, all at once he rode down the trail and approached the ceremony. Quickly, several braves drew down on him. He remained calm in his usual way, and showed no fear as he just walked his horse slowly toward Sad Hank and Chief Standing Man. He was saying something to them, but Retha could not make out the words. Chief Standing Man greeted Carl and pointed in the direction of the cliff dwelling where Retha and Cricket were hiding.

"They knew we were here all the time," she whispered. "That Carl," she smiled, "is the bravest man I know. Most people would be terrified, but he's as calm as a Sunday picnic. Damn, sometimes I think he's either a genius, or a complete idiot."

A slight sliver of the moon could now be seen rising in the east. The ceremony became very intense as the rising moon seem to trigger the real meaning of the ritual. The tribesmen were becoming trancelike in their ceremonial dance. One lit the brush under the man that was upside down on the post. The man screamed as the flames consumed his body. It was a terrifying thing to watch, and Retha bowed her head and turned from the gruesome spectacle.

As the moon slowly rose, the area was illuminated with a strange eerie glow. The tribesmen blindfolded the other five men, who were screaming with terror and begging. Several of the medicine men dressed in ghost-like clothing danced with pine torches around the helpless prisoners. From their vantage point above Moon Rock, on the highest wall Retha and Cricket could see the unearthly reflection move across the valley floor.

When the moon had fully shown itself, it had traveled to the first of the three peaks to the south just as Cricket had said. As the reflection faded, all the tribesmen slowly kneeled in prayer to the Great Spirit.

Retha could see Carl in the light of the bonfire stand up and mount his horse, Corky. He looked straight at the terrified Retha. As he rode up the only trail leading in, he motioned for them to meet him at the upper valley. Still in shock from watching a man burned alive, she was quick to oblige.

It was very quiet going up the trail except for the night birds in the distance. Retha expected any minute to hear the screams of the other five men bound to the tree snags, but never heard another sound. The night became very still. When they reached the valley, Carl was there waiting. Retha expected to find Carl angry, but it was exactly the opposite. He just hugged her and smiled. Cricket said he would ride on ahead and meet them later at the ranch.

"I thought they would kill you for sure, Carl! How did you know they wouldn't?" she gasped.

"I didn't," he grinned, "but I was determined to find you, and I had to do whatever it took. Somehow, I knew Sad Hank and Standing Man would be there. I guess you can say I just took a chance." As they turned their horses down the trail, he continued. "That light that shined across the valley and pointed to the first peak was the strangest thing I ever saw. I don't know, but I got a feeling that peak would also be a dangerous place to go."

Retha didn't respond, so Carl just chuckled. "When are you leaving?"

"As soon as I get a few provisions at home." She looked at him, returning his smile. "You already knew I was going, didn't you? But I can't get my mind off those poor ol' prospectors and especially the screams of the man they burned." Retha wiped tears from her eyes.

"That was no poor ol' prospector, sweetie, that was Rico Garza. Standing Man brought him here to be executed. Sad Hank is going to take his head to the Echo."

"Rico Garza?" Retha was confused. "Now I don't feel so bad. But when did they catch that bastard? If I knew that, I would have joined the party! But I couldn't stay another minute, thinking those other men were going to get fried at the stake."

"They weren't going to burn those prospectors; it was all a show with the intention of scaring the hell out of them. Standing Man told me of their plans before I left. They were told if they ever came back, they would receive the same fate as Rico Garza," he reassured her. "I knew that Sad Hank had captured him near Goat Head Mountain and took him to the village of Standing Man, but I had no idea he would wind up here. I thought they had killed him at the village. Charles told me about it, but things have been happening so fast, I guess I just forgot to tell you."

"Well, if Sad Hank knows where the Echo is, and he's your friend, why does he not show us the way?"

"I talked to him about that, and he said, now that we know where it is, that we could find our own way. He is forbidden to take us there. Besides, I think Cricket knows the way."

"If he does, why doesn't he say he does?" She shook her head in bewilderment. "Although I wouldn't doubt it. There are so many secrets hid in that boy. I'm going to just flat out ask him when we get home, if I can get close to him. He leaves every morning to check the cattle and find Puma Cass something to eat. Sometimes he comes home after dark and just goes to his cabin and I don't even see him. That lion follows him around like a faithful dog. I wouldn't be surprised if it sleeps in the cabin with him."

Carl tipped his hat back and chuckled. "Yeah, the darndest thing I ever saw. He comes around me sometimes and talks my ear off, sometimes in our language and sometimes in the language of the Pawnee. After that it may be two or three days before I see him again, but I know he's always there like a ghost in the night."

Carl and Retha traveled the trail very carefully down the switchbacks, sometimes walking their mounts. The trail was covered with loose rocks caused by the gathering at Moon Rock. At the bottom of the switchbacks the going was much easier, and they arrived at the Blue Moon Ranch around midnight. As they approached the cabins, they were surprised to see Cricket sitting in the open by the fire pit. The intimidating Puma Cass was lying a few feet from him. The big cat growled as they approached, then slowly walked away and disappeared into the brushy hillside.

"Well, I see you're well protected, Cricket, but your overgrown kitty cat scares the hell out of me sometimes." Carl greeted as they dismounted. He gave a sign from the chest as Cricket welcomed him home in the Pawnee language.

Then Cricket turned to Retha. "Want eat prairie chicken? I get some today in hills. Puma Cass not happy today – she get yucca thorn in foot, but she let me take it out."

"Well, isn't she sweet?" smiled Retha. "Yes, we will have a prairie chicken. We're both a little starved."

Carl bedded the horses down in their shed and slowly scanned the hill as he walked back to the fire. "Sure is a beautiful night. You would think that light from Moon Rock would still light the sky, wouldn't you? I see the moon, but there's no reflection now."

Speaking in perfect Pawnee, Cricket told Carl that the reflection could only be seen from Moon Rock. He said it shined all the time, but only one night of the year would it point to the Echo."

Carl, thinking this was a good time to ask, just asked the question. "Have you ever been to the Echo, Cricket?"

"Yes, I have been there more than once with my father. We lived just below there for a while when I was just a few seasons old. It's a sacred place and many tribesmen who have passed are there. It's a place of the dead. In the time of the Comanche many lived here in the valley. But we were only allowed to go to certain places on the mountain and never to the burial ground. Then one day they told us we had to leave; we never knew the reason. I think it was because I played with the yellow rock that was by our cabin. My father said it was the rock of fools, and would poison my spirit, and we left the area soon after. We were told never to come back. When we were a few miles away we could see the smoke from the cabin. The Comanche burned the cabin and any trace that might have been left there." He looked wistful as he continued. "I had a friend that I used to play with there. I really miss him, but I knew I must never go back."

When Carl translated to Retha, she looked at Cricket

sadly. "Why did you not tell me, Cricket? It seems like all this was for nothing when you already knew the way there. I really trusted you to tell me the truth."

"I want to, but I not want you get hurt," sighed Cricket as he stared at the ground.

"Well, it hurts me really bad, as I have been like a sister to you," Retha scolded, throwing the remaining part of the prairie chicken into the fire. "Damn," she yelled.

Cricket slowly walked to his horse with his head down and a hand over his face to hide the tears. Retha walked to the corral and stared up the canyon. Cricket looked at her for a minute, then with a broken voice called after her, "You are my sister."

Retha, hearing those words, stood paralyzed for a moment as thoughts and reflections raced through her mind. Cricket wheeled his horse around and quickly rode off into the darkness.

Carl stood shaking his head as if to think, "What the hell did I just hear? He just said you are his sister. Damn, I knew there was more to this than meets the eye."

When Retha realized what she had just heard, she ran after Cricket, but he had disappeared into the darkness. She paced the perimeter of the ranch until sunrise. When Carl tried to comfort her, she just pushed away and began to cry. She mounted her horse in the cool morning and scanned the surrounding hills, but Cricket was nowhere in sight.

# CHAPTER 16

Charles and Cat returned to the Cheyenne Wells ranch expecting to find a little peace and quiet but were surprised that the street was empty.

"What the hell is going on here?" questioned Cat. "All these people are peeking out the windows."

"You got me, but there damn sure is something wrong." Charles could see Pete riding from the hill to the east.

When Pete arrived, he explained that Nate and Jose had several of the hands stationed around the perimeter of the ranch. Tex Luna had ridden from the Triple A suffering from three gunshot wounds.

"What in the hell is happening here, Pete?" Charles nervously asked.

"Tex rode in yesterday and he's really bad. He said the Triple A was being held down by snipers in the hills. They've already shot several people. Everybody's afraid to come out of the buildings. According to Tex, they are demanding gold, and threatened to kill everyone if they didn't get it. He said there were several men in the bluffs surrounding the town with buffalo guns, shooting anybody that showed themselves. When the folks here heard of this they went into hiding, fearing the same thing would happen here."

"Has there been any trouble here, Pete?"

"No, and I told them not to panic, but they all are, and

they don't listen. I can't say if I blame them. We put the ranch hands and every available man that can shoot around the perimeter."

"What about Joe and his family? Did Tex say anything about them?"

"Just that Joe was trying to keep everyone inside and stationed lookouts in the dark of the night to search the area. It's a lot safer here, because we don't have the disadvantage of being in a valley where we can be looked down on. Those big bluffs along the river make it easy for snipers to pick them off. I was planning to go there right away, and now that you're back, we both can."

"Send a rider, Pete, to get Carl. Tell him we're on our way to the Triple A and for him to come running. We'll meet him on the north hill a couple of miles from the Triple A. Tell him to watch for a mirror reflection to mark our spot."

Pete quickly motioned for Jose and told him their plans. Jose dispatched one of his best riders to go to Carl.

Charles and Pete hurriedly packed a few supplies in their saddle bags and grabbed one of the pack mules from the stables and packed it with several boxes of ammunition. Leading the mule would be slower, so Charles told Jose to ride with the mule and meet them at the north hill. Then Charles grabbed his father's Hawkins rifle and rigged the scope.

"Cat, when Nate gets back, tell him to stay here and watch over things. He's out scouting for pasture." Charles hugged Cat, who was confused about why someone would want to do such a horrid deed. She watched as the men rode out of the township toward the south.

Cat scurried across the small street to where the girls were all huddling inside the new saloon and small hotel. When she entered the room, she saw that Big Sally was working over Tex and screaming at the others for hot water and supplies. Cat approached the bunk and could see the situation was bad, and Tex had become unconscious. Big Sally looked at Cat and shook her head.

~ ~ ~

Nate had been gone a couple of days scouting new grazing land for the herd. As he dismounted near the saloon, it was plain to see that something was wrong. He opened the door and was shocked to see his long-time friend covered with blood. He looked at Cat with questions in his eyes.

Cat explained that the Triple A had been attacked by snipers and somehow Tex had escaped and managed to get all the way to Cheyenne Wells. "Charles said to tell you to watch over things here and they will return when this is all over."

"What about Tex, Cat? Is he going to make it? We've been like brothers for years."

Cat said nothing, but slowly dropped her head and looked to the floor.

Sally walked away from the bedside and motioned for Nate to follow. "He's real bad, Nate," she said in a hushed voice. "He's lost a lot of blood. It's going to be a miracle if he makes it."

Nate walked out the door of the building and, muffling his mouth with his hand, yelled with frustration. Seeing Shorty across the street, he stumbled to him and the two fell into each other's arms.

"Damn, Shorty, have you ever thought we're always at the wrong place at the wrong time?"

"Damn right I have – that deal with that crazy Bo Jack that time, I thought I was going to die for sure." He wiped tears with the back of his hand, then changed the subject. "Yolanda is putting together some medication for Tex. She's good with that and if anybody can save ol' Tex, she can."

~ ~ ~

Charles and Pete arrived at the northern hill overlook late in the afternoon of the second day. It was Charles' plan to wait for Carl. After setting up a camp in a wash where it would be hard to see, Charles used the scope of the Hawkins rifle to scan the bluffs over the Triple A. The small township looked like a ghost town with the streets abandoned. He knew he would have to make contact to let Joe and the boys know they were there before they personally searched the hills. He needed to avoid being shot mistakenly by his own people. But he would wait for the cover of darkness to go into the town.

Soon after nightfall, Charles left Pete with the horses and traveled on foot to the edge of the settlement. He knew all the hands would be armed and watching for anything that moved. Every few minutes the roar of a buffalo gun would rattle or bust the windows from a building. The people had quickly learned to stay away from any windows, to avoid being shot.

As he slipped to the back of Joe's cabin, he made the sound of a whippoorwill. He knew Joe would know who it was. The Armstrong boys would always use the bird call they were taught many years before in the Mississippi swamp.

Joe carefully opened the back door, motioning for Earl and James to put their rifles down. "How many are they, brother?" Charles asked as he patted the young boys on the back.

"We don't know. They haven't shown themselves. We've had five people hit, luckily mostly by flying glass, but Mrs. Barrow was hit bad. We've got her at the school and the women are trying to help her. Those men on the hill have been shooting arrows into the street too, and some were flaming. One had a note attached demanding one thousand gold pieces. The others were aimed at the outbuildings, probably just to warn us. They want us to leave the gold by the river's edge or they will burn the town to the ground. I don't think they are tribesmen, but they have at least one bow, and the arrows have the markings of the Sioux. They warned us to stop trying to resist or they would burn the entire ranch to the ground. It's so easy for them to just sit up there and lob those arrows down on our buildings, so I told the hands to stand down and go to their families."

The words had rushed out of Joe, as if the shock of the situation was too much to contain. Finally, as he sat slumped in a chair in the center of the room, he looked up at Charles. "Is Tex all right? He rode off in a hail of bullets. I know he was hit at least one time," Joe asked, his face furrowed with worry.

"He was hit three times," replied Charles. "I don't know how he even made it to Cheyenne Wells. He's real bad, Joe. He was still alive when I left, but it damn sure doesn't look good."

Charles nodded as James offered him a chair and pulled it next to his brother's. "Joe, this gold thing keeps going on and on. The word has spread all across this land. We're getting every lowlife in this whole damn country showing up here. Tonight, Pete and I are going to search the bluffs and try to end this thing. Could you tell which way the shots came from?"

"No, but from the sound, they seem to be from the north across the river. They gave us until tomorrow night to deliver the gold to the river. It was my idea to put some of the coins in a saddle bag and let them actually get it. Then we could follow them back to where the others are hiding and take them all out. It's risky, but we can't let them get away with anything or more of them will be back first chance they get."

"I agree," said Charles. "Carl should be here by

morning, and we can put our plan in motion. There's a late moon tomorrow night and it's my guess that these yahoos will wait until the moon rises – if they don't, climbing down the canyon walls would be impossible. I bet they have horses on the ridge and will come on foot. About one hour before sunset, take the saddle bag of gold to the river's edge. Get one of the hands to help, but I hope he doesn't get shot at – we damn sure don't know who we're dealing with."

With the plan set, Charles rejoined Pete on the northern hill, explained their plan, and agreed they would wait for the arrival of Carl sometime during the night. If things went according to plan, they would fire three shots to say everything was ok.

Charles and Pete lay back on their saddles on the ground to try to get a little rest. It wasn't long before Charles heard the call of the whippoorwill and realized Carl was approaching. He answered and within minutes Carl emerged from the darkness. Charles explained their plan and the eager Carl settled down.

Charles scanned the bluffs with the scope on the Hawkins rifle and, to his surprise, saw a campfire. Several men appeared to be sharing a whisky bottle. He figured he could drop one dead, but in return the others would probably rain down fire arrows on the sleeping town. In the scope they appeared to be dressed like buffalo hunters. He saw no tribesmen.

The late moon was starting to rise over the east hills, shadowed by a few clouds.

"Well, boys, if my guess is right, those dirt bags are just about to make their way down the cliffs to the river," observed Charles. "They'll probably send one or two down while the rest watch from the bluffs. Joe and Tom Sheen will follow the ones with the saddle bag from below, if they can without being seen."

Knowing the terrain very well, Joe and Tom watched as

the outlaws slipped very carefully down the steep bluffs on two ropes the had tied and tossed far below to the river. One made it to the river, but the other fell into the swift current in the river bend. The first man just watched in silence as his partner was swept away, struggling in the swift current.

"Look at that," Tom whispered. "Life is cheap for this bunch. He's just going to let his buddy drown."

"Yeah, the greed for gold changes men. They become like a pack of wolves, fighting for the best part of the kill. Why don't you go downstream to the sand bar, Tom. If that ol' boy gets out of the river it will be there. Take him alive if you can, but if he acts dangerous just take him out."

Tom agreed and silently slipped to the sand bar. Joe watched as the other man opened the saddle bag.

Satisfied to see that it was gold, the man turned with the heavy bag and hurriedly he struggled to the bluff. Joe watched as he tied the heavy saddlebag to one of the ropes. Quickly the rope was hoisted from above toward the top of the bluff. The man then tied himself to the other rope. Everything went well for a while, but when the outlaws at the top had retrieved the gold, the man fell, screaming, to his death on the rocks below.

"They cut the rope," Joe thought. The words of his great friend Johnny One Horn flashed through his mind: many would die over the gold they had uncovered in the swamp.

In the dim light of the moon Tom Sheen approached the sand bar to find the second man dragging himself from the water. It appeared that the man had hit a submerged rock or something and was dragging his legs and moaning. Tom immediately asked the man to throw down his weapon. The outlaw slowly looked toward his legs, pointed his handgun, and fired at close range. The bullet landed at Tom's feet. Tom asked again for the man to comply, but when he pointed the large caliber pistol again toward Tom, Tom had no choice but to fire back, killing the man instantly.

He stared down at the man for a few seconds, then realized as he looked closely that the outlaw was very young. Shaking his head, he slowly walked away.

Charles, Pete, and Carl had made their way to the top of the bluff and watched the celebrating outlaws from the cover of a large rock. Pete had stationed himself on the back side, so as to get the outlaws in a crossfire. It wasn't long before the wicked power of greed showed its face, and the three men started arguing. One, dressed like a buffalo hunter, shot one of the others with a buffalo gun, dropping him, and then shot the other with his forty-four. One was apparently dead, but the other was begging for mercy as he lay moaning with pain. This made no difference to the greedy outlaw as he pumped two more bullets into the man, killing him too.

Charles ordered the man to stand down, but he mounted his horse, firing his forty-four wildly into the night. He wheeled the horse, not knowing exactly where the voice had come from, and ran in Carl's direction. Charles slipped noisily on a rock, and the man turned and pointed his buffalo gun at him as he tried to get to his feet.

Carl had been hesitant about killing the man, but he knew if they didn't stop him he would just bring others back for more gold. Now that he saw Charles in danger, from about forty feet away, he threw the big Arkansas toothpick knife and dead-centered the man's back. The man slowly slid out of the saddle to the ground.

As they looked at the man on the ground, they realized he was very young, and as they walked to the fire where the others lay dead, they could see that they were also just kids, probably less than twenty years old.

"Isn't this something?" Charles said, shaking his head. "These are just kids. They probably heard the story of the gold from some old man telling stories for drinks in a saloon somewhere out there. It's a damn shame that the curse has killed three more people, and some by their own hands."

"What a damn shame," Carl agreed, slowly turning his horse. "We better get down the bluffs and see what that other shot we heard was for. I sure hope Joe or Tom didn't end up with a bullet."

"Well, get the saddle bag, Pete. We'll get these boys' horses. It's a damn shame," sighed Charles.

Carl fired three shots in the air and Joe responded quickly from the river with three of his own.

"Well, I guess everything's ok down there," Carl remarked. "We can thank God for that."

An hour later the three, leading the outlaws' horses, reached ground level, and made their way around to the river's edge to check on Joe and Tom Sheen. As they approached, they could see them standing by a fire they had built. Joe and Tom were watching as the three appeared out of the dim, moonlit riverside.

"I see you're all right; we were worried when we heard all that shooting. Hell, these two here were just kids. I wish we would have known," Tom lamented as they emerged from the darkness. "I had to shoot one of them. I kind of think the kid wanted me to shoot him though. He was dragging his legs and he looked like he was in a lot of pain. He shot at me but it landed at my feet. Now I think he missed me on purpose. I had no way of knowing he was just a kid. I didn't shoot back until he backed the hammer again...." Tom was near tears, blinking them back as he continued. "Damn, I feel bad about this."

"The ones on the bluffs were just kids too – hell, probably not more the fifteen or so," Charles answered. "One of their own shot the other two of them. Carl took him out with his knife as he was about to blow my head off with that damn buffalo gun."

"Well, it's over for now," said Pete. We can bury these boys in the morning." He slapped Tom on the shoulder. "But don't feel so bad about these boys, Tom. Remember, they shot our friends and showed no mercy for them! Hell, Mrs. Barrow might still die, and Tex – we don't have any way of knowing if he's going to make it, or if he may be dead already."

~ ~ ~

As he'd become accustomed, Charles unrolled his bedroll and bedded down by the river, along with Carl.

Joe was still pretty upset at the thought of the outlaws being so young. He sat on the porch of his cabin and popped a bottle of whisky, then watched as the morning sun brightened the townsite.

Tom Sheen, still in shock about the shooting, had walked back to where the body of the young man was and sat down beside him. He stared at the river until the light of day.

Pete just slowly walked his horse into the night and disappeared.

~ ~ ~

Joe had dozed off as the sun rose in the sky. He jerked awake when his wife Cindy sat down beside him.

"Are you going to go to bed and get some rest? Or do you plan to sleep on the porch from now on?" Cindy jested. "We were all worried sick about you and the others. We heard a lot of shots during the night – hardly anybody slept. What happened?" She placed her hand on his shoulder. She could see he was troubled.

"They were all just kids, Cindy, about the same age as our boys! Now they are all dead. Three were killed by their own greed, turning them against each other. Tom Sheen killed one in self-defense and Carl had no choice but to kill the other. He saved Charles' life. That kid would have shot him with no hesitation." Joe pursed his lips, thinking. "It's that damn gold – the greed and the curse that comes with it. We should have listened to Johnny One Horn when he warned us many would die over what we found in that swamp."

Cindy sat next to him and stroked his arm soothingly. After two cups of coffee and a heavy dose of her calm support, he hugged her and thanked her

"Are you going to get some rest now?" she asked.

"No, I've got work to do. We've got to bury those boys, and then I got fences to ride. It ain't no holiday." Joe mounted his horse, still conveniently tied to the hitching post in front of the house.

As she watched him ride toward the river, Cindy wiped the tears from her eyes, sharing the pain she knew Joe had endured.

~ ~ ~

"Somebody somewhere is waiting for their boy to come home," Tom remarked as they finished burying the teens. "I feel bad for them. It's a hell of a deal."

Charles nodded. "Yup. But it was their bad choices that brought them here. Now let's all go and start where we left off, my friends. It's better if we just ride away – there's a new day out there. Let's get to it," he advised, hoisting himself into his saddle.

Carl followed suit. "Well, boys, it's about noon and I got a full twelve hours to ride to get home. Retha's not doing too good after finding out Cricket is her brother," he frowned.

"Brother?" Pete smiled. "How in the world did that happen?"

"Well, it did, and besides that, he rode off after a quarrel with Retha and never came back. Darndest thing I ever saw."

Pete tried to comfort him. "Well, he's just a kid, Carl.

He probably came back by now."

"Maybe, Pete, but I'll feel better seeing it with my own eyes." He turned his horse southward. "It's been good seeing you boys."

Pete had mounted up also. "Are you coming, Charles? That little Cat of yours is probably walking the floor by now."

"Yeah, but I'm going to stop by and see Cindy and the boys first. I'll catch you up the trail somewhere. I'll see the rest of you boys in a month or so, I hope."

# CHAPTER 17

## Cheyenne Wells

The rooming house was almost finished. Cat had added an upstairs, where she envisioned a haven for herself and Charles. Now she paced the floor, stopping at the window to stare across the valley as she wondered if Charles would ever return.

Tex was improving, but he had lost the use of his right arm. He was still in very poor condition, though. Yolanda, Shorty's wife, sat by him day and night to keep a careful eye on his condition.

The rest of the hands were still busily building cabins and a horse stable. Travelers on their way to Denver were becoming very frequent, and Cat's idea of a booming business was becoming a reality. Gold seekers heading for the gold fields in Denver were mostly men, but an occasional wagon group made its way into the small community too. Some drovers who came through were hired by Nate as temporary ranch hands. Riders and wagons made their way back and forth from the Triple A, and a steady stream of supplies was coming from Garden City and Abilene.

Since the saloon was so far from suppliers, Big Sally had constructed a moonshine still behind the new roadhouse. It wasn't uncommon for Sally to control the new rowdy crowd with an iron hand. She had already bested a rugged mountain man in the street outside of the roadhouse. In the muddy street after a downpour, they had rolled in the mud, kicking and gouging, until the exhausted man gave up. It appeared he enjoyed the conflict though, as well as Big Sally, and the two became friends afterward.

In fact, Harry Willie, the mountain man, liked the place so much that he acquired a job from Nate running the new livery stable still under construction. As it turned out, Harry was a very good blacksmith and great with horses. He visited Big Sally every day, sitting at the bar and drinking moonshine. Then she would accompany him back to the stable as he wobbled on shaky legs, dumping him in the straw to sober up.

Harry Willie hadn't gotten his name by accident; he was the hairiest man anyone there had ever seen. People teased him, but in a friendly way. He was well liked and offered to buy the livery stable from Nate and work out the debt by taking care of all the ranch horses. Nate, not having the right to sell it, just told him to talk to Charles when he returned.

The three card tables at the saloon were busy every day with gamblers passing by and a host of others. The girls entertained the patrons, and the place was becoming a well-known establishment with a classy reputation. Music was performed by two of the girls that were piano players. Word about the saloon spread very fast through the network of prospectors and families heading to the Colorado gold fields.

Along with the good people, the gold trail had attracted highwaymen looking to take advantage of the rush. It also brought a few U.S. Cavalry patrols trying to keep the peace. The patrols were small, amounting to five soldiers each. Altogether there were only three patrols that covered a range of more than eighty miles.

By now, there were nine cabins in the small village,

along with a bunkhouse, the livery stable, and the largest attraction, Cat's Place. Big Sally decided the community needed a jail, and quickly talked Cat into the idea. Cat appointed five of the hands to start the construction as soon as possible.

Nate, riding in from scouting the herd, was furious when he found out they had acted without him. He stopped by where the men were working and asked, "What in the hell is going on?"

One of the hands the others called "the Maestro" walked to his horse. "Just doing what we were told to do, boss. She said the town needed a jail, so we are just doing what we were told."

"Well, from now on, you men only take orders from me! Hell, this is a cattle ranch, not a damn town! Now get back to the cabin building. Anyone does anything without asking me again and they are fired, you hear? Now get to it."

The hands obediently gathered their tools and crossed the street to where the rest of the men were working.

Big Sally, watching from the saloon door, rushed over to Nate. "Cat's gonna be mad! She gave those men an order to build a jail," she hollered.

"This ain't no damn town, and we don't need no damn jail! Besides, Cat ain't the damn boss – I am!" he yelled back.

"Well, she's not gonna like it; I can tell you that, Nate."

"I don't really care, Sally. Until she's put in charge of me, I'm still the boss and what I say goes." He grabbed the reins and walked his horse toward the bunkhouse, muttering under his breath. "Holy crap."

"You're an ass," Sally yelled as Nate walked away.

"Not as big as yours," he angrily yelled back.

The hands were laughing, even though they were trying to hide their amusement from Nate.

Still, he noticed. "What the hell are you laughing at?" he challenged.

The workers guiltily wiped the smiles from their faces and continued working. Finally, Nate mounted up, wheeled his horse around, and headed toward the herd.

Late in the afternoon, Charles and Pete returned to the busy ranch. Carl had taken another route through Cricket Creek. As soon as Charles dismounted, he was met by a very mad Big Sally stomping out of Cat's Place. The fire in her eyes told him that something was up.

Pete, noticing the tension in the air, looked at Charles, slid his hat back and spoke. "I don't like the smell of this, boss. I think I'll just slide on out of here and check on those boys."

"Damn chicken," smiled Charles. "I'm still gonna shoot you one of these days."

"Yeah, well I might need to be put out of my misery after all this mess. I might not be able to bear it all," Pete laughed.

Charles turned to the big woman. "OK, Sally, what's the problem? From the sour look on your face, it must be pretty bad."

"It's that darn Nate, going around acting like he owns the place! He won't let us build a jail to lock up some of these yahoos. We need a place to sober them up, that's what we need," growled Sally.

"Well, Miss Sally, Nate and Pete are my long-time foremen, and I have given them a good-sized share of this ranch. So they are the bosses over the ranch even when I'm here. If Nate says he don't want a jail, then I guess this place won't have one."

"Well, your other half wants a jail. See if you can deal with that. I bet you change your mind then, Mr. Boss. I take my orders from Cat and no one else," Sally declared.

"Other half?" Charles mused. But he didn't respond; he knew it wouldn't help. He calmly tied Sachi to the hitching post and entered the newly finished saloon. He was amazed at the activity and all the strange faces. One of the girls called his name and pointed to the stairway.

As he reached the top of the stairway, he saw several rooms. Not knowing which room to enter, he knocked on the nearest door. A young lady cracked the door and pointed down the hall. "It's the room that overlooks the street."

A bit frustrated, Charles quickly walked to the room, opened the door, and entered. He found Cat busily rearranging things.

Surprised, she ran and embraced him. Then she excitedly began to tell him about how good the business had become. Charles listened, nodding and smiling, but thinking at the same time, "What the hell have I got myself into?" Then he interrupted. "But how is Tex? Has he been taken care of? Is he getting better?"

"Tex is healed from most of his wounds, but he's still bedridden. Yolanda is still taking care of him. He's in a room down the hall."

Charles followed Cat to the room to find Tex sitting up in bed and playing cards with Yolanda.

After talking to Tex for a while, Charles returned to the room with Cat, only to find Big Sally waiting for him.

"There are two drunks tied up behind the saloon, Charles. What are you going to do about it, Mr. Boss Man? And another thing, that damn horse of yours bit me on my backside while I wasn't watching. How do you put up with that alligator, anyway?"

As Big Sally stomped back down the stairs, Cat and Charles couldn't keep from laughing. Holding their hands over their mouths to keep Big Sally from hearing, they quickly closed the door.

Looking out the open window, Charles saw Jose walking out of the saloon and called down to him to take Sachi to the livery stable and care for him. Jose waved back, then escorted Sachi to the stable, keeping an eye on Sachi's teeth.

"Your horse bites people?" Cat laughed.

"Well, yeah. It's in his bloodline, I guess. He was sired by Coattail, Johnny One Horn's horse. His brother is Corky, Carl's horse. They both will bite if they're mad about something. I guess he didn't like being left tied on that hitching post. I know he doesn't like loud noises, and Sally was pretty loud today. But all in all, he's the sweetest horse you've ever seen."

Big Sally was in the back of the saloon with her dress pulled up while one of the girls was inspecting the horse bite. They hadn't noticed the ranch hands working on the roof next to the saloon, who began cheering and laughing. The first man that noticed was so shocked by what he had seen that he fell from the roof into the soft mud below.

"Damn Peeping Toms!" Big Sally yelled at the top of her voice as she huffed back into the saloon.

Charles and Cat heard all the commotion and decided to investigate. As they came down the stairs, they could still hear the hands laughing and jeering outside. Charles walked to the men, spread his hands, and asked what all the commotion was.

"Well, Manuel fell off the building into the mud," one of the men replied sheepishly.

"And that's funny?" Charles questioned. "He could have broken his neck." As he looked around, he saw Manuel, covered with mud, cleaning himself off by the watering trough. Charles walked over to him. "Are you all right, Manuel? I've never known you to fall off buildings you're building. You had anything to drink today?" he asked.

"No, boss, I was just doing my job. I was really close to the edge driving those shingles when I looked down and there it was."

"It? What was it?" Charles pressed.

Manuel was a shy young man, and his cheeks were flushed as he spoke. "Well, to be honest, boss, it was as big as the moon and staring me right in the face. It was the biggest ass I ever saw, and another girl was rubbing something on it. Some kind of black stuff."

"Well, Manuel, you lived. I mean, you didn't turn into salt or something worse," Charles grinned. "How big did you say that thing was?"

"I said the moon, I think, but I'm trying to forget it, boss."

"Mercy me, don't tell anybody, Manuel! Ol' Big Sally might come gunning for you – worse yet, may sit on you. I hear she's kind of got a boyfriend now, that Nate hired. From what I hear, he's got more hair than a grizzly bear. You might not want him to get wind of it, either. I'd advise you just to keep it to yourself, Manuel."

"Yeah, I know. I'll try to erase it from my mind, boss," Manuel smiled.

Cat, who had overheard most of the story, covered up her laugh with both hands to her face. "Lordy, Lordy, Lordy, seems like some kind of never-ending story since I've been here."

"Don't plan on it getting any better, my dear," smiled Charles. "Every day is a brand-new story – kind of fun, now that I think about it."

"Yeah, it's damn sure different. I'm having so much fun, my hair hurts," she laughed.

~ ~ ~

Carl arrived at his adopted home at the Blue Moon to find no one there. He didn't give it much thought, though, and started doing some of the usual chores that needed to be done. He told himself everything was ok, and he hoped that was true, until he noticed the sun sinking low in the sky.

After sundown, as he roasted a jackrabbit he had shot along the way, he looked around the place but couldn't find anything unusual. A couple of hours went by, and then he heard the shuffling of hooves approaching from the east hill. He sat very quietly as Retha dismounted her horse and removed the saddle.

"Need some help, gal?" he asked.

Carl had been expecting a warm welcome, but what he got was the exact opposite. Retha walked to the fire and sat down without saying a word. "Well, so much for, 'glad you're back, welcome home!' You want me to leave and come back again?"

"Carl, Cricket never came back."

"Retha, that boy was on his own for no telling how long. I'm not worried about him. Hell, when I was his age, I was a loner too, and back then this was a far more dangerous place than it is now, if you can believe that."

"But you at least had your brothers! He said I was his sister, and that's been tearing at me ever since. If he is my brother, then he knows my past, and probably knows more about me than I do."

"Ahh, he might have just made that up, babe. He's a wild cat and probably knows every trick in the book to get what he wants or to get attention. I wouldn't put much faith in that story. Hell, he'll probably show up in a few days. He just got his feathers ruffled. I'll ride over to Standing Man's village tomorrow and see if they've seen him, if that makes you feel any better. They've got hunting parties that cover a lot of this valley."

As the night passed, Retha settled down and the two shared a bottle of homemade wine from the Triple A.

The early morning came fast, and Carl was already tending the animals at sunrise. To his surprise, Shorty showed up from Cheyenne Wells.

"How in the world did Nate let you get away with shirking a day's work, old friend? How's Yolanda and the family? Hell, it seems like a long time since I've seen you."

"It has been," Shorty smiled. "They're all fine. I just told Nate I needed a few days to get away for a while. That Big

Sally struts around the ranch trying to run things, and it's just too much for me."

"That deal down at the Triple A was just about too much for me, you know, Shorty. Those were all kids that we had to kill down there. It was a bad deal all the way around." Carl sighed. He glanced toward the cabin. "Retha is still asleep, I think."

"Yeah, I heard what happened. It's a damn shame what greed will do to men, or, in this case, young boys." Shorty dismounted and looked hopefully toward the cabin. "I'll help you gather up some of those eggs from that hen house if I'm invited for breakfast!"

It wasn't long before Retha joined them outside as Carl whipped up some eggs and added some salt pork bacon he had brought back from the Triple A. As she joined them, she asked Shorty what brought him to the Blue Moon.

"Well, it won't be too long and I'll be leaving this country for good. I don't know, but I'm sure they are going to send somebody to look for ol' Marshal Tig. That old federal Judge still has a warrant out for me down in Dodge City. I got to go somewhere where no one knows me or my family. It's hard to be happy anymore when I'm always looking over my shoulder. I've been thinking about south Texas. There's a lot of space down there. I plan to get back into a cattle ranch down there somewhere and just try to blend in, maybe somewhere around Laredo." He wiped his brow as the sun blazed down. "I've been thinking about asking you and Charles for a little grubstake to help me get started down there. I thought I would ask you first, Carl. That's why I'm here."

"Well, my Lord, Shorty, I've known you all my life, just like family. You got my permission; just tell Charles I said yes. We don't have to prove anything to each other – he will take your word. I bet he'll be as sad to see you leave as I am, and the rest of the boys."

"Well, Yolanda has family down there she hasn't seen in

years, so it's all right with her. She knows sooner or later they will come for me if I stay here."

After reminiscing for a while about old times, Carl sadly watched his longtime friend disappear down the trail and into the valley below. "Damn," he said, "you never know in this life when the people you love, and even your family, will need to just ride away or be killed."

"I know," sighed Retha. "Sometimes it just doesn't seem fair, but nothing stays peaceful for very long in this country. I keep having these feelings of *déjà vu*, and it's driving me crazy." Absent-mindedly, she was tracing the letter 'C' on her leg as she spoke. "Cricket has something to do with that. I'm sure of it."

"Retha, you're letting yourself worry about the past and what happened then. You're not letting the future open the real doors for you. You might never learn what your past was, and that might be the best thing for your future. I'm trying not to nag, but just stating simple logic," Carl said gently.

When she didn't answer but instead continued tracing letters on her leg, a far-away look in her eyes, Carl stood up. "Well, I promised I'd ride over to Standing Man's village. Maybe they've seen Cricket. If I find him, I'll tell him you're worried, and he'd better get his butt home. But, Retha, if he won't come, I'm not going to force the issue. He made it on his own a long time before we met him. He's a lot more grown up than you think."

Retha looked up. "It's just that comment he made about me being his sister that I can't get out of my head. He knows where I came from, and that, I would give my life to know. If you see him, tell him I'm sorry."

Carl saddled Corky and mounted. He paused, searching Retha's face with a concerned expression. "There's an old saying out here and that is, 'be careful what you wish for; you may get it.' Hell, I don't even know what it means, but somebody out there must have found out."

As Carl walked Corky away, he stopped a few times and looked back, worried about the outcome of the situation.

~ ~ ~

A couple of hours later, Carl arrived at the village of Standing Man. He was quickly escorted to the chief's teepee and led inside. Standing Man was being pampered by several young women, but he immediately spoke when he saw who his visitor was.

"You look for Cricket, my friend? If that is why you're here, he has gone. He left a couple of days ago with Sad Hank. It seems he was angry at your woman, but he didn't tell us why."

The women all chuckled, and Standing Man smiled as he spoke.

"Yeah, I know that. He got his feathers ruffled a little, but she thought he would come home. She's worried, you know."

The chief nodded.

Do you know where he was going? Maybe I can find them and talk him into coming back," suggested Carl.

"I can't tell you this time, my friend. I would never keep anything else from you, but this time is different, and I am bound by the spirits. I regret that I cannot tell you, but I must not this time."

Carl thanked Chief Standing Man for his devotion and decided he had time to get back to the Blue Moon before sundown. As he made his way out of the village, some of the tribesmen eyed him with distrust, while as many waved, expressing their approval. This relationship was always a little stressful because you never knew when one warrior might decide to take revenge for the mistreatment and lies of the white man's army. Carl, being of native blood, tried never to show any fear.

The Chief didn't have to tell Carl where Sad Hank and

Cricket were going, it was clear they were headed to the Echo. Carl pondered not telling Retha, but his fondness for her told him he should never keep things from her. It lay heavy on his mind all the way back to the Blue Moon. On the way, Corky picked up a rock in his hoof and Carl dismounted. The trip would be long as he led the lame Corky down the rocky trail. It was sundown before he reached Cricket Creek, so he decided to make camp for the night. Rabbits were plentiful near the creek, and he knew he could at least eat. More frequent travelers, as well as bandits, were using the creek now, and left their trash cluttering the crystal-clear creek. He looked with disapproval at the mess and thought this was truly a shame.

Lighting up the white sand by the creek was a half-moon glimmering in the swift waters of the creek. He used his knife-throwing skills to get a rabbit with very short effort. As he sat by the fire, the sounds of coyotes echoed in the distance. Tired from the long day, he stripped Corky of the saddle and lay down, mesmerized by the celestial wheel in the sky. He dozed off, only to be awakened an hour later by the unmistakable scream of a mountain lion. Corky began to get nervous, and Carl quickly went to his side to comfort him. He wondered how the big predators knew when an animal was injured. He readied his rifle and fired a shot into the air. It crossed his mind that this might be the big Puma Cass, Cricket's pet.

Eventually, Corky calmed, and Carl once more lay down to rest. But an hour later he was awakened once more by something in the brush near the creek. He readied his rifle and saw, not more than thirty feet away, the glowing eyes of the big cat. He took careful aim, but then thought he should try to find out if this was the fearsome Puma Cass. He spoke to the big cat softly, saying her name. For a second the big cat stared at Carl, and then silently disappeared into the thick underbrush by the creek.

Carl managed to get a couple of hours' sleep without

any more interruption until sunrise. He knew for sure the Puma was Cass, or she would have attacked the crippled horse. He hid the saddle in the brush and decided he would return when he had Corky safely back to the ranch. Although Carl had removed the stone from the right front hoof, it had left a deep bruise that would take days to heal. Leading the injured Corky home consumed most of the day.

Retha had become worried, and was just leaving to search for Carl, but met him leading Corky only a few hundred yards down the trail. She dismounted and began walking with Carl back to the cabin.

"I thought I would come looking for you, cowboy," she smiled. "Picked up a rock, did he?"

Carl nodded. "Been walking all day."

"What did you find out at the village?"

"Well, he he did go there for a while, but then he left with Sad Hank. The chief wouldn't tell me where, but I assume that they're taking the head of Rico Garza to the Echo."

Retha became very quiet for a minute as she turned and looked at the mountain peaks to the east.

"Did I say something wrong, Retha?"

"No," she answered, "just that damn *déjà vu* feeling creeping up on me again. You know, Carl, the weather's been good and tracking them would be easy. If we leave right now, we could pick up their trail in no time."

"Yeah, good idea, but who would tend the stock while we're gone? I'll have to ride to the ranch tomorrow and see if I can get Jose or one of the hands to come watch the place."

She sighed. "You're right."

"Retha, are you doing this to find Cricket, or are you doing it for the gold that's supposedly there? Remember, that's a sacred place to the tribes, and I'm sure it's being watched all the time. I once heard that the tribes spent years covering the Echo with a mountain of dirt. It's just a story, but what if it's true?"

"My main reason is to find Cricket, but a little gold wouldn't be bad," she grinned.

"The power of greed is a curse on people – the more they get, the stronger the greed. Good men become evil. Johnny One Horn once said if you throw one piece of gold on the ground in front of good people, they might as a friend pick it up and hand it back to you. You throw a whole saddle bag of gold on the ground in front of the same people, and some would try to kill you for it. Greed grows and creates more evil," Carl explained.

"It's no different than what your uncles Charles and Joe did. They were desperate in that swamp, and they also were determined to get that gold. I've heard the story of how dangerous it was, diving into that snake-infested swamp, but they knew it would bring them a better life. It's no different here. I've been desperate all my life, so if I get a chance to help myself, I will."

"Ok, I'll ride to Cheyenne Wells tomorrow and get us a babysitter, but I think it's a bad idea. We could both be killed there. But if you must go, I'll go with you," sighed Carl.

# CHAPTER 18

Early the next morning Carl left for the Cheyenne Wells ranch. He promised he would try to return by late afternoon. As soon as he left, Retha packed her trail gear and a pack mule and left the ranch. Her plan was to be far ahead of Carl, in case he tried to follow her. She wanted to do this on her own. She was still searching for answers, and from what Cricket had explained, this Echo was somewhere close to where he – and she? – had once lived. She had to find out, and Carl seemed to be negative about her quest. Besides, if it was dangerous, she didn't want him to get hurt.

Being a well-experienced tracker, she picked up the trail of Sad Hank and Cricket within a few hours while crossing the valley floor. Sad Hank had known he might be followed and had kept backtracking to put anyone that tried on the wrong trail. Retha had the advantage of knowing on which mountain peak the Echo was located. It would have been better to have been able to follow them there, but the sly old Sad Hank hadn't left much of a trail. Then an unexpected windstorm further hampered the tracking, so Retha just set her sights on the third peak to the east.

When Carl returned to the Blue Moon late in the afternoon, it didn't take long to realize that Retha had taken a pack mule and had left without him. Looking over the valley toward the east, he could see a dust storm building.

Usually, hard winds like this at this time of year would be followed by rain. As he surveyed the dust-blown valley below, his anger changed to worry.

"Damn gal," he said as Jose looked on. "I've got to leave now, Jose. That looks bad down there!"

"Boss, maybe you better wait till morning. Could be that wind will die down when night falls," Jose urged.

"Well, either that, or there's a rain on the way. You're probably right. Either way, it would be useless to try to track her at night, and by now the wind has erased any trail she left. She's tough – she made it a long time before I came along." He dismounted and walked Corky to the enclosed stall. His limp was still pronounced, so it was obvious the stone bruise wasn't healed yet, and he was afraid Puma Cass might think him an easy meal.

"I'll gather the things I need tonight and leave at sunup; I don't have a choice." After he'd filled his saddlebags, Carl prepared to sleep for a few hours. Just before he closed his eyes, though, he remembered. "Jose, while I'm gone, you'll need to keep an eye out for Puma Cass. She doesn't know you, so stay close to the cabin when night falls. I'll be leaving at first light. Oh, and enjoy your stay, ol' friend – just consider it your days off."

"I will, boss, but the thought of being dinner for a mountain lion will not give me the restful days off I need," smiled Jose.

~ ~ ~

The next morning Carl awoke to the sound of thunder in the distance. He knew rain was going to hamper his progress, but he loaded the pack mule and picked a young paint horse from the corral to ride. Corky would be missed, but his hoof needed time to heal.

The rain worsened as Carl made his way down the trail to the valley. What had been unusually good weather had become bad weather overnight, and he wondered how anyone could possibly travel in these conditions. After a couple hours of watching the terrain, he noticed a small overhang in the bluffs. It was obvious that ancient cliff dwellers had once lived there, as their paintings were perfectly preserved on the sandstone walls. It seemed strange to him that after all the time he had spent in this valley, this was the first time he had ever seen them.

Thankfully, he made his way to the shelter and managed to build a small fire from some dry sage brush close to the mouth of the dwelling. He draped his wet clothes over a sage to dry and sat watching the fire and lightning flicker on the walls. The thunder grew louder, sounding like cannons echoing very close to him. The young paint horse became very nervous, and Carl had to comfort him often. The old pack mule paid no attention to the storm and grazed contentedly on the sage near the entrance.

As he waited, Carl wondered if Retha was all right. He hoped she had found some kind of shelter, but, remembering her impatience, reflected that she may not have tolerated the delay of waiting out a storm. He knew he wouldn't have been able to change her mind though. She would do what she had determined to do.

As his body gradually warmed by the flames, the flickering of the fire and the constant sound of rain pouring from the edge of the dwelling were mesmerizing. He would rest.

~ ~ ~

Sad Hank and Cricket had reached the foothills of the third mountain peak and holed up in a cave used by tribesmen from years past. Many posts holding dried human skulls marked the entrance path, as if to protect the cave. Cricket was very hesitant to enter, but Sad Hank assured him no harm would come to him if he kept his thoughts pure and free from evil. As their fire lit the cave, Cricket was intrigued by all the strange markings on the wall. He could hear the sounds of owls outside the entrance, combined with the howling wind through the huge pine trees. But in a short time, he started to appreciate the eerie sounds. They mingled beautifully with his thoughts and perceptions. The air was thick with the smell of pine and fresh rain. Clear, crystal water flowed from the cave wall into a beautiful blue water basin. Sad Hank told him to drink from the water for, "it is good and will cleanse the spirit."

Cricket spoke to Hank in his native tongue. "I don't remember seeing this when my family lived here. When I was younger, we lived at the bottom of the foothills. I would like to go there again before we leave this mountain."

"I will take you there, young Cricket, but all that remains of your home is part of the stone floor where the old cabin stood. This place was flooded with men that searched for gold. Many were killed and now their skulls and spirits guard the site."

Cricket confided, "I found the yellow iron in the creek that ran by our cabin. I was told I could play with it, but to leave it there. My father told me it was the rock of fools, and it was just a colored rock, so I did what I was told."

"Your father was a good man. He tried hard to protect this sacred place, but the numbers of gold seekers finally forced him to leave. I knew him well, and I have his killer's head with us. At the top of the peak is a portal to the dark world of the dead – there I will cast his head into the pit. He will spend his eternity there."

"You knew my father, Sad Hank?"

"Yes, I did, young Cricket, and your mother and sister. I am sad to think the monster in this bag took their lives from them. Your sister was kidnapped by buffalo hunters when she was about ten seasons old and was never seen again until she showed up with the Armstrongs and their cattle herds. She is exactly like I had visioned she would be. I heard that she has no memory of her past, and that might be the kindest thing the Great Spirit willed. There is no telling what she went through in those years."

"Then Retha is my sister," Cricket said, smiling, "I told her she was, but I really didn't know for sure. When I looked at her, I saw my mother looking back at me. She looks like her and somehow, I knew she was family."

"Well, your thoughts were right, but now we must rest. We will have a long, hard climb to the top of the Echo."

As Cricket lay on his bedroll, the storm settled down except for the lightning and rumble of thunder in the distance. What a strange place this was, he thought, enchanting in every way. As the rain passed, huge drops fell from the cave opening and the owls returned with their calls echoing from the massive pines. The lightning would light the skulls on the posts as the flickering from their fire dwindled. After an hour or so of listening to the hypnotizing night sounds, Cricket finally succumbed to his tiredness and fell fast asleep.

## The Triple A

The wagons full of coal that Charles had ordered were delivered to the Triple A and stockpiled. Joe was supposed to load the portion that the ranch in Cheyenne Springs needed, and so, having never seen the place, he decided to head the movement himself. His sons James and Earl begged to accompany him, but it was a hard decision. Even though they had become good horsemen and could handle a rifle as well as most men at the ranch, he felt the trip would still be too dangerous with highwaymen scoping the coach roads for victims. He felt it would be better if the boys stayed home.

After the recent rains, the coach roads were muddy, and

Joe instructed the ranch hands to add to the caravan six teams and two extra wagons and mules as insurance. One large schooner would carry fifteen coal stoves that would be much needed for the growing community at Cheyenne Wells. With the winter closing in, the coal would be a vital commodity in a few short weeks. The nights were already cool, and the wind was brisk. A light covering of frost in the early mornings was already warning that snow could be falling any time.

Joe would leave Tom Sheen in charge of the ranch, and if all went well, he would return in about ten days. He sat at the dinner table and explained to his wife Cindy and the boys his reasoning for wanting to deliver the coal and supplies himself. At first, Cindy was very opposed to the idea, but she knew that when Joe made up his mind to do something, there was no changing it. James and Earl still argued a little, but Joe convinced them they were needed at home.

"It won't be long, boys, until you will run this whole ranch," he explained, "but you still have a lot to learn. Another thing – until you do learn, you don't go around giving orders when I'm gone. Tom Sheen and your mother are still in charge." He winked at his wife, who hugged her sons lovingly as she nodded in agreement. "The other reason I'm going, by the way, is to bring Tex Luna home. I hear he's got a long road to recovery, and he belongs here."

James stood up after finishing his meal, draped his coat over his shoulder and picked up his rifle. "Talking about things to do, I seen some coyotes by the corrals earlier, and I better go check those steers." As he walked out the door, Earl was busy reading a news article from a newspaper the wagons had delivered from Abilene. He had no interest in coyote hunting.

"You know, Cindy, James is more like me, and Earl is more like Charles used to be. Looks like we got a cowboy and a scholar." Joe chuckled.

"Absolutely," Cindy smiled, "and that's not bad."

Since the wagons were still loaded from Abilene, the plan was to leave the next morning at daybreak. Not knowing how muddy the coach road would be, they loaded plenty of supplies into the cook wagon. With luck, they thought, the trip would take about five days, but if the road was wet it could take a lot longer. The six wagons loaded with the heavy coal were the ones to worry about. Their axles were already under a heavy strain, and with the pressure from the mud, the bearings would be the most vulnerable. For the moment the weather was clear, but a crisp wind cooled the area.

After saying goodbyes, Joe set off with the caravan toward Cheyenne Wells. Things went well the first day, with only a few wagons getting stuck. The second day, a wagon lost a wheel and axle. Joe had been smart to bring the extra wagons, as all the coal had to be unloaded and shoveled into the spare. All the hands and Joe were covered with sticky mud, making things extra difficult. But they tried to make the best of things, and several joked about their misfortunes.

On the fourth day of travel, they came across a prairie schooner with the mules still standing in their harness, but the schooner buried in the sticky mud. At first it looked abandoned but when they approached it, they saw a man sitting upright in the seat, dead.

"You boys look around," said Joe nervously. "See it there's anybody else in the brush. This looks like the work of bandits."

As the men were searching the brush, Joe inspected the wagon and its contents. The man in the seat appeared to have just died of an unknown cause and was still holding the reins to the mules with eyes wide open. Inside the schooner was a shepherd dog that just lay growling as the men walked around the wagon.

Pedro, a ranch hand who had temporarily moved up to

foreman status with the absence of Tex, stared at the unfortunate man with disbelief for a moment. "The look on his face, boss – he looks like he's been scared to death. Judging by all these flies and the smell, he must have been here a while. That sure is a faithful dog, though. I feel sorry for him. That kind of dog makes a good cattle dog, boss."

Joe grabbed some dried beef out of his poke and approached the back of the schooner. The dog growled a little at first, but after he smelled the beef, he walked to Joe in a very friendly way. After Joe fed him and stroked him for a few minutes, the frail dog jumped from the back of the wagon. Then Joe instructed the hands to unhitch the mules and give them water. "These animals would be dead in another day; it's amazing they've lived this long. We better get that poor man down and bury him. I'm surprised the buzzards haven't got him by now. He was probably headed for the gold fields in Colorado. That just goes to show you, you never know when your numbers are up."

After he thought a bit, Joe added, "You men hook up our extra mules to this schooner. We might as well take it. Thieves would get it anyway. And we can always use his mules; that is, if they survive."

When the crew had pulled the schooner from the mud, they buried the nameless man. They fed the shepherd dog and gave him plenty of water. But the dog was determined to stay with his owner's grave no matter how hard they tried to coax him into coming with them. Joe walked to the grave and sat beside the grieving dog, petting his head. The dog just lay down on the grave. Joe tried for what seemed to be forever, but the dog would not move. All the hands were saddened as they watched, and a few had to turn away.

"He's not going to move, boss. That ol' boy must have been a good man. Those dogs can feel the good in a person. I can hardly watch," sighed Pedro as he took off his hat out of respect.

"Well, there's nothing we can do, boys. We've got some coal to deliver. It's sad, but we need to be on our way." Joe said finally, shaking his head as he rose to his feet.

As the caravan moved out, Joe looked back several times to see if the dog was following. To his dismay, the faithful dog still lay on the grave with his head down.

~ ~ ~

A day later, the wagons arrived at the Cheyenne Wells ranch. Joe was amazed to see the bustling little community. The first thing on his agenda was to find Charles. As he walked into the saloon, he was met by Big Sally, and without knowing who he was, she tried to set him up with one of the saloon girls. Thankfully, Cat recognized Joe and quickly came to his rescue.

"Sally, take care of the other guys! This is Joe, Charles' brother! His wife Cindy would not be too damn happy with you trying to pawn him off like that."

Sally smiled and patted Joe on his backside. "Well now," she laughed, "if you change your mind, cowboy, just let us know. Now get those other mud-covered cowboys out of here and to the shower shed! I got enough dirt and mud to deal with inside here already." She shooed the men back out the door. "You men, get!" she growled as she pointed to the door.

"Better do as she says, boys! I've been told she bested a real tough ol' mountain man," Joe grinned.

Cat pointed Joe upstairs, where she said Charles was busy writing in his journal of continuing stories he loved so much.

But apparently, Charles had, out of curiosity, looked through some drawers beside the bed and found an envelope addressed to Cat from Denver, Colorado. In the letter, to his surprise, he found a businessman's offer asking Cat to come to Denver. It was an offer of partnership, offering Cat fifty percent of three large saloons and brothels. It also contained a contract signed by her which stated, 'as we agreed.' Charles hadn't been surprised when he read the letter; he just smiled and shook his head. He wrote a note and placed it with the contract. It just said, 'Good luck, Cat, you're a dandy, signed, Charles.'

Joe walked in to find Charles back at his desk. "You still writing, brother? I didn't think you would have time in all this hustle and bustle you've created."

"Yeah, it takes my mind off of it. Someday people may read all the junk I've written down – you never know. It's something different almost every day!" He smiled as he rose and grabbed Joe's hand. "How are you, brother?"

"Well, all right, except we ran into a dead man coming here. He had a dog with him. The dog was so faithful he wouldn't leave the grave after we buried the guy. Darndest thing I ever saw. He just lay there and watched us ride away."

"I'll have to hear that full, complete story. That would be a good one for my journal. Was the man just lying on the trail?"

"No, he was sitting in the driver's seat still holding the reins. His eyes were wide open. It was hard to tell at first if he was alive or dead, then we noticed the flies, and the smell was terrible. My guess is he'd been there a few days. We gave the old dog food and water and left a bucket of water beside him when we left. We brought the mules and the prairie schooner with us. It wouldn't have been long before scavengers would have taken it anyway." He shook his head regretfully. "I sure feel sorry for that dog, though. He would have made somebody a good companion."

Charles was making notes about the dog in his notebook. When he looked up, Joe continued. "Just asking, is Carl still around, or did he go back to the Blue Moon?"

"Well, he went back there, but when he got back, Retha was wanting to go off on that Echo goose chase. I think

they nicknamed her the Coyote Woman for a good reason!"
Charles grinned. "Carl's crazy about her anyway, so he was
wanting to go with her. I sent Jose over to their place a
couple days ago to watch over it while they're gone. I hope
he's not dinner for that big Puma Cass."

Charles put his notebook away, and he and Joe left Cat's
Place and walked towards the area where the hands were
unloading the coal.

"You know, Charles, that coach road's getting more
dangerous all the time. It worries me that Carl and Retha
are out there alone. What gave them the idea to go
searching for a mythical gold mine anyway?"

"Well, I think, after all I've seen, that it may exist, but
Sad Hank insisted we not go there," Charles answered.

Joe replied resolutely, "I'm going after him! That's my
son, and I can't just look the other way, Charles!"

"Leaving now, brother? Why don't you wait until
morning?"

"I can't, Charles. It would eat at me all night; you know
that."

Joe headed to the livery stable and readied his horse.
Harry Willie assisted him and introduced himself. "Leaving
so soon, Mr. Joe? That's a great looking buckskin."

As Joe and Harry chatted, Charles came into the stable
and instructed Harry to ready a pack mule. He took
supplies from the bag he was carrying and packed them
into the saddlebags. "Ready ol' Sachi, Harry, and tell
everybody I'll be back when I get back."

"You're going?" Joe asked, surprised. "You know you
don't have to do this. As for me, it's something I have to
do."

"Well, you didn't think you were going to leave without
paying me a proper visit, did you? Besides, this town life is
getting to me a little bit."

"I really didn't think you would want to go, with your
newfound business and all. Damn, that's amazing!" Joe

declared.

Charles just shook his head, then turned to the other man. "Harry, wait about an hour and then go tell Cat I had to take care of some family business, all right? Don't say anything else." Harry nodded and winked in reply.

After they mounted their horses, they stopped to talk to Pedro and the hands who were unloading the coal. "Pedro, tell Cindy and the boys I'll be back in a few days. I've got business to take care of with Charles."

Pedro agreed. He and the men would leave the next morning for the Triple A, taking the injured and still-healing Tex Luna with them.

## Two days later

The cool fall wind whipped through the sagebrush, making travel difficult. Late in the afternoon Joe stopped his horse and pointed to a small tree beside the trail. He motioned for Charles to follow without saying a word. They rode to where they had buried the man on the trail a few days before. To Joe's dismay, the dog lay dead atop the grave. Sadly, he dismounted.

He sat by the old dog and rubbed his head for a minute while wiping the tears from his eyes. "I tried to get you to leave, old fella. But somehow, I knew you would still be here," he said sadly. "You know, things just don't make sense sometimes."

Joe retrieved a small spade from the pack mule and began to dig the dog a grave. Charles was touched by what he witnessed and looked away while leaning on Sachi. "Damn," he finally said, "here, let me give you a hand, brother. That old dog loved that man so much he just lay there and died – holy cow."

They finished the grave and continued their journey toward the mountain peaks in the distance. Signs of a fire site that was a few days old caused them to suspect Carl might have made it, by the way the fire had been constructed. Traveling to the point of exhaustion, they finally made camp several hours after sunset. The menacing wind had calmed, and the night was still. The men hurriedly built a small fire to ward off the cold and thought they would get a few hours' sleep. They hoped they could pick up tracks to follow in the morning.

~ ~ ~

Retha had reached the foothills of the third mountain. She was amazed at how big the mountain was; it had seemed small from a distance. She decided to follow the base of the foothills and maybe find the cabin that Cricket had described. As the morning passed, she saw an outcropping of trees at the base of one of the many ridges extending down from the peak. She was thinking that it would be a perfect place for a homestead. It had a small creek and waterfall, and at the base of the tree line she saw the remains of a rock foundation of what was once a cabin. She dismounted and slowly scanned the area for any trace of something that would refresh her memory. The *déjà vu* feeling was strong here, and she realized she was on the right track.

She gazed across the valley for any trace of Carl. Though she didn't see him, she knew he would be following her, and that was a comforting thought. There was no sign of Sad Hank or Cricket either, but she wasn't surprised, knowing Hank would cover his tracks. From the cabin location she decided she would make her way up the mountain in her quest to find the Echo. But before she moved on, she searched the rubble of the old cabin for several hours and found several pieces of relics and broken glass. The most interesting thing was a carving on a rock by the creek. She brushed away the sand from the carving and read 'Seth and Mika Adams.' Cricket had the looks of the

Sioux, and Retha had known some Sioux women named Mika. This would explain his resemblance to them. As she glimpsed her reflection in the crystal-clear water, she stopped to stare. The long blonde ponytail stood out like the reflection of a mirror. She had always been complimented on the contrast between her bronze skin and blonde hair. Things were all coming together like pieces of a puzzle in her mind. Cricket was her brother, and the people whose names were carved in the stone were her parents. An easy feeling warmed her thoughts as she put her hands to her face and sat gazing at the water. The place was alive with the sounds of owls and the wind whistling through the pines. The natural scents sweetened the air as glimpses of the past flickered like a candle through her thoughts.

An hour or so before sunset, Retha had the idea to build a large fire in hopes that Carl would see the fire and find her. There were plenty of dried pinecones and limbs that had fallen around the area. That night she lay by the fire and listened to the peaceful sounds of the mountain. Excitement flooded her thoughts, but at the same time she felt more at peace than ever before. She fell into a deep, restful sleep and the night passed quickly.

Retha had tied her horse several feet away, but was awakened by a horse nudging her face with his nose. Startled, she quickly jumped from the ground to see Carl's horse, the young paint, standing beside her.

"Bobo, I told you to leave her alone," Carl smiled. "It's a good thing he likes you! You know he dislikes most people. Good morning," he chuckled. "So you thought you would just leave me home and I wouldn't come looking for you?"

"Well, I was kind of counting on you to follow me. I knew you would give me a problem if you were there, so, I do what I always do."

"Your way, I suppose."

"You got it. Isn't this a beautiful place, Carl? I used to live here! I'm certain now, and Cricket wasn't lying."

Retha showed Carl the rock she had found by the creek with the engraved names of Seth and Mika Adams.

"Makes sense, babe, but there have probably been a lot of prospectors here down through the years, don't you think? It could have been anybody."

"That could be, Carl, but the tribesmen were here guarding the place for years. It wasn't that long ago when they were still here. I don't think many have been here since. Besides, the gold seekers all think the gold is somewhere around Moon Rock, and the tribesmen still guard that place."

"Well, one thing is for certain, this is a beautiful place. I heard a story once from the old mountain man Earl Stockman of a lost mine somewhere in these mountains. He said the Spanish army – Conquistadors, he called them – once mined a fabulously rich gold mine somewhere in these mountains. I remember him telling that story when I was a very small boy and we were all gathered around the gazebo at the Triple A. That ol' boy had been around and still is a legend in these parts. You never knew when he was just telling a story to entertain us, or if it was really true."

"I would really like to hear the rest of that tale, so when we camp tonight I want to hear it, but for now let's go up the mountain and see what's in that neck of the woods," she smiled, touching his nose playfully.

"Well, I hope the day isn't too long, little lady – I was awake all night getting here."

Breaking the camp and readying the mules, they began their journey to the summit of the first peak. The pines were thick, and they had to backtrack several times to make any forward progress. Deer and elk were plentiful, and other critters of the mountain acted as though they had never been hunted.

They had tried to follow the creek bed, but the walls continued to rise, forcing them to take several different detours. Alongside the creek were many signs of native people from years past, and they noticed a few ancient dwellings in the bluffs along the way. Carl was marking their trail with an 'A' carved in some of the trees. He felt that anybody who tried to find them would recognize the initial.

Several warning signs along the way confirmed that at one time the natives meant business about wanting uninvited guests to stay clear. Human skulls were placed in several locations and draped in different colors. Some were placed within rocks, and some were placed on pine posts three to four feet high, staring across the valley floor.

If there ever was a clear trail, time had hidden the bigger part of it. As they ascended, the air became cooler to the point that they put on the heaviest clothing they had. Still, no trace of Sad Hank and Cricket appeared as they moved higher up the challenging mountain. They noticed what they thought to be smoke coming from the ground in several places high up above the tree line, but it turned out to be steam from fissures at the tree line near the summit. They were intrigued at the sight of steam drifting above the small creek in such an eerie fashion. Carl dismounted and walked cautiously to the creekside. Then Retha noticed what seemed to be a man sitting by one of the pines near the tree line. As she approached, she called to Carl and pointed to the figure. As they crept closer, they could tell it was a skeleton of a man clad in the garb of a mountain man.

"Look at that, Carl!" she exclaimed. "That old boy still has his old Hawkins rifle in his hands. Looks like he died sitting up staring down the mountain. It's a wonder wolves or other scavengers didn't get to him. Looks like he broke his leg."

Carl drew his knife and cut the wrapping from one leg.

They could clearly see the bone had been fractured.

"Yeah, no telling how long this ol' boy sat here before he died. Makes you wonder how it happened. This old gun's just a piece of rust. I'd bury him, but it looks like he's got a nice view of the valley. He probably crawled here to die, and he looks so peaceful. Let's just leave him be."

Retha picked up an old saddle bag lying near the body. "Holy Cow," she said, "I can't hardly carry this!"

As she dusted the old bag, she opened the rusted snap and was shocked to see huge gold nuggets glowing back at her.

"Carl, this bag is full of the largest nuggets I've ever saw! This old boy was mining the Echo."

Carl watched as Retha frantically searched the area with her eyes, then he walked to the bag and looked at the glowing nuggets inside. He scanned the surrounding area and rock formations but saw nothing in the formations except layers of shale and the remnants of lava that had been there for centuries.

"Retha, there is nothing here. These rocks here are not anything that would bear gold. It may be on this mountain somewhere, but not in this location," he said. "Settle down now. You act like you've got the fever and that's crazy."

While Retha was still searching the area, Carl built a fire and shot a couple of grey tree squirrels from the surrounding pine trees. He prepared the squirrels to cook and as he sat to rest, he took one of the large nuggets from the saddlebag and began to look at it. "Pure gold," he thought.

At the bottom of the bag was a small piece of flat shale. As he looked at it he noticed a few words etched on the flat surface. Dusting it off, he read, 'Look to the clowns.'

When Retha finally settled down, he called her to his side. "Look what I just found in the bottom of the bag, babe," he said, handing her the stone.

"It says to look to the clowns."

They were both confused by the etching. What could it mean? Night was closing in on the campsite and they sat for a while discussing it.

Unlike the lower mountain, here, there were very few sounds. As they talked and scanned their surroundings, they could see several hot spots in the summit above. Scattered small spots of glowing amber illuminated the mountainside. A few hundred feet up the creek, the steam suddenly stopped.

Carl washed his hands in the water and was amazed at its warmth. He grabbed a bottle of whisky from the pack mule poke and, to Retha's surprise, began removing his clothing. At first, she laughed, and then she realized he was getting in the creek.

"It's kind of hot, and smells like sulfur, but it damn sure feels good," he laughed.

Retha, pleased by what she had seen, quickly followed and the two sat in the soothing water.

"What do you think 'clowns' mean, Carl? I saw a circus once in Abilene that had what they called clowns that were making the children laugh, but I think this has a different meaning."

"I don't really know for sure, but I've seen pictures of clowns, and they all had painted faces, kind of like the tribal medicine men. It makes me think of those colored skulls we saw on the way up here. I do know one thing – we can't go any higher. That shale and crumbly rock above here is steep and slippery. I tried to walk up it a little way and it just collapsed underneath my feet. If you notice, the steam from this creek just stops a few hundred feet up there. My thinking is, that's the beginning of it. I've heard of hot springs where the water just bubbles from the ground."

"That ol' boy sitting by that tree keeps watching us," Retha chuckled. "I wonder why he was all the way up here, if the gold is somewhere else. Makes you think he was running from something – something that wouldn't follow him here, doesn't it?"

"Surely could be, babe, but that we will never know," agreed Carl.

# CHAPTER 19

## The following morning

Joe and Charles reached the old cabin site late in the morning and searched the area for signs of Carl and Retha. Embers still smoldered and smoked from the large signal fire Retha had used to alert Carl of her presence. While scanning the area, Joe spotted the 'A' carved into one of the large pine trees. The trail wasn't easy to follow as they made their way up the rugged mountainside.

By late afternoon they reached the warning of the painted skulls perched on the dried-out pine posts. The west side of the mountain was shaded from the sun, and it had been a relief when the sun finally rose at midday and warmed them. It was very difficult to see the summit, as the thick pine trees blocked their view. Every so often, they would notice the smell of sulfur coming from the adjacent creek. Before the sun had risen and warmed the west side, they had seen steam rising from the warm water of the creek.

After several hours they decided to make camp. The markers that Carl had left were not easy to follow, and Joe and Charles moved slowly, always on careful watch for any clue that would lead them to Carl and Retha. They were unaware that Carl and Retha were making their descent at the same time they were climbing up.

As they settled down for the night, the sun was getting very low in the western sky. "I can tell you one thing, Charles," Joe said, "it's really easy to build a fire with all the pine trees. It's a wonder they haven't been burned by now. These broken limbs we're using for firewood burn like kerosene."

"Joe, ol' Earl Stockman once told me of this place. Remember the skulls we found earlier, and the colored ones? He said in his story that everyone should avoid them and never disturb them. I didn't realize it was true that a place like this could ever exist until I saw it with my own eyes. He said the Spanish once mined the place hundreds of years ago. He had a steel helmet in his cabin, and a few old-looking swords. I asked him if he ever saw any gold, and he just smiled and said, 'No, I didn't have time to look for it.'"

Charles lay on his back, his arms under his head, looking at the sky through the trees as he recollected the stories he had heard. "Another thing he said, Joe, was that the skulls were staring right into the old mine. He said he and his partner, another mountain man named Scratchy Bill, were being chased by tribesmen and his partner retreated up the mountain and was never seen again. Earl was sad about it, but he had to leave in a hurry. He said when he camped that night he was visited by several tribesmen, and he was sure they were going to kill him. But one of the braves was the son of a chief that Earl knew, and that's what saved his life. The brave told him never to return to the burial ground or he would surely be skinned alive and left in the desert to die."

"Charles, your memory of these stories never ceases to amaze me," Joe remarked. "Do you think they're true?"

"You know, Joe, I always thought ol' Earl just made most of those stories up, but now, after putting all these things together, I'm beginning to believe most of them were probably true."

"How in the world do you remember all the stories, brother? I heard him tell at least fifty, but I don't remember most of them," Joe marveled.

"Well, you know I wrote all of them down in my books. Of course, I added a little flair to some. I sent some to a publisher in St. Louis as wild west stories. The publisher sent them to the east coast, and there, they love stories about the 'wild' west," he chuckled.

"I think we can reach the summit by tomorrow afternoon. I sure as hell hope Carl and Retha are ok. This place is just about as rugged as it gets," Joe said. "Since this creek is warm, this peak most likely has an active or ancient volcano. I read these places can be pretty dangerous. But, by the looks of this one, it hasn't erupted in hundreds of years." After a few minutes of silent contemplation, Joe pondered, "You know, this is where Standing Man should move his village. I never saw so many deer and wildlife in one spot. And all these owls keep the night full of sound."

Charles nodded. "You know, to the tribesmen, owls can mean a lot of good things, but some legends go on to say they can be messengers of death. That kind of spooks the hell out of me."

~ ~ ~

Sad Hank had finished three days of the ritual, praying to the Great Spirit all the time, and never leaving the cave of skulls. It was time to deliver the head of Rico Garza to the eternal inferno of the Echo. Cricket, painted in appropriate tribal fashion, watched silently as directed, intrigued by the ceremony.

Now, Sad Hank motioned that Cricket follow him deeper into the cave. The passage narrowed as they ventured deeper into the mountainside. Heat and the smell of sulfur thickened the humid air. Skulls had long ago been placed along the narrow walls. The heat was increasing.

Suddenly, Sad Hank instructed Cricket to go no further. Then he walked into the steamy air and disappeared. Cricket was becoming sick from the sulfur and unbearable heat. He waited several minutes before Hank reappeared out of the dense steam rising from the cave floor, this time without the head of Rico Garza.

A rumbling sound was emanating from deep in the mountain. Rocks and dust began falling from the top and sides of the ancient cave. Sad Hank grabbed Cricket, urging him to hurry, as they scrambled to exit the cave. Finally, outside of the cave, they could still hear a deep rumbling in the mountain as steam and heated air rushed from the opening.

"Let us go from this place, Cricket – our work is done here. We can now join your people down the mountain."

"What people?" Cricket asked, confused.

"Your sister and the Armstrongs," Hank answered, staring down the mountain trail.

"How do you know they are here, Hank? I have not seen anyone since we've been here."

"They are here, my young friend. The spirits told me of their presence. We will find them at the sacred clowns."

~ ~ ~

Early morning came to find Joe leaving the campsite to hunt some quail he had spotted near the creek.

Charles was busily building a fire for coffee. Several times during the night, he had awakened to feel the ground shaking. From his reading, he realized these were small earthquakes. As he worked, he watched the surrounding area closely, hoping the episodes would not worsen.

As he was cleaning a pot in the creek he heard the sound of horses, and people's voices. Looking up the mountain trail, he recognized Carl and Retha in the distance.

"Would you look at that, babe, we've been followed!" Carl smiled. As he and Retha arrived at the campsite and dismounted, she was greeted by a snug hug from Charles.

"Fancy meeting you here, Miss Retha," Charles joked. "Where did you get this yahoo?"

"I really don't know why, Charles, but he follows me wherever I go," Retha laughed.

Carl, amused by what he was hearing, noticed his dad's buckskin tied to the campsite post and started scanning the area for a sign of him.

"Looking for your old man?" Charles asked, still smiling. "He's hunting for the quail we saw down by the creek this morning. I swear, this place has more wildlife than any place I've ever seen, except for the swamp in Mississippi."

"Yeah, I got a couple of nice gray squirrels yesterday, but Retha wouldn't touch them. She said they were rodents, and it would remind her of eating a mouse." Carl grinned as he left in search of Joe.

Charles chuckled. "Well, I guess I'd eat a mouse if I had to. We used to eat muskrats in Mississippi – they taste damn good if you're hungry enough. By the way, did you kids find Sad Hank and Cricket?"

Retha smiled and reached for the saddlebag strapped to the pack mule. "No, not yet, but look at this, my friend. I never saw anything like it. There's a fortune in here."

"Wow!" Charles said, "Where in the world did you find this?"

"In the hands of a dead man," Retha explained. "What looked to be an old mountain man sitting underneath a big pine. It looked like he'd been there a long time, just a skeleton staring over the valley. We went as far up as we could, but above the tree line it got impossible to climb. Loose rocks and shale made the trail impassable."

"That ol' mountain man was probably Scratchy Bill," Charles smiled wryly. "Another legend proved true."

"Who in the hell is Scratchy Bill?" Retha asked, laughing.

"Well, I didn't know him, but Earl Stockman told me of a character he once befriended. Scratchy Bill told him about a rich vein of gold on this mountainside. They found some old swords and helmets of the Spanish that were once here. But they were discovered by the Comanche, and they ran for their lives. I guess ol' Scratchy Bill didn't make it out of here."

"Well," explained Retha, "the man we found had a broken leg. More than likely, he died from gangrene. He still had his old rifle in his hands. He also had this flat piece of shale in the bottom of the saddle bag that read, 'look to the clowns.' We don't know what it means, though."

Carl had found Joe and they returned to the camp with plenty of quail for everyone's breakfast.

As they ate, Charles explained, "The natives use the word 'clowns' to describe the skulls they've been using as trail warnings," Charles explained. "Have you seen those?"

"The skulls of the sacred clowns were a couple of hours down the ridge," Joe put in.

Carl and Retha had seen them, and the group agreed, after discussing the tale of Earl Stockman, to continue their search for the Echo.

## Cheyenne Wells

Cat was spending some time in her room, still contemplating the offer she had gotten from Denver, when she noticed a drawer that had been opened and not fully closed. As she sat down on the bed to reread the contract, she knew that Charles had seen the proposal. Her hands dropped to her lap. In shock, she realized that Charles already knew. It also dawned on her that he probably would not be back to Cheyenne Wells anytime soon. Now she knew why he hadn't said goodbye. Tears streamed down her face, and she locked the door to the room and stayed there through the night.

The following morning, she was down the stairs early and ordered Big Sally to pack all the girls' belongings because they were leaving for Denver. None of the girls had known anything about the Denver deal, and they were very confused.

Big Sally told Harry Willie to prepare a prairie schooner and team and bring it to the front of the saloon. Everybody on the street and all the workers that were still busy building the buildings were surprised as they watched Cat and company load their belongings into the schooner, leaving everything behind except their clothing and personal belongings.

Nate and Pete tried to talk Cat out of leaving without an escort of men, but she refused all their offers. They rode beside the wagon after Cat and the girls were loaded and ready. "Kind of sudden, isn't it, Cat? Don't you think you should have told Charles about this?" Nate commented.

"He already knows, Nate, and it's just business – he knows that. I got an offer in Denver I couldn't turn down."

Many of the workers and regular hands gathered around the schooner to say goodbye, saddened by the girls' sudden departure. As the wagon made its way out of the small village, there was an empty feeling that affected the whole population of Cheyenne Wells.

"Well, there goes the only thing that was fun in this place," Pete said, shaking his head. "Damn, just when things were getting good."

"Well, maybe someone will open the place back up one day, Pete. Why don't you do it? You know, get yourself one of them red dresses and call yourself the bearded lady! Hell, people would come from miles around."

"Oh yeah, well, I might make a dollar more than I do for

cow punching. One thing I've always said about this place is nothing stays the same for very long." He grinned back at Nate. "Red dress, huh? Red dress yourself! If you ask me, that's a perfect job for you, Nate."

"No, I'm going to be a politician one of these days – you know, get paid for bullshitting the people. I'll take all I have learned from you, Pete, and become President," Nate laughed.

"Well, Nate, all kidding aside, my brother, it still is sad to see them go."

"Yeah, it's not going to be the same, that's for sure." Nate looked wistfully after the departing prairie schooner, then turned back to his companion. "Well, I for one have got work to do, so I must part from your gracious company. That north fence won't fix itself."

"Before you leave my gracious company," smirked Pete, "look there, ol' Harry Willie is going with them! Just when I think we've got a good blacksmith, he up and leaves with a bunch of women headed for Denver!"

"There will be others to take his place, Pete. There always are." Nate wheeled his horse northward. "Work's waiting. See you later."

## Back to the Quest

Joe, Charles, Carl and Retha carefully made their way down the winding ridge until they reached the location of the sacred clowns. They dismounted and surveyed the landscape for any clue to the whereabouts of the elusive Echo. Hours passed without any results.

Carl finally tired of searching and decided to build a fire to cook a few sage hens he had shot along the way. Convinced there was no one around but them, he also thought the fire would alert Sad Hank and Cricket to their presence if they were nearby. He had no idea they were only a few hundred yards away at the time.

It wasn't long before Charles and the rest of the group joined him by the fire.

"Now," Charles said, "that shale ol' Scratchy Bill had with him said, 'look to the clowns.' Well, we looked at them, and we noticed they all look the same direction, over toward that small plateau over there." He pointed.

A few hundred yards from them was a flat plateau only about two hundred yards across and sparsely brush-covered. Charles and Joe had searched the plateau and found nothing, and there was no gold-bearing rock on the cliffs or walls around it. Retha and Carl had searched in the other direction and found nothing. As they sat around the fire, tired after an arduous day, they were amazed they had found nothing that even resembled a mine or traces of where any had ever existed.

# CHAPTER 20

J ust before sunset, Sad Hank and Cricket arrived at the campsite. Retha ran to Cricket's side and hugged him tightly with tears streaming down her face. He was a little shocked, but he also showed feelings of happiness.

"You are my brother; I should have known it by all the feelings I had," she told him. "Please promise me you'll never leave me again! It seems like I've searched all my life for answers, and I finally found a piece of my lost life."

Joe, Charles and Carl were touched by what they were seeing. Carl, not able to bear the hurt, walked away from the camp to the creek and stood staring across the canyon.

"Sad Hank, how did you find us? Was it the shots?" asked Charles.

"No, the spirits told me you were here." He looked at them soberly. "I see you still search for gold. This is a sacred place. Do not disturb the spirits of the clowns."

"We haven't touched anything around them, but legend says, and the slate ol' Scratchy Bill had in that saddle bag says, 'look to the clowns.'"

As the sun set, the group gathered around the campfire. Sad Hank sat cross-legged and burned a mixture of herbs to ward off any bad spirits. Everybody was busy for a few minutes, eating the roasted sage hens, before anyone spoke.

"Sad Hank," Retha finally asked, "I know you don't like to talk about it, but does this Echo really exist, or is it just an old wives' tale told by the drunks in the saloons to get free drinks and attention?"

"Before I tell you, I must give thanks to the spirits that you and your brother Cricket are once again together. I know you think you have found the answer to your missing past."

"Yes, but there are still years missing. Hank, do you know what happened?" she responded, a pleading expression in her eyes.

"Your father was a good man and a friend of mine. Many times, I would visit him in the old days when we were young. He was here on the mountain for years until some young Comanches took over the mountain and forced him to leave. I remember the day you disappeared. Oh, it wasn't the Comanches that took you. It was a couple of what you call mountain men. Your father said you were playing by the creek when they took you. We followed their tracks south, but then lost them in a blowing snowstorm. You were never seen again until you were guided back here by the spirits. Many times, I helped your father look for you, but after many moons he accepted the fact that you were gone."

Things got very quiet around the fire as Sad Hank continued. "This may be hard for you to hear, Miss Retha, but Rico Garza was raised by your parents also. He was rotten to the bone; many times, I should have killed him, but I made a promise to your mother that I would watch over him. As his crimes and murdering ways continued, I gave up my promise and knew he must be stopped. Your folks raised him as a son, and he ended up taking their lives for a few saddlebags of the yellow iron from this same mountain. The years I was in the far north scouting for the army, I used to hear about his foul deeds, and when I returned from the north and learned of your parents' murder, I knew I was going to have to take him down. I knew of Cricket and wondered how he survived by himself."

"Sad Hank, all this time you kept this from us. I really don't understand," she said sadly.

"Sometimes things should be left alone," explained Hank. "I was going to tell you one day, but I still don't know the answers to where you were for all the years. I really thought your memory might come back and I didn't want to interfere."

"Well, I'm still in the dark about that, but at least I've got Cricket now and things seem to be falling together – just in pieces. I'm shocked to know Rico was tied to my family – that's the worst thing I could ever hear."

"I threw his head in the eternal fire, and there he will burn forever for the bad things he did, Miss Retha. I am sorry I didn't tell you before this."

Sad Hank thought a long time before he continued. "This yellow rock you search for, Miss Retha, can destroy all that you have found. Maybe you should just take Cricket back to the Blue Moon and be happy building the ranch you always wanted. Many dangers follow those who seek the yellow rock."

"Well, Hank, you are so right." Retha smiled as she grabbed and hugged Cricket. "It doesn't seem so important now," she said as she emptied the saddlebag onto the ground.

Carl and the others were amazed at what they were hearing from Sad Hank. As the full moon rose over the summit, it lit the plateau in a mysterious glow. Carl turned to Hank and asked, "So, does the Echo really exist, or was the gold in the saddlebag just left on the mountain randomly?"

Again, everybody turned their attention to Hank as he stared at the fire. After a few seconds he spoke. "Oh, it's real, and it's here, and you're looking right at it, Carl."

"You mean the plateau? We searched the plateau and there's nothing there, not even any rock that could bear gold."

"Well, many years ago before any of us were born, the Spanish came here. They were fearsome people, with long knives and wearing armor made of steel. They mined the gold for years. They captured many tribesmen that were peaceful at the time and made slaves of them. They carried the ore down the mountain, and some said to the river that runs where the Triple A is now. There, they loaded it in large floating boats and took it down the river."

"It is said they did this for many years. According to my father before me, there was a huge vein rising from the plateau about thirty steps across and about forty steps high. It glistened with white quartz and large veins of yellow iron. The Spanish chipped away at the vein for many seasons. After the rock was mined to ground level, they continued, while all the time adding more warriors from where they came from. They were fearsome people and would kill anyone who interfered with their quest. After many years of digging, it became a large hole in the ground. As they got deeper, the heat from mother earth began to overcome them. The air became poison, and the smell of sulfur grew strong and poisonous. Many of the Spanish and the tribesmen died from breathing the poison air. A young Comanche chief named Saga rebelled against the Spanish and attacked them when they were weak. The Comanche killed them all. Their bodies were thrown into the hole that was at least fifty steps deep, and then the hole was covered. The Comanches worked for many more seasons carrying rocks and dirt and filled the hole as though it was never there. There were several more bands of the men of armor that came in search of the yellow iron. The Comanche had learned their ways and killed them all. Soon they were no more. Those skulls are a warning of death as they stare across to the plateau."

The group looked on quietly as Sad Hank softly told the incredible story.

"But what about the gold in the saddlebag of Scratchy Bill? He must have found it many years after the men came from across the sea," Retha queried.

"In the last days of the Spanish," Hank explained, "there were a few wagons that never made it to the river. It is said that they were attacked, and their drivers were also killed. Saga had a hatred for the Spanish like no other. It is my guess that Scratchy Bill found one of those wagons where it rested and gathered the gold. There may still be some, somewhere in the valley below, but if the Comanches hid it, it probably never be found. I think old Bill just stumbled on it. I ask you, my friends, never to tell anyone what you have heard here, and to keep the mountain sacred."

Hank stood and walked to the sacred clowns, chanting to the spirits. The others were almost speechless.

At last, Charles turned to Joe and Carl. "I've read about a gas that comes from this kind of activity. It's called sulfide, and it's extremely poisonous. Whatever is down there will probably stay there forever. Anyway, that's it. We have found the Echo and now let's just move on with what's left of this life."

"Yeah, I'm ready to go home," smiled Retha as she gave Cricket a sisterly hug. "We've got a cattle ranch to build. What about you, Charles? Have you got any plans with Cat Brink? I bet you are anxious to get home, aren't you?"

"Well, it might be nice, but Cat is probably on her way to Denver by now. Knowing her was fun, but I'm just not meant to be a man of the house. I'm not going back to Cheyenne Wells."

The group looked on in surprise as Charles walked a few steps away and stood staring across the valley in the direction of Cheyenne Wells.

Finally, seeing that Charles was sincere, Joe stood up and walked to his side. "What are you planning, brother? I thought you were really into that little Cat."

"Oh, I am, but for now I think I'll go back to the Triple

A and help get the place ready for winter. Then, if you'll go with me, Joe, I think I'd like to make a little journey back to visit our roots in old Mississippi. I want to visit my mother's resting place. Besides, I want to see what ol' Johnny One Horn has been up to."

Joe looked at Charles, who was smiling, and shook his head. "I'd love to do that too, but what about Cheyenne Wells? Who's going to run that operation?"

"Well, as far as I'm concerned, Nate and Pete and Carl can split it three ways – it's only fair, don't you think? Those two men have given us the best years of their lives, and Carl can have his fair share as well. You know, Joe, this place has brought a new realization of what life is all about to all of us. I've never seen a place that has so much life in it, even though it came from so much sorrow in the past."

They all sat by the warm fire and talked about the tremendous adventure they had just experienced. As the subject changed, Carl talked and joked with the rest of them, all of whom had become his family. The Echo was forgotten by them, but its stories and legends would be heard in the region for decades to come.

**To be continued...**

# ABOUT THE AUTHOR

Jim and Susan Armstrong

James (Jim) Armstrong, originally from Southeast Missouri, now makes his home in the Ozarks with wife Susan and countless creatures of the wild. He loves to spend time with grandkids, and when he's not doing that, he spends time in his music studio or writing.

As a, now retired, oil industry consultant and professional musician, through the ups and downs of the oil business, Jim spent many years bouncing back and forth between the two careers. His passion is music, and playing at Woodstock is one of his best all-time memories, yet that is a different story.

As the sixth son of a cotton sharecropper, he spent the first ten years of his life on a small farm near Steele, Missouri. Many spring storms rumbled across the boot heel of Missouri, and on those dark nights the family would spend time in their musty old dirt floored cellar. Jim remembers the smell from the kerosene lamp thickening the air. Aunts, uncles, and sometimes neighbors, would crowd in to weather the storms.

It was those nights that many stories were told. The tale of the Wisp intrigued Jim the most. He dreamed of one day writing it just as he'd heard it as a child, so he did, but the original manuscript was destroyed in a fire.

Jim rewrote the story and with the help of his friend Sharon, it was published as book 1 of this series, The Will and the Wisp.

JAMES D. ARMSTRONG

# ABOUT THE ARTIST

James H. Hussey

Jim Hussey is a native of New Orleans who has become one of the country's artists of note. Born in 1936 Jim was educated in New Orleans, and upon completion of his academic training he began a career in the world of business. Later, in the summer of 1970, he decided to leave that career.

Equipped only with the paints and brushes his mother had left him, an interest in art from early childhood, and inspired by his surroundings, his family, his friends, and prominent artists, he decided to leave his successful career as a salesman and merchant to pursue his love for art on a full-time basis.

In order to refine his ideas, skills and techniques, in 1972 he attended the John McCrady School of Fine Arts. The decision to pursue art proved to be a wise one for his renditions of the Old South. Its many lazy bayous, and life along the Mississippi, shortly became wanted by many art collectors, galleries and museums throughout the world.

His paintings reflect personal feelings in the nostalgic and romantic moods, settings, and history of the South as seen through the eyes of numerous novelists and historians. Like most true artists, Jim is constantly driven toward self-improvement and growth through better interpretation, increased skill and authenticity in subject matter and composition.

*"I believe when I display realism in a painting, it is as important to reflect my feeling on the mood of that subject, or to tell a story much as a poet, using all of the color and feeling of one's mind. Otherwise, one might just as well take a photograph.*